W9-AQA-639

TAKE HER DOWN

Kansas City, MO Public Library
00001188641385

Advance praise for *Take Her Down*

"Effortlessly transporting the halls of the Roman Forum to the halls of high school, *Take Her Down* grapples with questions of identity, community, and the public sphere. The personal is political while the political is personal—especially for teenagers—and Lauren Emily Whalen ensures that readers will question their own motivations, biases, and narratives as the story of Bronwyn, Jude, and their cadre of conspirators unfolds. Diversity only adds to the complexity and dynamics of the story—a brilliant realism where no character is an archetype, despite the source material. *Take Her Down* makes both history and Shakespearean Histories approachable for the reader."—*Emily Edwards, author and host of F*ckbois of Literature podcast*

"*Take Her Down* follows a cast of teens as they work through disappointment and betrayal amid a ruthless school election—all while experimenting and questioning who they might love. Whalen's writing asks the reader to examine how the boxes we put ourselves in don't always close, and how our capabilities for harm are as vast and far reaching as our abilities to heal and move on. The pace is fast; the stakes intense and breathtaking. I could not put it down."—*Jessica Cranberry, author of In The Trap*

Praise for *Two Winters*

"This retelling of *The Winter's Tale* follows parallel stories of family and forgiveness in two very different times...Finding the original play's resonance in the complicated kingdoms of high school while still appealingly down-to-earth, the specificity of place and slow build toward complication and tragedy work well in Paulina's section but less successfully in Perdita's. Readers need not be familiar with Shakespeare's original to appreciate this skillful adaptation. Unabashedly queer, moving, and sincere."—*Kirkus Reviews*

"*Two Winters* is an exceedingly clever adaptation that captures the heart of one of Shakespeare's most complex works—and it'll capture your heart, too. This multi-generational tale of self-discovery and the secrets we inherit needs a place on your bookshelf."—*Stephanie Kate Strohm, author of Love à la Mode and It's Not Me, It's You*

"*Two Winters* is a breath of fresh air; a sweet, nostalgic trip back to the 1990s, when music was everything, the angst was real and lifelong friendships were forged in the struggle of emerging identities. This modern retelling of Shakespeare's *The Winter's Tale* is a poignant and hopeful tale of love, tragedy and divided loyalties that will resonate with anyone who was ever a confused teenager. I just loved this book!"—*Lillah Lawson, author of Monarchs Under the Sassafras Tree, So Long, Bobby and the Deadrockstar trilogy*

"Compelling characters lead complicated lives whose twists and turns will keep you turning pages of *Two Winters*."—*Crystal Cestari, author of Super Adjacent and the Windy City Magic series*

"*Two Winters* somehow magically, skillfully pulls off the feat of balancing two independent but interrelated narratives that are equally compelling, with complex characters who we get to see learn and grow on the page. Both stories are funny and sharp and dramatic and heartbreaking, and the way they ultimately weave together makes for an encompassing and satisfying read."—*Michelle Falkoff, author of How to Pack for the End of the World and Pushing Perfect*

By the Author

Two Winters

Take Her Down

Visit us at www.boldstrokesbooks.com

TAKE HER DOWN

by

Lauren Emily Whalen

2022

TAKE HER DOWN
© 2022 By Lauren Emily Whalen. All Rights Reserved.

ISBN 13: 978-1-63679-089-3

This Trade Paperback Original Is Published By
Bold Strokes Books, Inc.
P.O. Box 249
Valley Falls, NY 12185

First Edition: March 2022

THIS IS A WORK OF FICTION. NAMES, CHARACTERS, PLACES, AND INCIDENTS ARE THE PRODUCT OF THE AUTHOR'S IMAGINATION OR ARE USED FICTITIOUSLY. ANY RESEMBLANCE TO ACTUAL PERSONS, LIVING OR DEAD, BUSINESS ESTABLISHMENTS, EVENTS, OR LOCALES IS ENTIRELY COINCIDENTAL.

THIS BOOK, OR PARTS THEREOF, MAY NOT BE REPRODUCED IN ANY FORM WITHOUT PERMISSION.

Credits
Editor: Cindy Cresap
Production Design: Stacia Seaman
Cover Design by Inkspiral Designs

Acknowledgments

For loving this story from its inception, allowing it to grow and putting it out there: the Bold Strokes Books team, including Sandy Lowe, Cindy Cresap, Ruth Sternglantz, and Carsen Taite.

For my absolute favorite cover ever: Inkspiral Designs.

For the best beta reading on the planet: Jess Moore.

For answering the tough questions: Hannah Mary Simpson, Andrea Berting, Zoë Mikel-Stites, Megan Pedersen, Allison Kirby, and Dan Scully.

For all my tarot needs, including Cass's spreads in the book: Avalon Dziak.

For letting me shamelessly plug on their podcasts: Emily Edwards (*Fuckbois of Lit*), Anita Kelly (*Lez Talk About Books, Baby*) and Brian Rowe (*Piece of Pie: The Queer Film Podcast*). Like and subscribe!

For letting me shamelessly plug in and out of their spaces: Jacksonville Public Library, Book Cellar Chicago, the Chicago YA Book Festival, and Our Town Books.

For constant inspiration and support: authors Lillah Lawson, Stephanie Kate Strohm, Jayne Renault, Dahlia Adler (and LGBTQReads) and countless others.

For everything: my fellow writers and performers, my family, and my friends.

For the B's in LGBTQ+.

I see you.

PROLOGUE

Dear Ms. Strohm,

For our senior AP English project, you asked us to sort out our experiences of the past three and a half years in whatever literary-adjacent way we felt appropriate. You wanted to give us the feeling of a thesis—in essence, something where research and writing would take an entire semester, that was physically impossible to throw together the night before or the morning of—before we got to college and grad school, which are in the business of theses. So, here you go.

We're on the verge of a new president of the United States, coming out of a global pandemic, and the world is (sometimes literally) on fire. I was a first-year at this school when the following events took place, with Mrs. Kirkpatrick droning through grammar lessons while I stared open-mouthed at the upperclasspeople sashaying through the hallways, gracefully and eloquently fighting over the power to...well, have power.

And then suddenly, a metaphorical bomb dropped.

Everything changed, under circumstances both well-known and mysterious, leaving more questions than answers. History was made, not only in the outside world but in our teenage microcosm. How could I *not* reflect on how we all felt then?

My senior project is an oral and written history of that semester, featuring interviews with the main players conducted in person and via phone/FaceTime, transcriptions of audio recordings, journal entries, and drafts of campaign speeches (school-approved and otherwise)—including the tiny but pivotal part I played in the whole ordeal. Though I've edited for brevity and compiled interviews into chunks for storytelling purposes, all important details are real.

To quote the old-school crime shows my grandpa loves, these are their stories. (*Too much?*)

Speaking of stories, with the subjects' permission, I've re-created certain scenes with dialogue. You know my affinity for creative writing, Ms. Strohm. So, with that in mind, I guess it's not a strict oral history. But stick with me. The things they said, they're important, and I want to put you right in the moment whenever I am able.

Everyone I profiled has graduated. I know you'll recognize your former students, but I've changed the names of most people and our school, to protect the innocent. I kept my full name and Cass's first name, with her encouragement. I thought a parallel to *Julius Caesar* would be especially appropriate not just because of my name, but the institution that was the center of our world, just like Rome was for Caesar, Brutus, and the conspirators.

Can't get more Shakespearean than that, huh? Not that I'm *looking* for extra credit, but I wouldn't turn it down either. Like everyone else at what I'm calling "Augustus High," I've got the Ivies in my sights.

More than anything, though, I'm proud of this project, the interviews I conducted, the informational *and* emotional gaps I was finally able to fill. When you're fourteen and entering a brave new world where "take 'em by the tits" is suddenly leadership language, plus you still have to take pre-calculus and remember where the bathroom that doesn't constantly, inexplicably smell like chili is located, you can miss a whole lot of what's around you. The kids above me seemed so... together, even when they were at each other's throats. Knowing that was far from the case is both comforting and strangely terrifying. Will we ever have it together? Do you?

I've rambled long enough, so I'll leave you to my oral history. My first thesis. A project I thought would never work, that started out as sort of a middle finger because you always say I "tell" when I should "show" but then, weirdly, came together and taught me more than almost anything in my four years here. If I were a suck-up I'd say "Thank you for this opportunity," but really...yes? Yes.

Yours truly,
Calpurnia Kennedy

The Players

Bronwyn St. James, she/her, junior at Augustus High, candidate for student body president

Cassandra "Cass" St. James, she/her, sophomore at Augustus High, Bronwyn's cousin, housemate, and campaign manager, club cheerleader and tarot enthusiast

Jude "JC" Cuthbert, she/her, junior at Augustus High, candidate for student body president, power lesbian and Bronwyn's ex-best friend

Porter "Pleaser" Kendrick, he/him, junior at Augustus High, Bronwyn's first boyfriend, Exploding Kittens devotee, straitlaced straight guy

Antonia "Tone" Marcus, she/they, sophomore at Augustus High, demigirl, Bronwyn's and Jude's ex-girlfriend, Jude's campaign manager

Scarlett (she/her), Nasim (he/him), and Declan (he/him), coconspirators and students at Augustus High whom Jude Cuthbert has alienated, ostracized, or busted over the years

Calpurnia Kennedy, she/her, unsuspecting baby gay and first-year student at Augustus High

Mr. Roman, he/him, teacher at Augustus High, idolized and/or lusted after by his students who are too young and/or dumb to know better

Principal Olive Murrell, she/her, principal of Augustus High. Has a PhD but prefers "principal." Stylish and authoritative. You don't mess with her, *ever.*

Augustus Magnet School, also known as Augustus High, technically the setting, but as you'll see, almost a character in itself. An exclusive magnet school, its motto is "*Ut est rerum omnium magister usus.*" Because of course it is.

Various revelers, coaches, and parents

ACT I

"…not that I loved Caesar less, but that I loved Rome more."
—Brutus, *Julius Caesar*

Chapter One

Bronwyn

Three thirty-five a.m. and my boyfriend was doing jumping jacks.

Is that a good place to start? I've never been part of an oral history before. No offense, I barely know *you* and now we're sitting together on my college campus. Thanks for the coffee, by the way.

And I'm your first interview? Wow. No pressure or anything. *And you want to re-create dialogue?* Yeah, I guess. Go for it.

Anyway, the jumping jacks.

For weeks, I'd jerked awake at that exact time, my body yanked out of REM tense and ready for a fight. Normally, the person next to me let out a small, satisfied snuffle-snort, turning over on their side to face me, eyes squeezed shut and mouth wide open. I didn't mind. It was the most peaceful they looked all day and all of the night. No way in hell I'd wake them up. I hoped their mind was quiet the same way mine raced with thoughts I wasn't ready to call regrets, with defensive responses no one in my waking life had even asked for. At that time, I was ready and waiting to be put on trial. Even at twenty-five to four in the morning.

Sometimes my fists even punched the air. Before I gave in to the shut-eye that would become *sleepus interruptus* a mere few hours later, I offered up an intercession to the Flying Spaghetti Monster that I wouldn't hit the precious one snoozing next to me. So far, so good.

After that initial body-jerk, I wouldn't move. Not only did I not want to interrupt their REM cycle, but it also felt wrong to interrupt the night. Barring climate change and/or natural disaster, of course. At that point I'd already done enough to disrupt what should have just unfolded in front of me, naturally as nightfall.

Every morning at three thirty-five a.m., my eyes popped open and stayed wide for at least an hour. I could kick all the way out of the sheets already mangled with my tossing and turning, pour a glass of water, stream *Full House* reruns on my phone. But because I stayed still, considering the inner peace of others, I tortured myself with my own thoughts. An apt punishment, really, for someone who used to think she could get inside everyone's head. Who always knew what she wanted and exactly how to make it so, to paraphrase my jailed father's paraphrasing of Jean-Luc Picard.

There's no head I wanted to be in less than my own.

Yet at three thirty-five a.m., that's what I was stuck with, no card games or kisses or blustery speechifying to distract me from the inevitable.

But that morning things were different because Porter was a jumping-jack bean. I could see a sheen of sweat on his brow, but his hair was pulled off his forehead by one of my cousin's hairbands she used when she was washing her face, doing an especially intense tarot reading or…doing jumping jacks. His breathing was like *huh. Huh. HUH.*

This was a guy who had his psychiatrist write him a note so he could do Yogilates instead of regular PE.

I remember rolling over on my side and patting the sheets next to me, trying to look as enticing as possible while hiding my alarm. I'm sure I read as constipated if he could even make me out in the dark. "Por. Come back to bed, hon. What are you doing?"

He ignored me, kept huffing and puffing, bare feet slapping against the old rug Cass and her mom had put over the concrete before I moved into their garage.

I tried again. I think I moved the strap of my cami down my shoulder. I've never been good at the seduction thing. It was then I knew he could see me because he rolled his eyes.

"What are you doing?" I asked again, but the dread was growing inside me.

He wasn't doing cardio at the ass-crack because he wanted to build stamina for whatever reason. No. My boyfriend's jumping jacks, when we should have been sleeping or screwing, were both a product of his beautifully messed-up brain—the messed-up was what made it beautiful, I want to be precise about that—and what we'd done, him and me and Cass, so I could win a stupid school election.

Jeez. Even just remembering the *jumping jacks* is hard. I hope you get an A.

Bronwyn

Our world ended the night he won.

Do you remember? Of course you do, you were like fourteen. Does your stomach still do funny shit when you think about that administration? Because mine does.

We were so excited. A woman president, the first in anyone's lifetimes. One who could trounce any sexist argument thrown her way, who'd already survived a world of hurt thanks to a philandering husband who denied he knew what a blow job even was, who had an amazing daughter, who was old enough to be our mom but still ambitious and cool. There was no way that November night wouldn't be a huge celebration, like when we were little and the previous president was elected and people partied in the streets—not like it was the end of the world, but like it was the very beginning.

The next morning, I woke up to dead silence.

This wasn't completely out of the ordinary, the quiet. Cass was a morning person but didn't bang around like my dads used to. Her mom, my aunt Deb, usually took early hours at the hospital so she was long gone, either that or she was asleep from the graveyard shift.

But this quiet was different. The entire world was still. I didn't want to check my phone because I knew what I'd see, what I'd dreaded since a stress headache had put me out of commission when we already knew what the results would be.

Not just a racist misogynist, but a rapist. No regard for any woman he couldn't fuck, and very little for the ones he could and did.

Jude and I were still speaking, very much so. The big rift that would happen soon wasn't even in my mind. And Cass and I weren't that close yet, still sussing each other out. The cheerleader and the overachiever, cousins who barely knew one another until one moved in with the other, like a wacky old-school sitcom except not nearly as funny in real life, just like the circumstances that led us to cohabitating in the first place.

So, like I had since we first got phones, I texted Jude.

You saw?

Bubbles right away. *We're fucked.*

School that day was surreal. I would have ditched—no adult was around to notice or care anymore, and even if I'd gotten caught, I'd have a worthy excuse. But what would I do, exactly? Keep refreshing my feeds as more bleak news popped up? Might as well sit through pre-calc and let formulas take my mind off things for forty-five minutes at a time.

The devastation hung over all of us like fog, dense and gray. Augustus High, through some weird combo of test results, population, or just plain fate, was primarily female (and increasingly, nonbinary). No one was sure why—it was a magnet school, not some single-sex private institution—but that's how it had been for decades.

We were heartbroken. The cishet boys, who usually stayed out of our way, were downright deferential. That day, not a one raised their hand or even appeared to speak, at least the ones in my (war) path.

Aside from a handful of seniors, none of us could vote. She'd crushed our school election just the week before. We trusted the adults in our lives to follow suit, to do the right thing. And they fucked us.

Jude and I didn't say the words. But that day we gave each other a look, the kind we could read in one another. Passing each other in the halls before my French class and her Portuguese independent study, we looked at each other and our eyes said, trust no one. Make this right.

That weekend, I met Porter.

CHAPTER TWO

Cass

I had no idea what a campaign manager does.

I still don't. You might want to google, for your project. Because I never did.

But Bronwyn asked, and just like when we were kids, she, the big four-year-old, and I, a puny almost-three, I'd do anything she asked. The tall blond queen and the tiny adopted Chinese servant, like one of those bad animated movies before people wised up to all the problems behind *that* power structure. And things were weird. She'd just moved in with me and my mom, and after all these years we barely knew each other. I had more in common with her new boyfriend. Her first ever.

But we'll get to that.

By sophomore year, I was lying to myself about Bronwyn. We were different. Our parents didn't speak anymore. Yeah, she was smart and popular, but I had my own strengths. I could lift human beings for shit's sake. I didn't need her approval. Her attention. Her anything.

Ha. That lie lasted until she moved in with us.

Not only did I crave her approval, I just wanted to get to know my cousin. Her pop and my mom were brother and sister but were ten years apart in age and had never been close. I think he never understood why Mom, single and childless and doing fine as a nurse but not exactly raking it in, would blow what was left of her trust fund, not to mention a ton of time and paperwork, to adopt a baby from another country. The families hung out a bit when we were little, but not much after.

When Bronwyn's pop got sent away and her other dad took to the Appalachian Trail to find himself, though, my cousin had nowhere else to go. She pretended it didn't bother her. But come on. I know going from a McMansion with her own personal wing to a tiny guest room with crappy carpet from the seventies had to come with major culture shock.

Technically, my cousin lived in a converted garage. Sure, there was insulation and stuff—renovations that took place way before my mom and I moved in. But yeah, she laid her head in a place where old cars coughed up God knows what. I never told her this, but I worried about the air in there.

I mean, maybe the leftover toxic fumes explained everything that happened after.

Anyway, the race for student body president was strange from the start. Used to be, no one cared about student government, but now that we had a certified asshole running the country, everyone did. We even had primaries for the first time ever after Christmas—only for the rising seniors; my class and the first-years didn't give a shit about our own class reps. The two frontrunners were not only at the top of the junior class, but two ex-best friends with a shared former girlfriend turned campaign manager and a whole lot of bones to pick with one another. Bronwyn said I was her first choice, but I suspect that's not true, she just didn't want to burden Porter, who…always had a lot going on, inside and out.

Like most everyone else, I admired Jude Cuthbert and feared her. Even before the election, she swaggered around the school in a way no one else could pull off. After President Dickhead was elected, she added slim-cut pantsuits that looked custom made just for her petite but somehow still lanky bod. The effect was stunning.

But I saw how she looked down on people like me, with ponytails that looked perky even outside the gym and well-developed calf muscles. She saw cheerleaders as unfocused, empty-headed, throwing our money at short skirts and goals that made no sense. Jude didn't have to tell me this. I was familiar with that contempt.

The tarot reading was my idea.

"You think she'll fall for it?' Bronwyn asked me when I proposed the plan. Her olive green eyes had a light in them I hadn't seen in a while, her round face open with both suspicion and intrigue. I was ready with an answer.

I leaned back on my nubby blue bedspread, running my fingers over the worn ridges. "I think she'll want to show off to her crew that she thinks it's all bullshit," I answered before glancing over at Bronwyn, who was lying next to me. "I also think she'll be curious but not wanting to let on, so she'll bite."

"Amazing." Bronwyn shook her head, rolling on her side to face me. "I was the one who hung out with her all these years, but you've summed her up to a T. How do you read people so well, Cass?"

I smiled. That was my secret.

Except for at cheer, I've always preferred blending into the woodwork. Even when you think about that expression, woodwork is way more interesting than people give it credit for. All those grains and layers—think of the rings that show a tree's age. And when it comes down to it, walls are what protect us, keep us safe. Blending into the woodwork is highly underrated.

Especially when it comes to learning about people. It's downright stunning what goes down in the girls' bathroom when the juniors and seniors think you're too much of a nobody to acknowledge. Just by keeping my ponytailed head down and washing my hands a little longer than the suggested thirty seconds, I learned enough about the inner workings of Augustus High to fill a book.

Bronwyn might not have had that skill set, but it's why I was useful to her. And I loved feeling useful.

The party swelled like they always did, or like they had since I started going to them, that is. Bronwyn might have been an outcast, but she still had enough clout that no one side-eyed her presence too much, especially with Porter by her side. As people quaffed trash can punch and gossiped about everything from Molly O'Brien's supposed abortion to whatever cute thing Mr. Roman did in the hallway this week, the three of us set a trap.

After finding enough space on a black leather couch to squeeze in, I brought out my cards and handed them to Porter to shuffle. He returned them to me with a sheepish grin and I smiled back before laying out three cards in front of him and Bronwyn. I wasn't really paying attention to what these ones said, it was just for show.

"So the major arcana is *here*," I began, when Jude strutted up to the couch, holding her red Solo cup as delicately as a champagne flute.

"The Three Musketeers," she murmured. Jude's short, five one in flats, I'd guess, but since she was standing and we were sitting, she was able to look down her nose at us. Even though I was pretending to ignore her, I could feel a blush spread over my face. Hey, I'm a cheerleader, not an actress.

"You sound like a supervillain. A cheesy one," Bronwyn retorted, never taking her eyes off me. She reached for Porter's hand and squeezed it. I saw Jude's ice blues turn into slits.

"Are you telling *fortunes*?" Jude asked, turning her steely gaze to me and flipping her short dark hair so I could see her fresh undercut. I took an *ujjayi* breath like my friend Morgan and I would do before comps, in through the nose and exhaling through my closed mouth like Darth Vader. Even without her pantsuit, in skinny jeans and a She-Hulk tee, Jude Cuthbert radiated power. Opposite me, I saw my cousin tense. Bronwyn wanted to project that power too, but as Jude's longtime also-ran, she hadn't quite gotten the hang of it.

That's where I came in.

"It's not fortunes, exactly." I willed the tremor out of my voice as I glanced up at Jude. "Tarot reflects back what's going on with the individual. What they're dealing with. It's open to interpretation more than anything. I'm still learning." All of this was true.

"Practicing on your cuz and the Pleaser." Jude smirked. "Sweet."

"She could do you," Bronwyn said, standing up and pulling Porter with her. "Cass does my readings all the time at home. She's really good at this." Even though we'd planned more or less this exact dialogue, her praise made me feel warm inside. I hoped it was real.

Jude folded her arms across her small chest, tipped her chin up at Bronwyn. "I know I'm going to win this election, Bronny. I don't need your cousin's cards to tell me."

Bronny. What Jude used to call her. No one else was allowed to.

Around us, the chatter silenced.

For a moment, Bronwyn didn't speak. Poor Porter looked like a deer in headlights. I willed my cousin not to back down. *I know she threw you off just then. But you have to be ready. She's a goddamn shark.*

People like Jude think cheerleaders are stupid. Still. They have no idea how we learn to size each other up when we're too young to know what that even means. Who's been doing the most push-ups. Who can lift and throw the highest, flip over the most times in the air. Who will let a twisted ankle at practice take them down and who will win championship on a broken back.

It's not too different from politics, in that way.

Then the fog on Bronwyn's face cleared, and she shrugged. "You do you, JC," she said to Jude. "C'mon, love," she murmured to Porter, kissing him right on the lips and leading him away. The look she gave me over her shoulder was brief, but the message was clear.

Fuck her up.

I gave the tiniest, most imperceptible nod. *Ready. Okay.*

"Sit," I said to Jude. The party volume resumed, the confrontation visibly over. I could almost hear everyone's sigh of relief tinged with disappointment there hadn't been actual bloodshed. I was on my own now, and I patted the spot in front of me, where the imprint of Bronwyn's ass was still visible on the leather.

She plopped down, slinging an arm over the top of the couch, taking up all the space that Bronwyn and Porter had shared. "Tell me something, Cass." Jude glanced over her shoulder, where Bronwyn and Porter were now holding their own cups, laughing about something. "When do you think she's gonna break out of that phase?"

I concentrated on reassembling my deck. The edges were fast becoming soft and worn from use and felt comforting against my fingers. "I think that's on my cousin, not me."

I wasn't going to take the "phase" bait like I knew Jude wanted me to. I still didn't get why she took Bronwyn's relationship with Porter so personally. Then again, I'd barely been kissed and was still figuring out who and what I liked. At this point I wasn't even sure who and what I *didn't* like, which mostly made me feel like even more of a freak. Kids at Augustus knew exactly who they were, and had since birth, it seemed. No margin of error, no room for gray areas. Got lonely.

Jude was still looking at Bronwyn and Porter, now holding hands and having one of those couple conversations where you can tell they feel like they're the only people in the room, even when everyone's getting drunk around them. For a second, I saw the slightest tinge of hurt cross her face. It was gone so fast, though, I might have hallucinated it. All the pot smoke in the air could have given me a contact high. I was still getting used to parties.

"Anyway," she said, turning back to me. "Do your thing."

I didn't dare look around for Bronwyn and Porter, but I knew wherever they were, they were watching. Observing me instead of the other way around. If I pulled this off, I'd truly be one of the three.

"Okay." I handed Jude the deck of cards. Despite the high stakes, I was feeling a little more confident now that we were officially underway. I knew something the great Jude Cuthbert didn't. "Shuffle these."

"Why don't you do it?" She tipped her chin at me.

"Because this way your energy's in them and I can give you a more accurate reading," I explained. "Shuffle, then cut the deck three times." Now Jude looked genuinely confused. "Split it into three separate stacks," I clarified, and she nodded.

My mother named me Cassandra on purpose. Before deciding on

nursing school, she'd told me, she considered going to school to study the classics, especially Greek mythology. Cassandra, the seer and the prophet, was always her favorite. Even though most of what Cassandra predicted was pretty freaking scary and understandably, no one really wanted to hear what she had to say.

"Why'd you name me something so dark?" I asked her then.

My mom pinched the bridge of her nose. I knew she wasn't impatient with me or anything, just tired from yet another graveyard shift in a wing where kids died. She leaned her head in her hand, gave me a sideways smile. "Wishful thinking, I guess. I want you to always know what's coming to you."

I've never been psychic or anything, no sixth sense and my boobs can't tell when it's going to rain. I don't even know why I googled "tarot" one random night last year, when my body was screaming at me from a double workout and even a hot shower and arnica gel weren't doing the magic they usually did. But ten minutes later, I was tiptoeing into Mom's room and begging for her credit card so I could order my first deck.

I had three. One just for me, one for me and special people like Bronwyn and Porter, and this one, which was new. It was simple, purple and gold and traditional, but gave off a more serious vibe. One I was hoping to project in tarot and in life.

Three stacks sat between me and Jude Cuthbert. Facedown. Even if she lost interest now, these were the most words we'd ever exchanged.

"I'm going to do a basic spread with you," I explained, wheels turning with what remained of the plan. "You can do more elaborate ones like the Celtic Cross, which would break down your entire situation." Around us, someone cranked up the bass and the floor started vibrating. I raised my voice to the level I usually only used for cheer. "But this one is just three cards. Your past, your present, and your future." I'd been concentrating on my deck, split into three, purple and gold winking up at me in the dim light, but now I looked up at Jude.

I thought she'd be rolling her eyes, so over this hippie-dippie bullshit. Or at the very least smirking at the dumb sophomore who didn't belong at the cool-people party and probably still smelled like the gym.

Instead, Jude's eyes were dead serious as they gazed into mine. Personally, I'd never felt drawn in by Jude Cuthbert. Intimidated, sure. But I never *got* how she could pull all of Augustus High under her spell.

Until that moment.

"Anyway." My voice cracked, and I swallowed hard before trying again. "I'm going to take one from each pile. Let's see what you're dealing with."

Then she put her hand on mine.

I wasn't expecting that.

"Hey." Her voice was low, urgent. I had to lean in to make out the next part, not just because of the cacophony around us, but because Jude's eyes were darting around and she was quiet. She didn't want anyone else to hear what she was about to say.

"Am I really going to win this?"

I looked for her telltale smirk, a joking light in her eyes. Played those six words back in my head, hunting for sarcasm. Nothing.

"I know she's your cousin," Jude said hastily. "I just…" She trailed off, and for the briefest moment I saw the same expression she'd worn when she watched Bronwyn kiss Porter. Not lovestruck. More lost. Hurt.

For the briefest possible moment, I questioned my own loyalty.

Then I lifted my chin. "In general, when you ask a question like that, you already know the answer."

"Fuck yeah I do," she said, grinning. The bravado was back. I had to refrain from rolling my eyes.

Slowly and deliberately, I set out the three cards. I had to make this count. For all of us.

"Three of swords," I said, tapping the first one. "You've had heartbreak in your past. Maybe…something recent?"

Jude rolled her eyes. "This is *high school*. Who hasn't?" I could tell I was losing her. She tipped her chin to the next one. "This is my present, huh?"

"Seven of swords." I concentrated on the design. These were handmade by a woman in Idaho who ran an online group called Witches' U. I didn't want Jude touching them anymore. It seemed disrespectful to this artist, who genuinely believed.

"Four more than three," she cracked. "So, more heartbreak?"

I shook my head. "More like deception. Betrayal." This time, I couldn't help but raise an eyebrow at Jude Cuthbert. "Sound familiar?"

Her eyes slit. "Your cousin did that to herself."

Someone coughed, and I looked up from our place on the couch. Apparently, my little reading had drawn a crowd. The music wasn't even playing anymore.

I thought about running. Forgoing the stupid plan, quitting my campaign manager post, getting away from all this bullshit. Running suicides, doing full push-ups, crunching until my abs begged for mercy—all the conditioning I hated but loved at the same time because it meant I got to be a part of something so much bigger than myself. What was I doing here, anyway?

Then I saw Bronwyn and Porter near the back of the crowd. Bronwyn half-smiled the way she'd done since we were toddlers. Porter gave me a discreet thumbs-up like the dork he was, the dork who made my cousin a real person and not some unattainable goal.

I turned back to Jude, gestured to the third card. Her future.

"Thank God it's not death, right?" she cracked, but I could hear a nervous tinge to her voice.

I shrugged, focusing on the deck, cool as a kid in a CW show about polyamorous teens where the cast is actually in their twenties. "Common misconception. The death card is more about new beginnings, but you do you."

Then I focused in on the card. Took a deep breath, and I swear the teenage drunkards around me did the same. I leaned in but made sure everyone could hear me.

"This is the Tower," I told Jude. "See how the lightning strikes it?" I pointed out the exquisite illustration, ran my finger up and down the painstakingly rendered bolts. "This one represents falling down. Collapse." I met her eyes. "Ruin." Leaning back against the arm of the couch, I didn't break my gaze. "But if the foundation's really bad, maybe the tower needs to, you know." I gave her my best cheer smile and enunciated the next two words for all they were worth. "Come down."

Silence.

Everyone was looking at Jude, to see how the junior class's reigning power lesbian would react to the sophomore nobody telling her she was in for a world of hurt.

Her face was unreadable. For a minute I worried she'd lean across the cards and slap me. Not that I couldn't take her, physically, but socially…I saw what she'd done to Bronwyn.

Instead, however, Jude burst out laughing. "Screw this," she said, "and screw you, cheer girl. C'mon, Antonia," she said to Bronwyn's ex, who had somehow materialized by her side. "I need a *drank*."

With that, someone hit Play. Imagine Dragons grooved their way around the room.

Shit.

I gathered up my cards. Then I elbowed my way to my cousin and her boyfriend, but before I could open my mouth and let loose the string of apologies, I was grabbed in a tight hug.

Bronwyn hadn't hugged me since…ever?

"You are a *star*," she breathed in my ear before releasing me, hand still on my arm, keeping me close.

"Uh…" Porter said.

"I'm pretty sure she just told me to fuck off," I said at the same time.

Bronwyn shook her head. "Nope. You scared the crap out of her." Noticing both of us looking dumbfounded, she leaned in closer to be heard over Billie purring about bad guys. "Look, no one knows Jude Cuthbert better than I do. I saw her face. And when she protests that much…" She trailed off before breaking into a full-on grin. "You guys feeling like blowing this Popsicle stand? McDonald's on me?"

The warmth of approval flooded through my body, but I tried not to look too ecstatic. "I could use some nuggets. Porter?"

He nodded, then grinned at me, held out his hand for a low-five. Oh, straight boys. "Good job." Bronwyn grinned at him as if he'd just done Euclidean geometry.

As we made our way to the door, Bronwyn glanced over at me. "Seriously, Cass, you're a master bullshitter. All that stuff about betrayal and coming down was *amazing*."

I smiled. We made our way to Bronwyn's Jeep—the one remaining token of her former life, as her dads had paid for it up-front—hit the drive-through, and chowed our Extra Value Meals before I begged off to bed (early practice) and the two of them went to Bronwyn's bedroom to do God knows what.

But I couldn't sleep.

It hadn't, after all, gone according to plan.

Here's the thing. I was going to make it all up. No matter what cards Jude drew, no matter what her energy-shuffled cut was *actually* telling me? I was supposed to spout a bunch of lies about how her downfall was coming. It's not like she, or anyone at the party, would know what the cards really meant, and even the really nosy ones would be too drunk to google.

Not exactly in the spirit of the tarot. At all. But I figured this was for a good cause.

Instead, I'd given her a real reading. I hadn't meant to. Those were the cards she had drawn, the ones that were supposed to reflect her situation, her arcanas.

Heartbreak.

Betrayal.

Downfall.

I didn't have the heart to tell Bronwyn and Porter that it was an actual, real reading I didn't mean to give. Jude was scared, hopefully paranoid, I'd messed with her the way we wanted. In that way, the plan had worked.

But now, I couldn't sleep.

What would happen to Jude Cuthbert?

And was I a part of it?

I gotta jump off this video call now. Practice. And if I'm being honest, I need to run around the track a few times.

Even now, it's hard to think about what I did.

CHAPTER THREE

Bronwyn

As I'm sure you remember, I got what I wanted.

And then it all went sideways.

Wanna hear a random anecdote? You can cut it out later if you want.

I remember getting my first pair of contacts in eighth grade, after a solid year of begging my dads, them finally giving in for my fourteenth birthday. The optometrist wouldn't let me leave until I could put them in by myself. It took a few tries and more than a few frustrated grunts I suppressed as best I could, with both Pop and Dad in the waiting room. I didn't want the eye doctor to think I was a baby, even though this was a random LensCrafters and I'd probably never see him again.

Once I was successful and they finally settled on my eyeballs like they were supposed to, though, my newly fourteen-year-old mind was officially blown. It wasn't just that everything in front of me—the sink for washing my hands before and after, the bottles of free sample contact solution, the doctor's bespectacled round mug—were finally clear. More so, I noticed my peripheral vision was now sharply, starkly clear. The door on the side of the room, the windows peeking into the lab, were practically pulsating at me. It was like I had a superpower.

After we did…what we did, everything came sharply into focus.

At that point I wished for blurrier vision. If I'd had it, maybe the three of us would still be playing Exploding Kittens and picking at that disgusting carpet instead of hiding vodka bottles like a drunk middle-aged woman in an HBO series. Maybe I would sleep at night instead of lying still and praying Porter was having good dreams. Maybe Cass's brow wouldn't have been perpetually furrowed instead of a mask of smooth concentration.

If we'd hit Delete instead of Send then, maybe I wouldn't see myself so clearly now.

From Porter Kendrick's journal (the one page he filled out before forgetting about it)

Hey, Porter, it's Porter.

This is such balls. My therapist—or at least, two therapists ago—says it'll help me to write myself notes from the future. Or, as she said with a wink like isn't she one of the cool kids, *texts* from the future. I don't bother to tell her that unless you're my girlfriend Bronwyn, texts are usually around two lines. Until Bronwyn and I got together I didn't *know* texts could be more than two lines.

But whatever. I'll pretend this is a text.

If I'm writing myself a text from the future, I guess I want Bronwyn to be president? I mean, I want her to be happy. I've never had a girlfriend like her before. Bronwyn has ideas. I get that. I want her to use them on the whole world.

What I want for myself is harder. I don't have the clear goals Bronwyn and Cass do. They've got their eyes on the shiny trophies and the perfect résumés and staying on top. I wouldn't say I wish Future Porter had no bipolar. It's part of what makes me, me. I always want to manage it better, but I don't want to get rid of it. Then I'd be even more of a blank slate.

I guess what I want Future Porter to know is what Future Porter wants for himself. Because right now, Future Porter has no fucking clue.

Chapter Four

Bronwyn

How do I explain Porter Kendrick?

I have to go back to before Porter. BP. Or Pre-Porter, PP. Whatever, you're the one writing this.

I'm not sure how much you know about my dads, considering the lawyers kept most everything out of the news. So this might take a while.

Everything fell apart at once for me. Everything. One morning, I was grabbing a granola bar en route to my morning Starbucks run, same as always. I might have yelled "bye" when I slammed out of the house, but definitely not "I love you." We weren't an "I love you" household anyway. Not like Cass and her mom, who practically say it in between bathroom trips.

Years later, I call it the day the bottom dropped out. When you lose everything, you can't help but think of it in terms of clichés. Maybe someday, for me at least, that'll make it hurt less.

School was its usual blur of pop quizzes and boring lectures. A little extra worry that permeated the air nowadays. This was before the election, and we were still *pretty* sure she was going to win, but the energy even on social media was…aggressive. And that second debate was straight-up scary, the stuff the male candidate was proposing while people in baseball caps cheered. But other than calling our congresspeople, donating to Planned Parenthood, and side-eyeing our male classmates even more often than we had before, we still weren't sure what to do.

This is before the student government frenzy took hold, by the way.

That day, I got home from school and saw police cars outside.

I can't tell you what I said, except I remember thinking my parents were dead. A car crash, maybe? Or something more sinister like one of those crime podcasts the girls in my lit class loved but I could never get into? Was *I* going to be on a podcast now?

No one was dead, it turned out. My pop, who'd provided the big bucks for the house, the Jeep Grand Cherokees, the life we all loved, had been embezzling and insider trading and about every other white-collar money-grabbing offense you can imagine. Despite the highest profile lawyer he could find, Pop didn't have a leg to stand on. My oldest brother, Dylan, was already living on his own all the way in Colorado, wife and family, didn't affect him much. My other brother John was at University of Michigan and had to scramble for financial aid. Got his first-ever job that was actually to pay the bills and not teach him a lesson about money. But at least he has an apartment that Pop paid for in full as a graduation gift. A place to call his own.

That left me, the baby; and Dad, the college professor. Who immediately took a sabbatical from the one class he was teaching—I don't even know how he did it that fast—and took off for the Appalachian Trail. Supposedly something he'd always wanted to do, though I'd never heard him talk about it. I wasn't sure he'd even read *Wild* or seen the movie. Now all I got was the occasional postcard in chicken scratch handwriting, reminding me to keep my grades up.

Here's what I knew: I was closer to Dad (the house husband) than Pop (the breadwinner).

I'm the youngest. My older brothers are straight, I should mention that, I'm the lone queer offspring. Anyway, they live in different states, we only see them on holidays if that. I have vague memories of one swinging me above his head while I giggled. The other always let me have M&Ms when Dad wasn't looking. Then they went to boarding school, then college, their own lives. We barely feel like siblings, and there was never a question of my moving in with them when…it all went down.

My dad, mostly stay at home, I said that.

My pop, though. He made all the money. And there was a lot of it. He *worked* in money, as a financial planner. And not one of those strip mall types. Pop had a corner office, downtown in the city, where all of the big deals work. You know those guys on MSNBC, CNN, or Fox—ugh—telling people to invest their money? Yeah? I was gonna say, if you don't, your parents probably do.

I hope they didn't listen to him, is all I can say.

So yeah, I never questioned why we all had our own wings of our gigantic house, why I had my own credit card at ten. Why Dad didn't have to work at all. Why *I* didn't have to work at all, not even for the semblance of responsibility like some of our classmates, how their parents, like, foisted jobs or internships on them.

He grew up poor. I knew that much.

I guess that's kinda why he got greedy.

Which leads into what I didn't know: my pop had pretty much always stolen from his clients.

Almost all of them.

Including a family with an autistic daughter who'd trusted him with their life savings.

And before he got caught, he tried to run. Like that morning after he sent me off to school.

Yeah.

Ugh. I swear I didn't know about it. And people asked. Not just police and the SEC, but Augustus people. I think even before I started dating Porter, they were ready for...some excuse. Gotta knock me down from that pedestal, you know?

Anyway, amid the police chaos—they were cutting our mattresses open, in case he left cash there, I guess? No cash, but they found a letter from Dad to me.

Essentially pouring his heart out like I was some sort of emotional support human. Not his only daughter. His pride and joy. The one he drove to SAT prep, three different times, and piano lessons and piled leaves on me when I was little and every time I'd pop up and he'd shriek and we'd both laugh our asses off.

Turns out, he was resentful AF for having to stay home all those years, only working as an adjunct professor on occasion. Talk about a shit job, little pay and even less respect. Pop had "encouraged" him to not work, and really "encouraged" meant threatened, almost. Not like, abuse, but control. And now he was broke and I was almost grown and...I'll never forget the way he closed out the note:

"You get it, kid. Right? I need a break from all of this."

How's that for a kicker?

Then I had two cop cars following me and my Jeep to Cass's house.

I'm sorry, her *garage.* Converted, but still. Where I would be living for the foreseeable future.

I still think about that family, with the autistic daughter. I want to apologize, send them cash I don't have, or a lifetime supply of her favorite ice cream or something. Provided they don't want to murder me in my sleep.

But what, exactly, would that accomplish?

Daddio, I don't get a break from *any* of this, but have fun in the wild I guess.

That's what I would've texted him.

I wish I could remember more of this weird time, for my eventual memoir if nothing else. Even now I couldn't tell you what it's like to have the bottom drop out in the span of a school day, between the first granola bar and the forgotten afternoon snack. Between the a.m. Starbucks run and the p.m. Crown Vic you'd never seen outside of an elementary school field trip to the local police station that, since it's the burbs, hasn't seen this much action since the one murder took place in 1967.

I couldn't take much with me to Cass's house. Condos of my father's associates where I'd spent glittery but boring Christmas parties had more room. And when you have a couple of hours at most to pack, the sheer amount of *stuff* looks an awful lot like trash. I got to keep my phone and my car. I took jeans, flannels, and button-downs. What was the point of dressing to impress anymore? I remember running my hands through my perfect bob, thinking I had no choice but to grow my hair out now.

Cass and Aunt Deb, they tried in those early days to make the garage a home. They found a double bed with the thinnest possible mattress, a worn quilt my great-grandma had made. Because this was considered the wrong side of the tracks, but still a fancy suburb, the garage was heated. And the house was small so I didn't have to go far to pee or shower.

But still. A garage. I might slip up later and call it my room, but don't forget: garage.

This was where Pop's stealing, his hubris in believing he'd never get caught, had landed his only daughter, his pride and joy who was supposed to be the next great hope, after two handsome but decidedly mediocre sons.

His words, I swear, not mine.

Then there were my aunt and cousin, who I'd barely spent any time with since I was a little kid and Pop's major job I never quite understood, took off and we moved to a better neighborhood. Our high school was magnet, so I saw Cass there when she hit ninth grade, but she wasn't the star student, super involved in activities, the way I was.

Cass was, is, a cheerleader. Her and Aunt Deb's house is a shrine to perky bows and cheap plastic trophies with that horrible fake gold. Pictures of Cass at every age hang all over the walls, my cousin grinning while wearing tiny, pleated skirts in a rainbow of colors and more lipstick than JonBenét Ramsey. At least she didn't wear those fake teeth things like little kids in beauty pageants.

To say my dads didn't laugh at that would be a barefaced lie.

I get it now, why she spent most of her waking hours at the gym that housed her club team, why she spent all her time perfecting stunts and yells and choreography for a sports team that didn't exist, why the fridge almost overflowed with ice packs she'd alternate with heat. Back then, Cass was the former playmate I didn't understand, the lowly sophomore who didn't party and who did fine grades-wise but didn't really seem to care about being at the top of her class and getting into a prestigious school. We spoke two different languages: mine was GPAs and elaborate answers to essay questions, hers was short, barked commands, sharp gestures and gravity-defying ass-over-head flips.

Though secretly, I envied the fact that she had a mom who hung pictures of her all over the house. We had carefully chosen coordinated family photos whose places in the house were dictated by my parents' decorator Stan, who I'd privately thought of as a dictator because he wouldn't let me hang My Little Pony posters on my bedroom walls when I was little. Cass's mom was devoted to her, but not in a creepy way. I never got the impression she was living out her childhood ambitions through her daughter or anything weird like that. She just seemed…really and truly proud.

As for Aunt Deb, I barely saw her. After spending what was left of her trust fund on Cass's adoption and becoming a nurse, she also took random odd jobs—including an Uber driver, probably for most of our classmates—to help pay for Cass's gym. Apparently, cheerleading was not only a time-sensitive extracurricular, but an expensive one. The Disney print scrubs she wore to cheer up the kids in the cancer ward where she worked took up space in their laundry hampers along with Cass's practice clothes, and soon enough, my flannel shirts.

So yeah, I went from *Gossip Girl, Suburban Style* to *Shameless*. Only without the boisterousness, giant family, and morally ambiguous shenanigans.

Though that last part would come soon enough.

The first few weeks, Cass and I skirted around each other. We never exchanged more words than "Are you done in the bathroom?" or

"Did you eat the last PowerBar?" She still took the bus to school, not that I offered to drive her, or even thought to offer, I'm ashamed to say now. Kind of a weird thing to say about someone who's now my best friend. One of my only friends, really.

On the night after we officially had a new president, she came into my garage room for the first time ever. I was lying on my uncomfortable bed, staring at the ceiling. She lay down with me and squeezed my hand, and we stayed that way for a while. But the next day, we went back to school and cheer and pretending we weren't roommates. Business as usual.

Really, Porter brought me and Cass together.

It's not like he was new to Augustus High. He'd been there since the first day of first year, had tested into the school in eighth grade and won a coveted spot. Porter was smart as hell just like all of us, even though his grades were up and down sometimes. Rode the bus just like Cass until he got his own car. His mom was a nurse too, but psychiatric, changed her career from teaching when he was little and banging his head against the wall. My mom was a surrogate from Florida, who'd also given birth to my brothers and had a huge family of her own.

Sometimes I wondered what it would be like, having a mom like Aunt Deb, who took extra jobs so Cass could cheer as much as she wanted. Or like Porter's mother, who made his mental health her priority, which wasn't always easy, and he knew it too. Even Jude's mom, the country club queen, was dedicated to her daughter in her own way, ensuring she'd be successful and confident. I knew my dads loved me, or I thought they did until the bottom dropped out, but mom-love seemed...different. Special.

Anyway, I was aware of Porter the way you are with something in your peripheral vision, or like the thing you put on the coffee table and always mean to take up to your room but you forget until it basically becomes part of the scenery. You know? An object you notice, but not really.

Until one night shortly after the bottom dropped out, when I hardly knew Cass at all and hadn't bothered to change that, when Jude and I were still friends, and Antonia and I were together. When I was secure in my queerness and I understood Jude's mission to bring back the lesbian label and all the power it held, thanks to our foremothers in the lavender mafia.

It was after the national election, and the shitshow of an inauguration. We were holding court at a party, as usual. I don't even remember who was hosting, it all ran together in those days. Probably talking politics, how our beloved candidate had fucked off into the woods after losing the electoral vote, and who could blame her, really?

I was listening to Jude talk about how it was more important than ever that the student body president be a girl. A girl who loved other girls. Naturally, we were all in agreement. We always agreed with Jude, but to be fair, she was usually right. And how could you *dis*agree with the concept of queer representation in leadership?

Student government was largely bullshit, of course, and we knew it. The adults, frustratingly, held all the power when it came to school stuff that mattered. But we could make a *statement*, Jude said, about *representation*. Why not use everything we had at our disposal, and start with some bullshit office that usually went unopposed? Even figureheads mattered right now, and we could start setting an example for other schools in rural areas that weren't nearly as progressive as Augustus. All it would take was a couple of stunts that went viral and we could make closeted kids feel less alone, inspire out kids to be the change at their own schools.

Later, Jude would bring up this very party and accuse me of stealing her ideas. (What she didn't know was that our almost-prez had been a student body president too. In college, not high school, but still. When I found that out in a random Google search when election grief was still fresh, I could feel the seed of the idea implant in my brain.) Pinpoint what happened next for my defection, as she called it. Jude got old-school Soviet when she was especially upset. Of course, she wasn't saying anything we all didn't already know, but that's Jude Cuthbert. If she spins an argument a certain way, or publicly has an idea, it's hers forever. Her own personal copyright.

But I'm getting ahead of myself.

As Jude spoke, spinning a tale of lesbian-led peace and harmony everywhere, her blue eyes glowed, and as I stood listening, my arm around Antonia, feeling my girlfriend's warm, bare shoulder under my hand, I was rapt as any little first-year. Jude made you hang on to every one of her words for dear life.

"Yeah. I agree."

I have a low voice. I mean, you know that now by talking to me, but since you're going to be writing this down, I assume, I should probably describe it, huh? Rough and scratchy, though I've never smoked a cigarette in my life. I got teased a bunch in grade school, before I tested into Augustus High, with its mostly nonmale population.

Jude had always told me it was distinctive, a thing of beauty. In ninth grade, everyone else seemed to back her up on that.

I guess you know this now too, but Porter's tone is only about an octave lower than mine, but smooth as an old-school radio DJ's. (My pop was still a fan of the Sirius oldies shows, which is where most of those dudes are living out the rest of their days.) The syllables, the way he drew them out, were tentative but confident. Breaking into this group of power queers, he had to be.

All of us glanced over, confused by this curly-topped guy, as tall as I was. He hadn't talked over anyone, merely asserted his agreement, but it was unusual he'd approached us all the same. Our heads swiveled back to our fearless leader, to see how she'd react.

Jude didn't leave us in suspense. Rolling her eyes and scoffing, she took a glug of her beer, muscles of her throat moving, delicate but strong, like a ballet. "You agree, huh?" she said once she'd swallowed. "If you're trying to get laid, Pleaser, you're at the wrong party."

Ah yes. *Pleaser.* That nickname.

Porter Kendrick was quiet. Solidly in the middle of our class, mostly kept to himself. But he had a nickname, and a rep among the straight girls. Let's just say he didn't earn that nickname from sucking up to teachers. We had no idea whether the rumors were true or whether one girl had just had a *really* good experience, and we didn't really care. Cishet guys weren't in our orbit.

This time, though, Porter didn't back down. "Not trying to get laid," he said. "Just a hard agree."

Then he smiled and faded back into the crowd, taking a sip from his Coke. The Pleaser, as I'd soon learn, didn't drink because it interfered with his meds.

And something happened to me.

Even now I'm not sure I can explain.

My whole life, heterosexual was never the default. I realize that's a world away from most of our very backwards culture, where kids get kicked out of their own homes every day for being queer and trans. And it's not just in the small farm towns you'd expect. That crap is everywhere. Jude and I ended up disagreeing on a lot, but we're still in sync about the important things, mainly that people should be who they are without fear.

Well. According to Jude, that doesn't apply to people like me. But I'll get to that.

I grew up with two gay dads who were open about where me and my brothers came from. They were legally married. Nothing shady about coming from a surrogate and the adoption that followed. Even though I wondered about having a mother, I never wished for anything more than what I had. I didn't even have to come out. My brothers liked girls and so did I. If anything, I think my dads were disappointed that only *one* of their kids was gay.

Maybe it's better they weren't around to see what happened next.

That night, after Antonia and I had our usual post-party sex in their car and they dropped me off at Cass's house—my new reality—I didn't go right to sleep. Something bugged me about Porter's storm-gray eyes, and that smile that seemed to take over his whole face. So open.

Where did he get off?

I went over that brief conversation, one that hadn't even involved me, again and again in my mind, going over every syllable. Jude, being Jude, had laughed it off, a guy who didn't deserve a voice having the audacity to agree with her. He wasn't in her orbit, so he didn't matter.

And he hadn't done anything wrong, not like some of the guys in our class, who had previously been deferential but now that the Titty Grabber in Chief was in office seemed to hold a new sort of power that was scary. Like before, they'd been in check, but now they believed they could run the world. Talking over the female teachers, strutting around the hallways with their teenage-boy chests puffed out like roosters, that kind of thing. Our crowd wasn't bothered, but I knew some of the straight girls were.

And secretly, it was the first time at Augustus High that I was afraid a guy would grab my ass out of nowhere, that I'd go from feeling totally safe to completely violated in the span of a microsecond, with the touch of just one hand.

But Porter had been respectful. Said his piece and fucked off like a good boy. So why couldn't I stop thinking about that smile?

I think even then, I knew why. Just didn't want to admit it to myself. Even then, I knew what that would mean.

I woke up with my sheets twisted around me like vines in a fairy tale and the usual Sunday morning hangover. Realized I was still clutching my phone, which was now cool to the touch, its battery drained. Again, nothing out of the ordinary, as I often fell asleep texting. Only today, something was different, and while my pop was having breakfast on a tray or whatever they do in white-collar prison and my dad was cooking beans or whatever they do on hiking trails, I was barging into the house that still didn't feel like mine knocking on Cass's doorframe.

She looked up, dark brown eyes wide, from where she was sitting at her desk with a deck of cards with weird drawings on them.

"Hey," I said, hesitantly. This was new for both of us. "Starbucks? My treat."

I knew my cousin very little, but I could practically hear her thoughts: *Bronwyn, who's said fuck-all to me since she moved in here, wants to take me out for coffee?*

But Cass is a much nicer person than I am, so she shrugged and said, "Sure, why not?"

There he was again, standing behind the counter in a green apron and a name tag festooned with, of all things, tiny stickers that looked like kittens. "Hey, Bronwyn," Porter said, and there was that smile again.

Fuck.

"I'm Cass," said my cousin, standing up straight like she always did. "Bronwyn's cousin."

"Cheerleader, right? I saw you doing those…flip things after gym. Tight." What?

Here was *my* contribution to this conversation:

"Uhhhhhh."

So much for two years of debate team.

Now they were both staring at me. "Bronwyn?" Cass said. "You want anything?" Oh great, so apparently she'd ordered and I was standing there with my mouth open like a psycho.

"Venti iced coffee, unsweetened, almond milk," I managed to mumble before brandishing my credit card that, thankfully, still worked.

"Good to see you." Now he was looking right at me.

I felt a tug on my sweatshirt and realized Cass was basically dragging me to the other side of the counter. Looking over my shoulder, I saw a line had formed behind us. Probably because I was an idiot.

"That was a vibe," said Cass when we were back in the security of my Jeep, my seventeenth birthday present. The best my pop could buy.

I scoffed and rolled my eyes, a perfect imitation of what I'd seen Jude do last night. "I'm hungover, Cass. My reflexes are shit."

She took a long drink of her Frappuccino and set it in the cupholder, fixing her ponytail before regarding me again. "He's really nice."

He's a guy, I wanted to say. *I have a girlfriend. I'm gay.*

"He's okay," was all I said before fitting my key into the ignition and driving us back home in silence.

Bar none, that was the longest conversation Cass and I had had since we were little.

Even though I didn't tell her the worst part until much, much later:

I knew Porter Kendrick worked at that Starbucks.

(*laughs*) That was a long one, huh? I kinda wish we left it at that, and this would be a story about how my life changed so fast and hard, and how I ended up changing fast and hard with it.

But then you wouldn't be interviewing me. Writing a whole damn thesis.

Would you?

CHAPTER FIVE

Porter

No one knows what it's like in my head. Most days, I don't even know.

It's always been this way.

I'm lucky, I know that. I could have been born into a family where no one takes me and my weird-ass brain seriously, or people just yell at me to calm down. Note to everyone: *don't yell at an anxious person to calm down.* It has the opposite effect, even on normal people probably.

Instead, I have a dad who will never understand me—someone who likes card games instead of soccer and who still cries more than what's comfortable—but loves me anyway, and a mom who's a psychiatric nurse and my advocate. And at that point, we were expecting my surprise baby sister.

I mean, my mom went to nursing school because of me! Some days I didn't know what to do with that. My mom's career stemmed from my brain. If that doesn't mess you up, nothing will. I was happy when she and Dad told me she was pregnant. Not just because I'm a softy who had always wanted to be a big brother.

But also, that meant less attention focused on me. More time to get away with anything.

We all know how that turned out.

Even now, I'm a worst-case scenario guy. Not like someone with a bunch of canned food and assault rifles in an underground bunker. More like, I've never known what it's like *not* to worry constantly. I get anxiety attacks at the most random times, when it feels like my head's in one of those medieval torture vises and I can't breathe, and I can barely raise my hand to go to the bathroom where I can feel the judgment of some rando pissing in the urinal. Judgment that might not even exist outside of my own head.

Got my first attack in kindergarten. Good times.

But what we—me, my parents, and all the docs we've seen over the years—discovered was that it wasn't just anxiety. Not that anxiety is *just* anything, but you know what I mean. We cycled through the different ways I'm different, and pretty quickly settled on bipolar II.

Some say they *have* bipolar, and others say they *are* bipolar. I'm in the first camp. It's as much a part of me as the holey T-shirts I really should replace but just love so much. Or the cards with funny names. I used to call myself an unstable unicorn while we were playing that game, but I stopped because I could tell it was making Bronwyn and Cass uncomfortable. And at that point, we were each other's lifelines. We may have pulled some terrible shit, but I don't regret the togetherness.

I don't know what being neurotypical is like. My first memory is of banging my two-year-old head against the wall because my vocabulary was limited to words like "cookie." But the rest of me knew *something was very wrong.*

I'm even lucky. A lot of folks with bipolar II are misdiagnosed for years, decades even, but aside from one antidepressant that briefly made me suicidal, I'd been on the right path since I hit puberty. In fact, most people at Augustus High would have bought my pills off me if, you know, I didn't need them.

Junior year, some of them had an effect that doesn't go well with having a regular girlfriend, which may be the meds or may be in my head, but I didn't know the difference because I was way too embarrassed to ask my doctor or, God freaking forbid, my own mother.

With Bronwyn, I faked a confidence I didn't feel, at first. I'd been aware of her since we were first-years, but that's not anything special. *Everyone* knew Bronwyn St. James, the queer queen of our class, second in command only to Jude Cuthbert, who everyone feared more than they loved.

The two of them weren't dating, but they were tight, besties but too cool to use that word. They weren't into student government or anything like that, but they had the best grades and were super active in the LGBTQ+ Alliance. Anyone could tell Augustus High was just a warm-up for Jude, Bronwyn, and their group—eventually, they'd rule the world with iron fists painted like rainbows and we'd all be better for it.

Jude was straight-up scary, but the kind you respected. If she called you out, you shaped up. Who doesn't want that kind of crowd control?

But Bronwyn was different. More accessible. You got the feeling she was the brains behind the whole operation, while Jude was the bluster. Bronwyn St. James was the fixer, like in any movie with a mob hit or a high-stakes bank heist. She got shit *done.*

And she looked good doing it. Tall with that blond hair that always looked messy in a way that you could tell she'd engineered every strand. Her hair bent to her will and didn't stand a chance against the force that was Bronwyn St. James. Her green eyes looked straight out of a Disney movie—you could see her long eyelashes when she slow-blinked at some guy's idiocy, which was often. Her mouth turned down perpetually like a sad clown's. And the way she moved through the halls, like she knew she was the shit but didn't have to prove anything, unlike Jude, who constantly seemed to overcompensate.

I was a goner from day one.

So pathetic. Bronwyn didn't date cis guys. How does a dude in worn T-shirts and jeans compete with Antonia Marcus? Even if Tone weren't so stunning, I was a straight guy pining after a gay girl, like *Chasing Amy* but without the misogyny.

Have you watched that movie? Good. Don't. Ever.

After the election, they all openly hated on straight guys, which pissed off most of the guys I knew. I got it, though. Douchebag in Chief never met a skinny blonde he didn't want to fuck, including his own daughter. Anyone online would tell you about the uptick in racist and sexist microaggressions and aggression-aggressions too. I may be a straight white guy with a broken brain, but I'm not stupid.

It even started happening at our school. I wasn't really close to anyone, but guys I'd previously said 'sup to were now openly commenting on girls' asses. Wondering if a trans sophomore would finally pick a side. It was gross, and yet I didn't have the spine to speak up. I'd just roll my eyes and walk away. Later, Bronwyn would say I was part of the problem. She was right.

That night at the party, though, I'd promised myself to do better. When I overheard Jude talking about representation, I was careful. I didn't want to talk over her, just show my support. Evidently, I did it wrong and she laughed at me like always.

Then Bronwyn and I locked gazes and something clicked.

If we were on some bad teen drama where high school is nothing like the real deal, this is when the song would cue up. The one you couldn't get out of your head after the episode was over and would later download and stream over and over. And while you listened, you'd dream about having that moment with someone too.

Then she showed up at Starbucks, and if I hadn't been a goner before, I sure as hell was now. Could barely make her cousin's Frappuccino.

Even looking back, even knowing what comes next, I still can't believe my luck.

CHAPTER SIX

Bronwyn St. James: Candidate Speech Draft #1

Hello, Augustus High. My name is Bronwyn St. James, and I'm campaigning for next year's student body president. I was a 4.0 student until my grades took a hit when my dad was arrested and my other dad fucked off to go hiking. I was also heavily involved in the LGBTQ+ Alliance before my opponent, Jude Cuthbert, told everyone I was a slut and blacklisted me. That was after she stuffed my locker with condoms, by the way. Never mind that there's a B in LGBTQ. In Jude's world, I'm a traitor.

Okay, I'll level with you. I don't know if I'm bisexual, if I'm queer, or what. Probably bi? I'm not straight, but that's not an answer so much as it only leads to more questions. I'm starting to think I'll never get sexuality right. Isn't the point of a better world that we don't have to constantly explain who we are?

Because this is more than about who I'm dating. That might be the most outside indicator, but I've never been sure in my sexuality the way everyone else here seems to be. I'm not saying I want people to go back in the closet or be scared of their own selves because they're constantly being told by their parents or church or whoever that they're not okay. Can you be okay and still not know everything about yourself? I hope so.

We're taught to be badasses. Look around you: superheroes are everywhere, and they're not just boys anymore. I know that's supposed to be a good thing, and it is. Mostly.

But what if you don't feel kickass twenty-four seven? What if you're scared and confused more often than not? What if your life's been upended, everything from the people you call your family, to the roof over your head, to the person you're starting to think you love even though you make no sense on paper, and even stranger, you suspect that even if nothing in your outside world changed, everything on the inside still would?

Who exactly is the superhero for that?

Maybe it could be me.

(Oh God, I can use exactly none of this. I'm not even showing Cass. What a time-wasting puddle of navel-gazing word vomit trash. Next thing you know I'll be keeping a journal instead of running the school.)

CHAPTER SEVEN

Bronwyn

I was the one who came up with student government.

Not student government per se. But it wasn't really a *thing* at Augustus High, just a sad booth at first-year orientation week's activities fair, that you could practically see the dust motes gathering around before it was put away for another, more optimistic year. Even the banner was faded, looked like it was from about 1984.

But sophomore year, something changed in me. For one, it looked like the president of the United States might, for the first time, be a woman. How could you *not* get excited about that? How could you not want to be a part of something much larger than yourself even at the most micro of microlevels? This is back when I had my own wing, when my dads were around, when I was still basking in their carefully curated plans for me, their beliefs that for me, the sky was the limit, and I could do anything. More so than my brothers. I was the most wanted.

I was *special.*

Of all people, it was Jude who laughed off my inspirations.

"Seriously?" she said, leaning against her locker and popping her starched collar like a frat boy in one of those old college movies Pop used to watch when I was little and he thought I'd gone to bed. "Why would you waste your time on like, school dances?" Her latest conquest passed by, a cute little first-year with pink hair that I'd seen talking to my cousin Cass once or twice. Jude winked at her, and the move would have looked cheesy on anyone else, but the girl giggled her way into Mr. Miller's English class.

"Will you focus?" I snapped my fingers at her, and she glared at me, but at least I had her attention again. "It's not, *like*, school dances," I said, imitating her signature drawl that no one could quite figure out considering she was born and raised in the suburbs of Chicago like the rest of us, but was so *Jude* no one could hear her without it. "I mean, right now it's school dances," I corrected myself. "But we could really change things. Big things."

"Like what?" I had half her attention. I'd take it.

"Like, liaising with the PTA to negotiate the amount of homework we have with teachers. Those kids not far from here used to make *suicide pacts* because they were so overwhelmed. Why should that be us? Being busy doesn't guarantee we're going to get into our first-choice colleges, and what if we're so stressed, we don't even *make* it to college?"

Jude raised an eyebrow. "You've thought about this."

I was just getting warmed up. Literally. My jaw started shaking a little bit, the way it only did when I was either very excited or deathly nervous. Maybe I was both. "I hate to sound like a Broadway musical, JC, but there's like…a whole world outside of Augustus. Yeah, we bust our asses to get into college, but then what? People will still have inadequate health care—our president is doing what he can, but there's still so much more. And at the risk of sounding like a hippie, what about the planet? Are people *really* recycling?"

"So join the Earth Club or whatever." Augustus High did, in fact, have an Earth Club. They met after school, often outside, and got stoned when the faculty supervisor left for the day.

"They're doing the groundwork," I lowered my voice, "when they're not smoking up." Jude snorted, but I could tell she was warming up to this. "But the people in power, they're the ones who make the real change." I leaned closer. "That could be *us.*"

I should have led with "power," because there was nothing Jude Cuthbert coveted more. It didn't matter that she had the inherent charm that made her one of the most unintentionally popular (the only acceptable kind) at Augustus. You didn't stay on top by kicking back.

Jude took my hand and we went to Principal Olive Murrell's office.

I always think of her as that: Principal Olive Murrell. Between the crisp suits and Louboutins, she is worthy of three names. Right? You know what I mean. She never lets anyone see her sweat. Except, now that I think about it, in the days after the presidential election. She wore flats instead of her usual heels. Didn't exactly tiptoe around, but seemed to be looking over her shoulder, constantly on guard.

Anyway, a year later, student government was the place to be, to *do.* We did, in fact, negotiate less homework after a series of meetings with parents, teachers, and the Augustus Magnet school board. We got written up in some educational magazine or another, even. A framed copy was in my old room, in pride of place on the wall. I wonder where it is now.

But it's Jude they remember. And at first, I leaned on that. Who better to recruit Augustus High's best and brightest to get shit done? Now, though, I almost wish I'd gone to the principal's office myself. Learned to really speak up without her quite literally holding my hand.

After the bottom dropped out, we got a horrible new president and Jude and I were no longer friends, my thought process went like this:

What's more powerful than president of the whole fucking school?
I want this. I need this.
The only problem is, so does Jude Cuthbert.

CHAPTER EIGHT

Cass

My mom says I've always been fearless.

I don't know about that. But I do know that one of my first memories was standing in our yard—different one than we have now—crunching brown grass under my pink-and-white sneakers as I figured out how to do a back handspring.

I was three years old.

I asked her about it once, when we were driving home from a competition.

And okay, most of what I'm about to tell you is what my mom's told *me*, over the years. Because, again, three years old.

I didn't know it was called a back handspring, of course. I just knew it was the first warm-ish day in a long time and I was finally allowed out to play. My cousin couldn't come over, and I later realized it was because my mom and uncle had had one of their many arguments that caused them not to speak for a while, before starting the whole cycle over again. Mom was doing her nursing homework. So like it usually was, it was just me and the courtyard of our apartment building where there were no other kids my age, only some older boys who would sometimes chase me. But I didn't see them now.

I didn't know it then, but my mom watched me through the window that day, the daughter she'd traveled miles and time zones and spent a crapton of money to bring back from a faraway land. My mom, who didn't have an athletic bone in her soft, squishy body that was perfect for hugs, regarded me in awe. She never hid that.

"I probably should have come outside too," she told me once, driving back from a comp when I was ten. We'd stopped at the McDonald's drive-through. I remember my lipstick, bright red to match our team gear, the same shade as everyone else, making a ring on the straw of my Coke. Looking at that lipstick ring, I felt so grown-up.

This memory's clearer, obviously.

Mom reached into the bag we were sharing, pulled out two long fries, and munched. "That's what any mom would do, right?" she said, more to herself than me. "Get out there and protect you from breaking your neck."

"So why didn't you?" I asked when she handed me a fry. I wasn't mad, just curious.

She looked over at me the way she always did, like she'd just opened the best present ever that she wasn't expecting and couldn't believe her luck. I thought all parents looked at their kids that way back then. "I don't know," Mom said, looking back at the road. "Wait. Yes, I do." She smiled softly, the ribbon of gray highway stretching out before us. "You were so tiny, and yet you clearly had a handle on things. You had that same determined look you get in practice now." She glanced over again and furrowed her brow.

I burst out laughing. "That's what I look like?" I was ten and still a year away from learning what "self-conscious" meant.

Mom nodded thoughtfully, not laughing. "You look strong," she said. "You're going to do what you do, and you don't need anyone's help to get there."

That day, she said, I shivered a little, putting the long sleeves of my purple sweatshirt over my hands like paws, and wondered what it would be like to touch the grass with my hands. Not the normal way, like bending over, but like the girls in *Bring It On*, the movie my mom and I saw on TV, and she later bought for me because I couldn't stop talking about it. The boys and girls throwing each other around and flipping in their colorful outfits were fascinating to me.

I couldn't say why then, but it wasn't just the athletics. They were friends. Part of a group. There was more of them than just two. They didn't have to deal with people who asked why they looked different from their moms, or last names like mine that felt way too fancy, like a princess in a castle instead of an apartment that felt tiny even to a little kid. I guess with my three-year-old logic, I figured I could get there, and I could start with flipping over myself.

That first time, there was just me and the dry grass and my hands and feet, and I had to make them all work together.

I fell down a lot. I remember that much. I could do a standing backbend easily, and it wasn't a big deal to walk over myself until I was upright again. But how to flip? Hop and then throw yourself back, hoping for the best? The ground wasn't soft, and even then I knew to protect my head and what I'd just learned was called my "spine." In later years, every cheer coach I had would compliment those instincts. My current coach John called me Tack, as in "sharp as a." My teammates had another nickname for me. One much less cute.

That day, right before the sun set and Mom called me in for SpaghettiOs, I figured out how to flip over myself.

The next day, Mom googled "cheerleading for three-year-olds" and found me a gym.

I don't know what it's like not to have a goal. A purpose. In that way, I guess I wasn't that different from anyone else at Augustus High. Only instead of wildly expensive colleges that *U.S. News and World Report,* or more likely, their own parents, say are the very best, I had shiny trophies in my sights. Perfect bows. That unmistakable spike of adrenaline when we placed at a national comp. And a college that wasn't Ivy League but would see my potential and throw money at me for it.

At that point I even had a social media following. Cheerlebrities—yeah, that's an actual term—were mostly a thing of the past, but sometimes I posted a pic and got free sneakers. Which was nice because cheerleading is fucking expensive. I modeled new uniforms once in a while. A company sent them, I posted, done.

I didn't love the extra attention, especially from old guys. Some of them had an Asian fetish. Grosser than gross. And that type got even worse after the presidential election. More persistent, like I owed them. I did a lot of blocking, and I didn't tell my mom.

Cheer is my identity, but I'm also not delusional. Even now I'm very aware of how finite the sport is, how every stunt could be my last if I'm not careful. How the "career" span is shorter than that of a professional ballerina's, even.

Here was my plan, sophomore year at Augustus: I'd get a scholarship to a school—or two schools, if I did community college first—with a good team and cheer my ass off while earning my degree for free. And hopefully by the end, I'd have some kind of idea of what I wanted to do next. What that was I wasn't sure, except I knew it wouldn't involve working multiple jobs so my kid could achieve her dream.

My grades were good. I'd studied by the dim glow of our car's back seat and the harsh overhead fluorescence of the gym since I was old enough to have homework at all. Keeping the required GPA for both my club team and Augustus was never an issue. I actually *like* to read, so I wouldn't sound like a bubblehead on applications, and I tested pretty well. My mom never hovered over me like a lot of cheer moms (don't get me started), but we planned out the important stuff together.

I owe her everything, because she's the one who looked out the window when she should have been studying and planned for what she saw, based solely on a three-year-old's determination.

When I heard Bronwyn and Porter laughing in her room, I could feel my face furrow again. That same determination, different kind of backyard.

They'd hooked up shortly after our trip to Starbucks, just like I knew they would. I'm still figuring out who and what I like, but I know chemistry when I see it. When we stood at the counter, Porter's goo-goo eyes were so pronounced, I knew there was a fifty percent chance he'd gotten my order right. (He had. It was a perfect caramel Frapp.) And Bronwyn was trying to be cool, but I knew my cousin, and she wasn't as subtle as she thought she was.

Besides, she'd had the rug pulled out from under her. I loved our crumbling little bungalow with my tiny bedroom and ugly carpet we didn't bother replacing because it was too expensive, but she'd come from a mansion with her own wing and polished hardwood and marble floors, and was living in a *garage*. She'd never invited Jude Cuthbert over, even when they were still tight. I was used to being alone while my mom helped sick kids and drove around strangers so I could stay in cheer. She was used to her dads and tutors constantly pushing her to be the best. I knew how to be driven on my own, but Bronwyn was adrift.

It was nice to hear her laugh.

And one night I saw an opening.

Head high and eyes forward like I'd learned to do in competitions even when I was shaking like a leaf on the inside, I marched through the door from house to garage, and plopped down on the beige carpet right next to her boyfriend. They were on the floor, with a pile of colorful cards between them.

"Cuz!" Porter exclaimed, even though I'm Bronwyn's cousin and not his and we'd only exchanged a handful of words, all involving coffee drinks. He bumped my shoulder, warm under his T-shirt. I'd learn Porter always ran a little hot.

"H-hey," Bronwyn said. Her face said *shocked*, her tone *amused*. I called it a draw and stayed put.

"Hi," I said. Best to start simple. "What are we playing?"

And that was that.

A lot was working in my favor, I knew. Bronwyn was lonely. Not only had her home life disappeared during one school day, but she who'd always been loudly and proudly queer was dating a guy.

And maybe that would have flown outside of Augustus, but not with Jude Cuthbert in charge. I knew Jude was ghosting her former right-hand woman: ignoring her texts, putting condoms in her locker, basically saying "you can't sit with us!" like we were in *Mean Girls: Lesbian Edition.* I also knew that Bronwyn could probably make it all go away—the *Mean Girls* part, that is—just by dumping Porter, preferably in front of the whole school with Jude telling her exactly what to say.

I also saw the energy between them, watching from a distance as Porter came by more and more, catching a glimpse of them in the hallways between classes. They didn't kiss or grope. They didn't have to. Instead, they held hands, fingers laced together all sweet and old-school. Bronwyn couldn't put her head on Porter's shoulder or vice versa since they were the same height. So instead, they touched their heads together, Bronwyn's blond hair that she was growing out against Porter's wild chestnut curls. If she hadn't been the former reigning bitch of Augustus High, it would have been laughable.

Instead, I found it…sweet.

Like I'd tell Jude later, at the party that was the beginning of the end, Bronwyn's sexuality was Bronwyn's to figure out. I didn't think she'd suddenly turned straight or whatever. But even if she had, I didn't exactly understand the gatekeeping. Jude and that clique had always been about accepting people for exactly who they were. I guess, though, gay girls with boyfriends didn't apply.

Anyway, from then on it was the three of us. I suddenly had people to sit with at lunch who maybe didn't understand my cheer obsession but were more open to hearing about stunting drama and finally nailing my full-full the way the other sophomores who'd graciously let me sit at their table were not. I liked Porter's obsession with card games with weird names and how he said they calmed the shit raging inside his head. Even though sometimes he used the name of a card game and called himself an "unstable unicorn," and Bronwyn and I were never sure how to respond to that, so we just kinda laughed.

Maybe most of all, I liked how my cousin was becoming more of a human to me every day and less of a paragon. She was funny, with her scratchy voice and surprisingly high-pitched giggle, and loved dumb jokes, which probably shocked me more than anything. Sometimes she asked if she could braid my hair, and I had this visceral memory of her doing the same thing when we were little before our parents fell out. Her hands were slightly rough. I welcomed the contact, even when she pulled at the roots.

Do you see where I'm going here? I finally felt like I belonged. I didn't know how to talk to guys outside of cheer, until Porter. And Bronwyn wasn't just a reluctant roommate, a distant relative, anymore. She was a *friend*.

That explains my part in everything that happened after.

If I'm really being honest, I would have gone even further.

All Bronwyn had to do was ask.

CHAPTER NINE

Porter

The state of my brain isn't good or bad, it just is. Bipolar is definitely not like you see on TV, with people throwing violent tantrums or whatever. There are two different variations, even. But all you see in the media are people rocking back and forth and acting their version of insane. So can you blame me for not being ashamed, but not wearing my diagnosis on a T-shirt either?

I was kind of a rebel in that way. Everyone at Augustus was all about broadcasting, from their sexual identity to what they ate for lunch. I think that's why Jude gave Bronwyn so much crap. For the first time, Bronwyn wasn't super clear on where she stood, or at least where Jude wanted her to stand.

In the beginning, I probably panted "I have bipolar II" into Bronwyn's mouth, and she mumbled "okay" and then we were all over each other again. I remember I could taste caramel Frapp on her even though I knew that was Cass's drink. She must have sneaked a sip and I remember I loved that.

I'm sure I'll talk more about it. In fact, I *know* I will because I did some really stupid shit after the other stupid shit we pulled. I knew better.

At this point in junior year, I was doing good. Like, really good. I'd figured out my coping mechanisms, and they weren't just card games. I worked at Starbucks some weekends. I was actually remembering to brush my teeth and put on deodorant, and in the past I had to write reminders on index cards and tape them to my bathroom mirror. I was running around the Augustus track when I felt squirrelly, which is sometimes what I called hypomanic when I wanted it to sound less clinical.

Because of all this, I persuaded my mom to let me take a break from CBT. I felt okay not having a therapist for a while. Maybe more than that, I wanted privacy. Less probing into my innermost thoughts. And at that point I was dangerously close to talking about…things, that weren't working. I was fucking embarrassed. I didn't want a crowdsourced solution for once.

Basically, I was this horny idiot who didn't think. But we'll get to that.

Back to my cards. When I met Cass, we sort of connected on that front. Not that I was trying to read people's personalities or futures or whatever. But it's the whole sensory appeal. The idea that you can hold these delicate pieces of paper and they'll tell you something, even if it's just "you have an exploding kitten and therefore you've lost this game."

At that point I had at least three decks on me at all times. The basic one, kings and queens and all that. Maybe an Uno if I was feeling nostalgic that day. Then one of those with really elaborate rules that calmed me when my brain was going in a thousand different directions. Never a Boy Scout, but I was always prepared.

By junior year I was dating. A lot. I never had problems with girls. Not just the "Pleaser" nickname I pretended to find stupid but secretly found really cool because I was a dumb, horny seventeen-year-old boy. Like I said, I didn't yell my diagnosis, but I didn't hide it either. My mom always said going to therapy from an early age made me more empathetic, a better listener and in touch with my emotions or whatever. I know there's nothing wrong with child therapy, but I still got insecure about it. So it's not like I was desperate that day at Starbucks. I was coming into this relationship from a place of wanting, but not needing, you know.

And at this point my mom was pregnant.

Maybe other people would be grossed out that their parents were still having sex. I wasn't. I was excited. Not just to get to know a whole new person from day one—how many times do you get to do that?—but to have some of the attention off me, my brain, and my body. That last part got more embarrassing as I got older.

But maybe it explains a lot about what happened to me. To Jude. To all of us.

Even after the shit hit the fan, Bronwyn stuck by me.

In fact, it's *that* that started to bother me when things got really bad. When our actions, my bad judgment and my headspace collided, she stayed, and it started to bother me. My girlfriend was a fixer, after all. That was obvious.

Did she love me because she saw me as broken?

Ugh, I promise I'll be more straightforward during our next call. Wanna schedule it now?

CHAPTER TEN

Cass

It was my idea to tear down the posters.

It was Porter who went along with it.

Sometimes I stayed after school to work out, on the days I couldn't get to cheer for whatever reason. It seemed so obvious. I think because of that, Bronwyn was kind of annoyed she wasn't the one with the idea.

Do you know the Augustus election rules? Your posters have to be handmade, not professionally printed or anything like that. *We,* Bronwyn and I, took it seriously. Honestly, it was the first time we had fun together without Porter as a buffer—I think he was at his last therapy appointment before he stopped going entirely. We got frappés, went to the craft store, went crazy with the glitter. Even did purple and blue and pink, the bisexual flag colors, as a fuck you to Jude.

Of course, Jude made fun of them. She did that kind of sneer-laugh she was known for, but I could see her fury in the way her brows scrunched together. The anger that made me take a step back, like she was going to take a swing at me.

The next day she showed up with these giant—I don't even want to call them posters, they were more like billboards, pretty much ordering you to vote for her. JUDE CUTHBERT 2017 with no slogan, screaming from every part of the hallway. If our aggressively cute posters were the sweet, tiny flyer in a cheer squad, Jude's signs were the base. Not to be fucked with. And she most definitely did not make them herself. It was laughable, really.

Anyway, one day before Spanish, one of Jude's posters assaulted my eyes for the millionth time and I had an idea.

I wanted to surprise Bronwyn. I was still in cousin-pleasing mode. We were getting closer at home, playing Exploding Kittens, even watching old sitcoms from the nineties after finishing our homework.

We loved *Full House* because it was so over-the-top corny but still kinda sweet when the music came on and the dads taught the daughters a valuable lesson. She started driving me to cheer sometimes, without my mom even having to ask. I liked our little cocoon, with and without Porter.

It's not that I was jealous of Bronwyn because of Porter. I was jealous of Bronwyn *and* Porter. Yes, she was getting a world of crap because of their relationship, but they just…fit together. You know? The way you don't often see in high school because everybody's got their heads up their own asses. But they weren't like, rom-com cheesy. They were just real.

And at this point, the new president was a couple of months into real office, posting the craziest shit on social media. He wasn't a fan of queer people. Or women. Or anyone who remotely looked Asian. One of his favorite targets was a congresswoman who was part Japanese. I'm not going to repeat the words he was somehow allowed to use, but they kept me up at night. We learned about internment camps during World War II in middle school social studies. My classmates were mostly white at the time, and I bet you a hundred bucks they forgot about the internment camps after the test, only to be reminded years later in AP History. I'm not Japanese, but I never forgot.

Speaking of Porter, he was totally into the plan. Even when I told him I'd need to sit on his shoulders. He got this little smile on his face, let out his weird bark of a laugh that sometimes I'd think about long after he left the house. Which was confusing and exciting at the same time, like the first time I nailed a back tuck without even trying.

"Yeah," he said, nodding like one of those bobblehead dolls. "Let's do it."

We picked a time when we could easily lie to Bronwyn and tell her I had cheer and I'd get another ride, and Porter had to take his mom to a doctor's appointment. Then we killed time until people drifted out of Augustus, done with their various clubs and teams to pad their college applications. Okay, we hid in the girls' locker room. Porter bought a feast from the vending machine and we sat on the floor, getting Nutty Buddy wrappers everywhere and trading the stupidest jokes we could remember.

We didn't tell Bronwyn about that part.

Anyway, I don't know how Jude got her posters that high—she probably had an in with the custodial staff, knowing her. I looked at Porter, and he looked at me. I told him I could sit on his shoulders if he was up for it. Like playing chicken in the swimming pool, I told him, not that I ever felt cute enough to do that. I didn't tell him that last part.

He gave me a boost. I was a little worried in the second before I got up on his shoulders. I don't think I'm fat or anything, but I'm… compact, as you can see. A lot of muscles I started developing early because I was never a flyer. And Porter wasn't emaciated, but he was skinny.

I didn't expect his shoulders to feel so strong under me.

I tried to push that out of my mind.

I wasn't quite successful.

Once my hands closed around the thick posterboard—again, this was print-shop quality shit—it wasn't hard to pull. The *rrrrrip* was so satisfying, I can still hear it. Surprisingly loud too—Porter barked out that laugh again, which made *me* laugh, as he walked me up and down the hallway. *Rrrrrip.* Bark. *Rrrrip.* Bark.

Most fun I ever had in that building.

We repeated the process, going through every hallway, every nook and cranny, until we had this pile of huge, thick, aggressive orders to VOTE FOR JUDE. By this time Porter and I were on either side of the pile. We looked at each other and said "What do we do?" Not at the exact same time, but that sort of overlapping way that means you're really in sync with someone, and we cracked up all over again.

I looked away first.

We were going to leave the posters, but we didn't want to be classist and make the custodians clean up our mess, so we hauled them out to the dumpsters.

"You think she'll like it?" Porter asked me, meaning Bronwyn.

He didn't say her name but even just that *she* sent me slamming back down to earth, tearing away that giddiness I'd felt while on his shoulders.

Rrrip.

Here's the thing. I know who I am now, in terms of who and what I like and who and what I don't. Back then, not so much.

It was…hard, sometimes. Everyone at Augustus had been out since they were like, three, or at least it felt that way. People were queer or they weren't, and either way they were out and proud and loud about it. Which is great, but when you're not sure you have romantic or sexual feelings for anyone, or at all, life's a little confusing.

I didn't know anyone asexual, and I didn't know if I *was* asexual or just a late bloomer, stunted by stunts and gym time and pleated skirts. When everyone around you act like adults running for Congress, the real Congress and not our little student government, you wonder if you're just a baby.

More than that, back then I saw asexual as absolute. You felt nothing approaching attraction, ever. My understanding now is way more nuanced, but back then I was still figuring it out for myself, and… not ashamed, exactly? But left out. Why didn't I know exactly who I was?

Those little frissons of *something*, with Porter. Part of me relished them. The other, bigger part knew to keep it all to myself.

This was my cousin's boyfriend, after all.

When we got to school the next day, Bronwyn saw the big blank spots in the hallway. We all heard Jude throwing a tantrum down the hall, Antonia trying to calm her down in that steady, Antonia way. Principal Murrell would make an announcement later: unacceptable and inappropriate, anyone who had information should come forward, blah blah blah. Of course no one ever did.

Looking up at those big blank spots, Bronwyn threw an arm around each of us, me and Porter. "You two are the *best*," she whispered, crushing us into her.

Porter looked at me sideways and winked.

CHAPTER ELEVEN

Bronwyn St. James Campaign Speech, Draft 2 (never submitted for approval)

Hello, my name is Bronwyn St. James. I'm a junior at Augustus and I'd like to be your student body president for the 2017-18 school year. I am the best candidate for the position because I adapt to the changes around me. And in the past several months alone, there have been many.

Ever wake up and find your entire life was basically a lie? That the money you once used for gas and clothes and endless iced coffees really belonged in innocent people's retirement accounts? That you never thought you liked cis boys because gross, ew, they smell and they're reprehensible and even the nice ones do nothing for you? That there's no way in hell you'd ever live in a garage?

Yeah.

I rolled with these major changes—more than some of you will ever see in your entire privileged lives—and then some, while our country went from a strong and kind commander in chief to someone who makes fun of disabled people. My grades never faltered. Okay, they did. I only stopped my involvement in the LGBTQ+ Alliance because I was forced out.

Which brings me to my opponent, who's never been unsure of anything in her whole goddamn life. Trust me, I know. Everything in Jude's life has been deliberate and has gone exactly her way. Do you want this person to be leading you? What will she do if the bottom drops out for her? What will happen if she falls for someone she didn't expect? Will her GPA stay impeccable, will she make good on her grand plans, or will she completely fall apart?

If it happened to me, fellow students, it could happen to anyone.

(Goddammit, Bronwyn. You can't use this. Try again.)

Chapter Twelve

Bronwyn

"Okay, what's the plan?"

Cass sat next to me, drumming the eraser of her pencil on a blank page in her geometry notebook. The constant *tap tap tap* might have annoyed someone else, but I found it comforting. Gave my mind something to focus on, just like Porter and his cards.

For the first time, the race for Augustus High student body president was crowded. From Jason Ramirez, a slacker straight boy who was mainly known for dealing Adderall in the parking lot, to Willow Parker, a drama queen who *always* slept with the set designer of whatever show she was in, suddenly people were clamoring for the title.

In the outside world, the election results had lit a fire under all our asses. Most of us didn't want to see the increasingly scary pattern our country was taken repeated inside the walls we could control. Though I suspected a few people wouldn't have minded.

Anyway, there was a primary. Even with my current outcast status from Jude's group of power queers, I was able to garner a win. The top two candidates would proceed, just like real primaries except without the two-party system.

The top two candidates? Me, Bronwyn St. James; and my former best friend, Jude Cuthbert.

Thunder clapped outside Cass's bedroom window and we both jumped. "I hope my mom's staying safe," she murmured. I bumped her shoulder with mine gently.

Since that first Starbucks trip, it was like we'd pressed a button for Instant Cousin Bonding. We hadn't hung out in so long and our parents weren't close, so I'd forgotten how Cass's quiet intensity, just like pink rubber tapping blue lined page, was so reassuring. I'd always thought of myself as a fixer, but it was my cousin who truly got things done, from tossing some tiny girl in the air to helping me figure out campaign strategies. It didn't matter that she'd never even thought about student government before. Now, she was all in.

"Here's what I need to know," Cass said. Setting her notebook aside, she turned to me. Now *I* was the subject of her laser focus, and honestly, it was a little uncomfortable. Maybe it was her tarot card hobby—like cheer, I didn't quite understand the fascination—but more often than not, it felt like Cass could see parts of me I couldn't.

Or maybe I just didn't want to.

"Why do you want this so badly?"

There it was.

I swallowed hard, stalling for time, then concentrated on my socked feet. Cass and her mom were a shoes-off house, just like mine used to be. Only instead of scuffing hardwood floors like my dads had worried about, they didn't want to muck up the already disgusting carpet. Navy with white snowflakes knitted in, they were J.Crew and way more expensive than anyone should pay for socks. But then, that was the life I had.

"I..." I started to say, then lost my voice and had to try again.

Of course, Cass would ask this. Any campaign manager would absolutely start with the way, and strategy would stem from there. And while Jude had Antonia, who'd wanted to be a political speechwriter since sixth grade, Cass was flying blind, and she knew it.

That didn't make the question any easier to answer.

"It's all I have, you know?" The words rushed out before I could catch them, shape them, make them sound sharper and brighter. Just because my cousin and I were growing closer didn't mean I was completely ready to let my guard down.

But when I looked up from my socks, she was studying me intently. "Keep going."

I bit my lip. "This stays between us." Her face went pale, and I rushed to reassure her. "There's no big secret or anything, I'm just about to do an emotion dump and I can't have it going around school that I'm some whiny little bitch, especially now. Jude and Antonia know my weaknesses already and this..." I took a breath. "This could ruin me."

"I get it," Cass said. I wasn't sure she did, completely, but her dark brown eyes brimmed with loyalty. This was my family. I could trust her.

I wiggled my toes, felt warm wool on my skin as the sky raged outside.

"Jude has everything," I said. "Two parents who didn't abandon her. She didn't lose her house and have to move in with…" I trailed off, realizing how offensive this was to my family member who'd always just had one parent and lived in apartments until she was five.

Holy privilege, Bronwyn.

I sneaked a guilty glance at Cass, who rolled her eyes. "Chill. Go on."

"It's not just that," I said in a rush. "Really. But she's always had it so *easy*. Her grades are amazing, she's super involved and she's going to stand out to colleges no matter what. She's been bred for this shit." I had been bred for this shit too, but then the bottom dropped out.

Now I had nothing.

I pushed on. "So why does she need yet another line on her résumé? I know better than anyone that Jude Cuthbert's set for life. And I used to think I was too, but I'm not anymore. Student body president could help. My grades dropped a lot once…everything happened. I'm working to get them back up again, but junior year's crucial. It might be a meaningless title, but winning this election could make the difference between Dartmouth and Plywood U."

Cass was nodding. "I get it. I really do." Rain beat on her windows, a *tap tap tap* not unlike what she'd been doing with her pencil. "Not in the same way, exactly, but I want a cheer scholarship, and the competition is fucking fierce."

I must have looked surprised because she shook her head. "There's a *reason* my mom works her ass off so I can go to the gym whenever I want. But even then, what if I get hurt? And that happens *all* the time."

She looked away, and we were sitting close enough I could feel her strong body tense. "If I get injured, I can kiss college buh-bye." She looked at me with a sheepish grin. "Might sound like a foreign language, but I can see where you're coming from here."

Sitting on a bed in a thunderstorm, exchanging confidences and vulnerabilities like in some kind of Netflix show about pretty people with problems. Maybe it was that sudden rush of warmth, of sheer closeness, that made me say what I did next.

"Also? I just really want to bring her down."

I didn't know what Cass would do or say next. She was a rules girl, always had been. Her path was strong and true with clear, achievable goals. Tumbling passes. As and Bs: not a perfect GPA but one to show colleges she was serious. Now, a senior class presidency for me.

In contrast, I was a mess.

As thunder rumbled, I waited for Cass's decree. She was my only friend then if you didn't count the person I was dating. I half expected her to kick me out, stay loyal and muscular and always ready to do the right thing, guide her one-woman team to a personal best.

Instead, something came over Cass. Her normally perfect posture went ramrod straight. She rolled her shoulders back and set them down, almost growing a foot. I was intimidated by the mask of smooth concentration that took over her face, making her look ten years older than fifteen. I'd find out later that this was the persona her cheer team called Killer, and one she adopted in the moments before competitions when nerves and emotions were at their very highest.

You don't fuck with the Killer.

"Tell me how," she said.

And I did.

Chapter Thirteen

Bronwyn

At Augustus High, no one cares if you're queer. In fact, they expect it. Of course you know that. Is it still that way? Not surprised.

I don't know what it is about that place, but other than the fact that people who identify as male are in the minority, so are those who identify as straight. This isn't like the places I've heard of downstate, where football player thugs wait outside to beat up the one gay kid who likes to draw and isn't even out yet. Teachers, administration, faculty, school board: you're either not straight or half your family isn't and there's no way in hell you'd even utter a *syllable* that could possibly be seen as oppressing someone else, if you can help it.

And I was grateful. Really. Since I was little, I've been aware that I could have been born or adopted into precisely that kind of town, that kind of family, that hates people for just being who they are.

But it's not utopia.

The problem with Augustus High is, there's no margin for error. We're a magnet school, meaning you have to test into it and maintain a certain GPA. The rivalry is nuts, and money don't buy you shit. Even though my grades have worsened significantly since the bottom dropped out, they're still way better than most of the public schools around here, and that's with tougher work. Freelance tutors in this suburb make *bank*.

And when I was a junior, those standards were even stricter for sexual identity. It's not in the Augustus handbook, of course. It doesn't need to be. Once you're there, you know the rules.

I never even came out in the traditional sense. It's not like I grew up in a heteronormative household. My brothers liked girls and so did I. That simple. When I met Jude, we always had our little crushes, the way kids do, before we started dating for real. They just weren't boys, or at least they hadn't been born that way.

No one questioned us and neither did we. And when we both tested into Augustus, it was queer girl heaven on earth because almost *everyone* was like us, cis and trans, just one big not-straight happy family. Jude and I didn't even have an ex in common until Antonia. The dating pool went that far and wide.

Porter said he always noticed me. I can't say the same was true on my end.

It wasn't like that creepy nineties movie where the comic book nerd guy gets all obsessed with the lesbian. Until he tried to talk to us all at that party, I'd never interacted with him outside of classes. I had brothers and dads, I wasn't a stranger to the cis male species, but high school boys I wasn't related to were…unfamiliar. Foreign. Their T-shirts were more worn, their hair messier. With girls I'd gone out with in the past, that had been their choice, their statement not to care about looking perfect all the time.

But Porter was different. There was something unfinished about his mop of curls, his jeans that were threadbare on the bottom from dragging on the ground even though he was as tall as I am. I couldn't verbalize it at the time, but it's like I wanted to be that finishing touch. That missing piece.

So gross, I know, but that's how I felt that first time I really looked at Porter Kendrick.

I've read books, seen movies, where someone (usually in a small town or at the very least an extremely heteronormative environment) who always thought they liked another gender, realizes they like the same gender and oh no! What do they do? A valid journey, for sure, and one a lot of people go through.

But there's no real instruction manual for what happens when the opposite is true.

When I told Jude, she glared at me and said, "I love treason, but hate a traitor."

Seriously. She *Julius Caesar*'d me.

"What is this, sophomore Honors English?" I joked, trying to keep it light.

"So you're straight now," Jude said. She slammed her locker shut and leaned her back against it, looking like James Dean in that movie my dads loved. All she needed was a cigarette dangling from her mouth.

The bell rang. Everyone scattered but Jude went nowhere. She stayed in place, expression cool, waiting for my answer.

At first, I couldn't form the words. "What? No!" was all I could come up with. "Just because I'm with a straight guy now doesn't mean *I'm* straight."

"I'm pretty sure that's *exactly* what it means."

"Come *onnnnn*," I wheedled, glad Porter wasn't here to witness this. "Bisexuality? Hello?"

"A myth." She pointed her finger at me. Jude never wore polish, but her nails were always cut short and buffed smooth. Her undercut looked fresh, and with her skinny jeans and short-sleeved button-down, she was a lesbian on a mission. A lesbian who'd recently reclaimed the label with a vengeance.

Only now, the vengeance was directed at me.

"I can't believe you're saying this."

She shrugged. "I guess it makes sense that you're acting out," Jude said in a measured tone, like some kind of reverse-conversion therapist. "Your pop got arrested, your dad went apeshit—"

"Hey!" I cut in, but Jude put her hand in my face. Which she'd never done before. I took a step back, wobbling like she'd hit me.

Now her ice blue eyes were steely. "I thought the Pleaser was a *joke.*"

I looked down at my sneakers.

The thing is it had started exactly that way.

Back then, Jude and I were still tight. Okay, she was pulling away ever so slightly, but I chalked that up to my own major life shifts that happened literally overnight. Jude was never good with change. I figured once the dust settled, we'd be back to normal.

Monday after the party, I'd huddled with Jude and Antonia doing our usual post-party postmortem. Only Porter happened to walk by. He rewarded me with that same grin he'd given me at Starbucks the day before, when Cass sensed a vibe and I shut her down.

There it was again, that unfamiliar flash that I didn't usually experience around straight boys because *I did not like them that way.* Except…

"What was that?"

Antonia was gazing at me. They've always caught on way quicker than Jude. Who was now also scrutinizing me, wondering what I'd say next.

I barked out a laugh that didn't quite sound like me. "The Pleaser? Whatever. I think he's in love with me."

Jude visibly shuddered. "Ugh. He probably wants to ask you to *prom* or some shit." Our crowd did not do prom. Way too straight, even at Augustus.

It wasn't until way later I realized Jude had a point. Maybe neither of us could articulate it at the time, but if I were to date a guy, I *could* pass as straight. That would afford me a kind of privilege. That bothered Jude.

And looking back, I can understand why.

"Yeah," I said. "Like the Pleaser has anything to offer me." I reached for Antonia's hand, threaded our fingers together, offered them a saucy grin.

They didn't smile back, just studied me with that penetrating gaze of theirs. "Right," they agreed, tone flat.

Luckily, the bell rang right then. Jude and Antonia were off, and I'd been in front of my locker, so I used the excuse to fumble around, sticking my head into the dark space. I realized my eyes were welling up.

It wasn't my best friend and girlfriend I was trying to convince just then.

It was me.

I first kissed Porter in the safety of my car when I'd picked him up after a Starbucks shift, ostensibly getting a caramel Frapp for Cass, neither of us knowing who really started it but crawling into the back seat to finish it. I told myself I was allowed a one-time experiment. Only one time turned into twice, then three times, then I realized I wanted to be seen in public with him. Not grope in the hallways but at least say hey and smile and not act like this was a fling.

I don't know when it happened, but between that second and third makeout, I knew I wanted to be Porter Kendrick's girlfriend.

"...and now you want to date one?" Jude's voice jerked me back to the present, in front of our lockers. Her stare burned a hole into me as she repeated herself. "The epitome of everything that's wrong with straight men was just elected our *president*, and now you want to *date one?*"

I folded my arms. "You're comparing a racist, sexist pig to a guy who likes card games?"

Jude snorted. "Now you're not-all-men-ing me? You really don't get it, do you? What about Antonia?"

"Antonia and I broke up," I said. "Which you should remember, seeing as she's *your* girlfriend now. So clearly you're reaching." I braced my hand against the locker so I wouldn't slap Jude. "It wasn't working, and we both knew it. I only got with Porter after." The day after, but she didn't need to know that. "It's not like I cheated."

"Maybe not on Antonia," Jude shot back. She straightened her cuffs like a power guy on Wall Street and crossed her arms over her chest. "Just on your identity."

"Okay, what the *fuck*," I said, heat flooding my face. I could feel the rash breaking out on my upper chest, which only happened when I was really stressed out. Like PSAT stressed out. "You don't get to tell me who I am."

"Maybe not." Jude advanced toward me. Only a few steps and she was considerably shorter, but I still held my breath, wondering what would happen next. "But think about this, Bronny. We were at Stonewall, after we were kicked out of our houses and had to sneak around even to meet other people like us at bars. We took care of gay men with AIDS. And even then, the white, male-dominated gay community didn't give a crap."

Now she was breathing quicker, the way Jude did when she was especially fired up. "We were outcasts, the butt of a joke. We didn't go through that so you could go to fucking *prom.*"

"Um, *we* didn't do any of that," I said, gesturing between myself and Jude. "Did you even have to come out to your parents? I know for a fact you didn't." She rolled her eyes, which she knew I hated. "And why are you always bringing up prom? It's not like *you* can't go with whoever you want. You're just choosing not to like it's some sort of statement when really, Jude? No one fucking cares."

"You know, I get if you wanted to kiss him to prove a point or whatever, but you can't be a self-respecting queer woman and date the most basic of *men*," Jude said, as if I hadn't even answered her, tried to be reasonable, at least at first. "Either you're one of us or you're not." She held up her hands like I was pointing a gun at her. "And clearly, you've chosen *not.*"

"Ladies." Principal Olive Murrell's voice boomed off the empty hallway walls. She looked exactly like Viola Davis and was just as intimidating. Her high heels click-clacked as she made her way toward us. "Why are we not in class?"

Jude gave me a look that could have stopped traffic, that blazing and commanding. "Have fun at prom," she said, before shouldering her backpack and walking off, knowing full well I was watching.

The next day, she and Antonia kissed in front of her locker. Antonia had never been into PDA that I knew of, but I guess Jude changed her mind. Two weeks later, they mutually ended things. Jude, whose every word and action had to be a *statement*, as I was seeing now very clearly, said that monogamy was for boring people, but friends would outlast any high school bullshit. Antonia, as Antonia always did, went along with all of it.

I heard all this secondhand, in between classes, from the few of Jude's minions who still deigned to talk to me. First-years and sophomores who used to hang on to my every word now snickered when Porter and I passed them in the hallway. Someone even tripped me once, and I knew it wasn't an accident.

Must have taken a lot of effort for Jude to rally her army like that.

The truth is, I didn't know who I was. Or more precisely, I *did* know, and I knew it wouldn't go over well with my best friend.

If there was a way I could have kept dating Antonia just to keep up appearances, or hell, even to maintain some sort of consistency in my ever-changing circumstances, don't you think I would have? I didn't ask to fall for a straight guy who was proudly average. Who didn't live to assert himself, who let me take the lead more often than not. Knowing Jude, she saw all of this as weak.

Honestly, I think Jude would have understood—or at least been more tolerant of the whole situation—if Porter himself had been queer or trans. If he'd been anything other than a straight white guy with mental health stuff he didn't keep a secret but didn't exactly broadcast either, figuring it was his business and no one else's. Jude didn't get people who didn't loudly proclaim who they were every goddamn second of the day. And she thought he was boring, with his T-shirts and card games and his hair that he obviously didn't care about. She genuinely didn't understand why I wanted to spend all my time with him and my cheerleader cousin.

Granted, she didn't know the extent of how my life had changed. Yes, she was aware I'd moved houses. And everyone in town knew about my dad's arrest. But Jude didn't know everything that was going on inside, how strange I felt every day, yanked out of my natural environment, because I just didn't feel comfortable telling her anymore.

You can see why.

The week after our fight, I opened my locker door and a shower of condoms flooded out. My sneakers were invisible under a sea of foil in candy colors. I can still see them, so shiny under the Augustus hallway light. Winking like they were making fun of me, like everyone else was now.

When I opened the front pocket of my backpack later for a pen? Same thing. I still don't know how Jude got in *there.* Everyone laughed. Jude Cuthbert laughed the loudest.

I stopped speaking to her after that. Probably just what she wanted.

The truth is, loud and proud is great. But for some of us, it gets exhausting. And confusing.

I didn't choose to fall in love with a boy, any more than I chose to live with the cousin I'd barely spoken to since I was eight.

But there we were.

CHAPTER FOURTEEN

Cass

Do you remember the whole "girlboss" thing? In the 2010s? Of course you do, sorry. It's not like you were in preschool at the time.

It's kinda what got us in trouble in the first place.

Basically, and I'm sorry, I'm about to be super binary, girls were expected to be guys. Antiquated stereotypes and all.

Everything online was aspirational. As a girl, you had to show the best possible version of yourself at all times. Now we're all about relatability, showing yourself without makeup, crying videos, the whole thing. That can be fake too, but I don't miss the aspirational days.

It was like empowerment on steroids. No room for vulnerability. "Real talk" often meant hurting feelings in the name of being cool, and writing it off as "that's just the way I am."

Of course, it's good to feel powerful, to take steps toward the gender equity we still don't have. It's not like I want us to go back to when women couldn't vote. But the girlboss stuff, it was extreme. Rather than make me more comfortable, it put me constantly on guard.

You were a superhero, or you were nothing, and shit got worse after the presidential election. The female candidate was eviscerated at every turn. In the first debate, the asshole who ended up winning physically *followed her around*. Looking all threatening. And people thought it was funny. That's what she got for trying to be a person, for not yelling back, for not pulling out one of the AR-15s she was trying to make illegal.

At that time, any semblance of weakness was your fault. You were a little baby girl who couldn't take it. And any issue you had was yours alone. You just weren't strong enough.

Of course, Jude Cuthbert embraced this. And eventually, it almost killed her.

Bronwyn

Jude Cuthbert was a superhero in her own mind.

Okay, in everyone's minds.

At this point, if you were a girl, there were two choices. You were strong, driven, all those muscular adjectives. Or you were dumb, didn't try hard enough, fight hard enough. Guess what category Jude decided I fell into, once I started dating Porter?

Originally, I was hurt. Once the student body president race heated up, I decided to exploit it.

She wasn't the boss everyone thought she was. How could I show the world?

How could I take her down?

CHAPTER FIFTEEN

Bronwyn

I wanted her to die. I just did.

I couldn't tell anyone once that thought occurred to me. Cass appeared all things stoic, but underneath, she was an empathy machine, a Cancer if I'd ever seen one. Tough as hell, but ask her how she felt when some rando on an opposing squad or team or whatever twisted their ankle during a comp, and her face would crumple in shared pain.

Same with Porter. My boyfriend's bipolar made him empathetic too. He wouldn't even trash the guys who used to call him a pussy and pants him in the hallways of his elementary school. Though he did admit he wished they used a less misogynistic insult. Good boy.

I was the resident asshole of our trio and I owned it. I mean, I was looking to take down my former best friend. And I knew, I *knew*, it was about more than future financial aid. But even I wouldn't voice out loud the deep desire that jolted me awake in the middle of the night, syllables loud and jangly as any alarm:

I want Jude Cuthbert to die.

Who would miss her after the initial mourning? Death is a part of life, they tell all of us as soon as we're four and lose the wizened grandparent or great-aunt with crepey skin who smelled like pee, who we didn't know that intimately to begin with because, well, we were four. You grieve, you go on. Death is natural. It happens to all of us eventually.

So why wasn't it happening to my ex-best friend and current rival *when I wanted it to*?

I wasn't wishing for her murder. Even I'm not that diabolical. I'd want it to be quick and painless. A car accident. A brain aneurysm, out of nowhere and maybe only a little pain before she went under forever.

A coma followed by a DNR, during which she faded away without knowing the difference.

And then it occurred to me: we couldn't assassinate Jude for real, but we sure as hell could assassinate the reputation she'd worked her ass off to curate.

She was asking for it.

I know how bad that sounds.

I also knew my own mind. This wasn't a passing thought.

What Jude didn't realize was the day of our blowout fight, right before she single-handedly blackballed me from the LGBTQ+ Alliance, was that I saw her phone.

A picture of a guy I'd never seen and a *love u.*

He didn't even spell it out, so I knew he was straight.

CHAPTER SIXTEEN

Cass

Catfishing. It was kinda brilliant.
    I had the idea. And we took it from there.

Bronwyn

Almost gross how easy the whole thing was. Cass said it came to her one night in that weird place right before your subconscious takes over. You know how that is? I still get my best ideas that way. Guess it's a family thing.
    And I had the perfect catfish, thanks to this tiny flash of memory. First year, spring, debate team. The pollen was really acting up like it does in northern Illinois. So half my teammates were sneezing and blowing their noses.
    Not Jude though. Allergies were for mortals.
    Anyway.
    There she was, all pocket-size in her navy blazer, giggling with…a boy.
    I knew he was a guy because I'd watched him eviscerate his opponent earlier, biting off clear syllables in this sexy baritone. He had clear, tawny skin and the craziest black curly hair and looked straight off a CW show, except our age and not, like, a thirty-year-old playing a teenager. Even his burgundy blazer looked extra sharp, like he'd just stepped off the J.Crew website.
    Jude never giggled. She chuckled. Or cackled occasionally if she was feeling extra bitchy. But I could see her glowing from six feet away. I saw her gesturing with her hands as she explained something. Jude only did that when she was extra excited or horny. Or both.

We never saw him again. I think he transferred? I don't even remember his name.

But I remember the way she looked up, up, up at him. He was so tall. And she came off in just those ten seconds or whatever, as very, very straight.

Anyway, we won the whole tournament and I forgot about him. Until I realized I needed to step it up and suss out her weaknesses. Tearing down her supposedly handmade posters wasn't going to cut it.

So we'd catfish.

Porter

Even then I wondered if we were going too far.

Pretending to be someone else is funny when you're watching that smug guy with the cameraman friend surprise unsuspecting souls on MTV. Maybe not when it's your girlfriend's former best friend. And when you wonder if they should just, I don't know. Talk?

I didn't say anything. You and I have been talking for a while now. You get how deep my feelings went.

Bronwyn wanted this. Bad. Of course I was going to help her.

She and Cass needed me.

Because I know how guys talk. Especially when they want something.

Cass

We should have made a YouTube video. Catfishing in a few easy steps!

First, get a burner phone. From anywhere. I think you can even use an app now, but we wanted to go all in. Me and Bronwyn. I was fully invested now, a campaign manager with bonus content.

Then you text your…catfishee? Whatever. Say you met her at debate a long time ago. Give her a few details, nothing too concrete, but enough that she'll form a picture in her mind of the boy who made her giggle. The boy who Bronwyn assures you she is not connected to in any way on social media. The great Jude Cuthbert wouldn't risk following a *straight guy.*

And then…let your catfishee run with the illusion.
Jude was really into him. I remember that much.
Like. Really into him.
Really.

CHAPTER SEVENTEEN

Porter

The Saturday night after we started the catfish, I woke up screaming.

At first I didn't know where I was, except that the screaming wasn't an incredibly realistic dream but a high-pitched sound I was actually making.

Something soft covered my mouth.

I saw her eyes, almost glowing with worry, her round, pretty face lying sideways across from me, and I remembered. I'd crashed at Bronwyn's like I usually did at least once a week. Her aunt worked so much she never checked, and my parents didn't care as long as I called them and was home for our weekly Sunday breakfast the next day. Sometimes I even brought Bronwyn. They loved her.

It wasn't even about sex then. I just liked feeling Bronwyn's body next to mine. Hearing her soft snuffles when she was in a deep sleep. Seeing her open her eyes when the sun came up.

"Hey." Her scratchy whisper immediately sent my blood pressure down a few notches. She took her hand away from my mouth. "I'm sorry," she said, showing her hand to me. "I just didn't want you to wake anyone up. My aunt has super early shifts this week."

I shook my head, trying to get the demons out, and sat up.

"Bad dream?" Now she was sitting up too, pushing my hair out of my face like my mom used to.

"Yeah." I pinched the bridge of my nose with my fingers, felt her reach under my T-shirt and rub my back. "Oh, that feels good." She smiled and for just a second, I forgot about everything else except how happy I was to be here, with Bronwyn St. James. In terms of dreams, this one had come true.

If only all my dreams were that nice.

"Want to talk about it?" Bronwyn scooched closer to me, slid her arm around my waist, and rested her head on my shoulder.

"It was Jude." I squeezed my eyes shut, trying to piece together the terrible shit my REM cycle had thrown at me. Next to me I could feel Bronwyn stiffen. Well, she'd asked. "Lying on the ground. I couldn't see her face." Breathe in, breathe out, just like I'd done since I was four and woke up thinking the walls were closing in on me, about to squeeze me to death like Han Solo in the trash compactor. "Um, there was blood. A lot of it."

Silence. I was too exhausted to try to backpedal, to make Bronwyn happy. Normally, that was all I wanted, and I knew how she felt about Jude. Hell, I knew how Jude felt about *me*. Her glares in the hallway were like a thousand knives. She never spoke to me, but that was almost worse. The girl was vicious.

Bronwyn lay back down and turned her back to me. Now there was a cloud of tension over us so thick I could almost see it hovering. No way was I going back to sleep.

Then she turned over.

"Was she dead?"

There was something about her voice I couldn't place at first. Then I realized: it was completely flat. No affect. She was usually so expressive.

Without thinking about it, I scooted away. Just an inch or so. I always loved being close to her, but right then? I needed that space.

Then she laughed, just a short puff of air, followed by a little giggle. Like I'd just told her one of the dumb jokes she secretly loved.

"Ugh, I'm sorry," she said, flopping onto her back and looking up at me, face completely open. "I think this election's making me insane."

I lay back down and then propped myself up on one elbow. I kissed her forehead. She tasted a little salty. Bronwyn sometimes got sweaty in her sleep, always active even when her body was still.

Is she going to see this? Eh. She's heard it all by now anyway.

"It's fine," I said, then waggled my eyebrows in the way that always made her laugh. "Want a distraction?"

Bronwyn slung her leg over mine. "Hell yeah," she murmured, leaning in. She reached inside my boxers, but that was a no-go like always, and I tried to ignore the look of disappointment on her face as I scooted underneath the covers, grinning up at her one more time.

They don't call me the Pleaser for nothing.

But even when we finally lay back in bed and I tried to sleep, I saw blood.

Chapter Eighteen

Bronwyn

Porter and I couldn't have sex.

Well, we couldn't have *that* kind of sex. The kind that a cisgender guy and a cisgender girl normally have. The kind you have to get birth control for, either by grabbing condoms at the drugstore while praying to the Flying Spaghetti Monster that your judgmental former friends don't see you, or by driving to Planned Parenthood with your cousin, still undecided about her own sexuality, embarrassing the hell out of you both.

The kind of sex that is privileged, I would realize much, much later. The hard-core Christian types might quibble with your motivation. Procreation versus pleasure. But otherwise, no one even blinks, let alone passes a law against it. When I realized I was bi, I didn't think about that.

The lack of sex wasn't because of nerves. This wouldn't be my first time with sex, or with the equipment Porter was working with. You don't *have* to have sex to know your sexual identity, but I wanted to so badly.

For Porter, it was a medication thing.

"I have some, uh…" he said to me after our first hookup. "*Performance* issues."

I turned over on my side to face my first boyfriend. We were in my bed, half-dressed, and one of us (okay, me) was very satisfied, albeit frustrated she couldn't make him feel the same way. "Nerves?" I asked. I wasn't shy, never have been.

"C'mere," he said, pulling me close so we were bare skin to bare skin. I closed my eyes, breathing him in and relishing the contact, the intimacy. Tone had a gorgeous body, but I never felt as safe with them, or with anyone, as I did right now with Porter.

He slid one arm around my waist, ran the other hand up and down my back, making slow circles. "My meds," he rumbled in my ear. "They make it so…you know. Certain things don't work the way they should."

"Ohhhhh," I said, pulling away just enough so we were face-to-face. His face, by the way, was an odd shade of purple. I didn't need straight As to know that this wasn't info Porter broadcasted.

Then it occurred to me. "Wait. Is *that* why you're the Pleaser?"

I'd done a fair amount of…stuff by this point, but I hadn't found anyone who was this focused on showing me a good time, as it were. He was both in tune with my body *and* experienced enough to know when to go hard and soft. When enough was enough, and when there was never too much.

Rolling me on my back, Porter placed a smacking kiss on my forehead. I freaking *giggled*. I'd never heard myself giggle like that before. "It didn't start out that way, but…" He grinned and blew a stray curl off his forehead.

I smoothed it back. "Well, I'd give you a stellar Yelp review."

"Thanks," he said, and we kissed again. "Um, are you okay with that?"

"Oh. Yeah!" I said, meaning it. Apparently, that's all it took for Porter to show me, once again, how he'd earned that notorious moniker.

By the time of the election, though, I think it bothered both of us in different ways. And while we could talk about so many things—his anxiety, my pop's fucked-up stealing and whether I'd inherit that level of sociopathy, what would happen if Jude continued her reign of non-inclusive terror—that particular topic was off the table. I didn't want to trigger him with my feelings or make him feel inadequate. Porter didn't want to stress me out with any more of what he called his "inner monologue bullshit."

The thing is, I was a fixer. And I couldn't fix this. It didn't matter how beautiful I was, how sexy. And if I believed Porter or looked in the mirror, I knew both were true. But it's hard to *not* take…that personally after a while. My brain could understand I wasn't the reason behind it, but my body and heart were a whole other story.

At times, Porter had to stop me from trying to make him feel the way he made me feel. He was gentle and understanding in a way that made me think he'd had this talk with other girlfriends. But I was *special*. I was supposed to be *better* than them, goddammit.

Part of me appreciated that, thought we were mature for not letting a perfectly normal side effect get in the way of our otherwise lovely relationship.

The other part really, really wanted to please my boyfriend, in *that* way.

Don't get me wrong. I loved what we *did* do. I never saw Porter as broken. It's not like mental illness was an unusual thing: half our school was neurodiverse in some way, most likely.

But I did want him in that way. A lot. A *whole* lot.

And in some ways, maybe I did want to prove myself. I could have a boyfriend. I could have it all.

CHAPTER NINETEEN

Cass

We decided Annie Murphy's party was it.

Not the party with the tarot reading. It's weird. I get the feeling you thought I went to a lot of parties. And I didn't. Just those two, that year.

Jude invited "him" on her own. We always did that dumb finger-quote thing when we talked about her catfish guy. I'm doing it again right now.

Granted, this party was supposed to be more of a blowout. Annie Murphy's parents were going out of town for the weekend, and they lived in a giant house on the lake. No supervision, unlimited funds for booze, pills, and general debauchery. The premise was straight out of an eighties movie, but real. Everyone who was anyone was going.

Did I mention that before Bronwyn moved in, I wasn't part of that *anyone*? Most of my cheer friends went to the public school, and their GPA requirements were way less harsh than mine. Most of us had gone to the same middle school, but when it came time, Mom insisted I test at Augustus. She never said exactly why. Other than "You're smart, honey."

I think part of it was some unspoken competition with Bronwyn's dad. Like, *look at what my daughter can do with a single parent and a tenth of the resources you have.* Not that we were really in touch, but Mom's never stopped trying to prove herself.

Anyway, I got in, but I'd mostly kept to myself.

My classmates liked to make me do tricks, flip over again and again after PE. They were temporarily impressed, I got to soak up a little attention and goodwill, win-win. No one complimented me, though, until Porter, that day at Starbucks. If you asked me, he was the best thing to happen to Bronwyn. She was…different when he was around, hanging in her room playing Exploding Kittens. Softer. Happier.

It's crazy looking back, how much Porter and I went along with Bronwyn. Questioning nothing. Taking those critical thinking skills we were supposedly learning at Augustus and flushing them down the toilet.

She was powerful like that, but power over us wasn't enough.

It never was.

Porter

I was assigned "him" duty for the party.

We'd take turns being "him." Have they told you about the finger quote thing? Yeah. It was dumb. But it made us laugh. In a different way than we laughed playing cards or watching Netflix. A meaner way.

It's hard to look you in the face when I talk about this.

Annie Murphy's blowouts were legendary. I'd never been. Neither had Cass. Of course Bronwyn had gone the year before. She told us it wasn't the typical stupid high school party with trash on the floor and barf in the bathrooms. When that didn't work, she said she'd buy us McDonald's if we really hated it. We were easy like that.

That was before Jude invited "him."

I jokingly texted something like, *Where does Augustus hang out on the weekends?* At that point, it had been going on for a couple of weeks. Getting less friendly, more…more than friendly. Way more. She was interested, no doubt about it.

And she was the aggressor! We didn't have to do all that much, just encourage her to tell "him" how cute he was when he presented his rebuttal. And then joke about the word "rebuttal" and how he had a nice butt or something. Really. This was Augustus High's power lesbian, complimenting a guy's ass and not in an ironic way. We never even gave him a *name*, Calpurnia.

By then, we figured we could ruin her on screenshots alone.

Bronwyn

I wanted more. I always did. And I knew how to make them get it for me.

Cass

Once Jude invited "him," Bronwyn decided to step it up.

Jude made it clear that Annie Murphy had guest rooms. As in multiple. Nice ones. And this was their lake house! The girl's family was loaded, way more so than Bronwyn had been.

Jude also said straight out—ha, *straight*—that she wanted to be alone with him in one of those guest rooms.

Of course, we'd be waiting. With our phones out.

But the way Bronwyn saw it, we could destroy her a whole lot easier—and faster—if we had help.

CHAPTER TWENTY

Bronwyn

You were a first-year, Calpurnia. You were there. You *know* she had more enemies than just me.

What's that old saying about an omelet? Anyway, someone that high in the social status didn't get there by being nice.

At Augustus, Jude Cuthbert decided who was different enough to be cool. But there was another kind of different…the outcast, freaky kind.

If we're calling them coconspirators, well.

Finding them was so, so easy. At that point everything was coming together. I convinced myself that student body president was not only my fate, but my destiny.

I could change the school. The world. And these three could help.

I didn't even need to say that, though. Turns out taking down Jude Cuthbert was the easiest sale in the world.

CHAPTER TWENTY-ONE

Scarlett

Fuck. I haven't thought about *that* in a while.

It's, oh, going to bring back some stuff for me, probably. That whole deal was traumatic, and I was only the on the fringes. Is everyone doing okay now? Good.

Seriously.

I should probably start at the beginning, right?

I went all the way through Montessori with Jude and Bronwyn. It was whatever. Not nearly as diverse as Augustus, so there were years when I was one of like two Black students in this baby prep school, basically. Gotta love those northern suburbs.

Anyway, those two were tight. Of course, we all knew that. Fixated on those books about the prairie girl. Whatever makes you happy, and from early on, for me that was soccer.

I applied to Augustus because their team was amazing. State championships several times over, the works. It didn't get a ton of attention because that place was way more about academics, leadership, anything that wasn't sports, really. The team didn't get a ton of funding as a result.

But I didn't care. On the field, that's where I felt at home. And my grades were excellent, so I was a good fit.

Jude and I…

So first year, we're all a little out of sorts. A lot of Augustus students come from small private schools or really big public ones. Either way, you're the star of your class in this tiny little rarefied environment or this giant place when no one gives a shit. Augustus is right in the middle size-wise and the expectations are high high high.

But yeah, you know this. Your first year is nuts. Everyone's the smart kid, and everyone has something to prove.

It was first semester when Jude and I started…talking a little bit. I think she didn't have quite as many classes with Bronwyn back then. We'd never really been friends, but we had that shared K-8 history. And when you're new and lonely and you just got a D on a quiz for the first time ever, sometimes that's enough.

She was always gay. I know we're lucky. We'd always been in places where that wasn't a big deal. It was celebrated, even. A lot of the upperclasspeople went to Chicago Pride in June, because the parade was wild, and they'd let you into bars as long as you weren't getting into fights. All queer love, eff the police on Halsted Street.

What people like Jude don't always get, though, is that for a lot of us, it's not gay or straight. I knew what had happened with Bronwyn junior year, even before she came to me. You couldn't *not* know. They were like a power couple without the sex, and their breakup was *news*.

What Bronwyn didn't know, though, was that it happened to me first.

Back to first year, that very first semester. I think it was only October. It wasn't like Jude and I were eating lunch together or anything. That time was for Bronwyn. She didn't even have to tell me. But before and after class, we'd chat. And soon it was less about how late we were up finishing that Western Civ essay the night before and more about…what we did on the weekends.

You see where this is going, right?

I could tell she was gearing up to ask me out. You just get that energy, right? Almost better than before the first kiss. So much possibility.

And then I let it slip that I'd broken up with a boyfriend the summer before.

A boyfriend.

I don't even remember his name now. I was thirteen going on fourteen and it was at soccer camp. One of those things that didn't matter.

But it mattered to Jude because she never spoke to me again.

Completely iced me out the next day and all the days after. This was before she was quite so popular. Again, we were first-years.

I knew why, though. I'd gone out with a guy and offended her gay sensibilities. So much for inclusion.

Of course, it turned out fine. Ish. She was able to align her schedule more with Bronwyn's the next semester. I bonded with my teammates on long bus rides and two-a-days.

I never forgot how it made me feel, though. Like I was less than. I like who I like—labels aren't that big of a deal to me—but that feeling that you just don't belong, well, *anywhere*? It stays with you.

If Bronwyn hadn't explained the situation to me, hadn't asked me to be on hand, at the party, to text out whatever would bring the great Jude Cuthbert down to earth with the rest of us? I would've volunteered.

Raised my hand.

Oh, and we had to make sure she was *at* the party in the first place. That she had reasons to be there, just in case she chickened out on the meetup.

The trap was my idea. I think it's called a honeypot? My dad watched way too much James Bond when I was growing up. So sexist, but also made an impression.

See, Jude Cuthbert still had a thing for me.

She never said as much, but I saw her checking me out in the hallway. More than she checked out my friends, or the underclasspeople. Usually I tried to avoid her watchful eye, still smarting from her early judgment of me.

But before the party, I embraced it.

Wore the tightest tops I owned and could get away with—not *that* revealing because that's just not how I dressed, but they did the trick. I could feel her eyes on me as I swished by in the hall, strategically applying ChapStick so she'd look at my lips. Remember how she once called them "luscious" before blushing and giggling.

Yes, Jude Cuthbert was known to giggle from time to time. I thought it was cute…before.

The day before Annie Murphy's party, I made sure to loudly mention to my soccer teammate how excited I was to go. How I was specifically going to be looking for someone to kiss.

Yeah. It was stupid. I won't ever know if it actually got her there. But at the time I was still really, really mad at Jude.

I wanted to take her down.

Nasim

It was simple, really. I wasn't the right kind of gay.

I knew even then, there's no right and wrong kind. Of course there isn't. But it's a good thing Jude Cuthbert was so persuasive, huh?

Otherwise, we all could have just...been who we were. Maybe that whole mess would have turned out differently.

You and I are the same age. I'm sure you remember I was a theater kid. A Thespian. I applied to Augustus because my parents wanted me to, but I was sold when I saw that badass auditorium. Velvet curtain and seats, the works. A far cry from the converted cafeteria at my Catholic grade school. We weren't even Catholic, but saying "public school" to my parents was the equivalent of "dog shit."

So.

I was gay, out since seventh grade. I was a theater kid. But I wasn't Jude Cuthbert's idea of "gay theater kid."

And for some reason that bothered her.

What does "gay theater kid" bring to mind? You won't hurt my feelings.

Right, exactly! Super flamboyant. Out since birth. Loves glitter and feathers and knows Stephen Sondheim's entire repertoire by heart. Including the scores that have been released, like, once.

I was the opposite. Thick glasses that didn't come off until junior year. Not because my parents wouldn't let me. Because I was too lazy to learn how to touch my eyeball.

I wore a lot of striped polo shirts. And khakis.

I *know!* I was so unfortunate. It wasn't until college when my roommate was a fashion major that I learned how to not dress like a blind toddler.

And I love the classics. Shakespeare. Molière. Hansberry. Musicals I can take or leave.

Jude was in my drama class that first semester and she kind of...zeroed in on me. Asked a bunch of questions about why I was mostly about the dead white guys and was I trying to blend in with *that* wardrobe?

Okay, she had a point about the wardrobe.

But otherwise, shut up. You know? Not everyone is HEY, I'M A BIG HOMO all the time. I knew, I'd always known to an extent. Who else loves the Kenneth Branagh *Hamlet* as a five-year-old? But I dressed how I dressed, I liked what I liked. The Thespians had no problem with it. Why was this random junior who thought she was the shit so obsessed with making me fit into a little box of her own making?

Every time I passed her in the hallways, she'd incline her head toward me with my striped shirts and my Shakespeare texts. Whisper to her little minions. And laugh.

I heard they were looking to ruin Jude Cuthbert. I said I'd share out whatever humiliation Bronwyn and her cronies got on camera. No problem. Then Bronwyn leaned in, asked if I'd try something else too. Anything I could think of, to put her in that place of humiliation.

Why the heck not, you know?

The next time Jude rolled her eyes in my direction, I took the bait.

"Say it to my face," I said, crossing my arms. I was taller—most everyone was—and it felt good to physically look down on Jude Cuthbert. She opened her mouth to speak, and I said, "Yeah, but not now. At Annie Murphy's party. Embarrass me to your heart's content in front of our drunk classmates."

Then I flounced away, swaying my hips in a way I never did usually, just to tee her off.

Of course she'd take the bait. At least, that's what my dumbass self thought that day. I considered it a brilliant move.

Why'd I do it? Jude Cuthbert was never as open-minded as she pretended to be—and why did she even care that I didn't fit her definition of a theater fag? Because Augustus was all about her. She just wanted every not-straight person to like, fall in line. And fuck you if you didn't.

Yeah, I said yes to her ex-best friend. If that's what I'd gone through in a semester, with her as my classmate, I couldn't imagine what Bronwyn had endured.

Of course, I didn't know the whole story.

Does anyone, ever?

Declan

Oh. That name.

Jude Cuthbert is a good alias. You're welcome. She was a tyrant, that one.

I was always good with big words. Literary references. I could get every question on *Jeopardy* as my burnout mom smoked and weighed dime bags. The night before testing into Augustus, I was up all night with a screaming baby that wasn't even mine. Or my mom's. And my scores were still off the charts.

Not that she'd ever given a shit, but I wanted to prove her wrong by getting into this big fancy magnet school. Maybe even college.

I'd be the smart one you see in all those inspirational movies. And it worked, but at one point it almost didn't.

Because of *her.*

[redacted]…Jude, sorry, I keep using her real name. I know you don't want it in here. Sorry again.

She had never known what it was like to use a SNAP card at the organic grocery store because your kid sister went through a period where she would only eat kale. I have no idea where that little girl tasted kale in the first place. She, Jude, okay I'm getting used to it…I knew what her house looked like. She'd been primed for good schools, good plans, good life.

The opposite of me.

The day of that test, we were sophomores, taking junior pre-calc. I'd had a tough time, the teacher, I don't remember his name, was a real dick. Yeah, Mr. Pollack. Always gave me tardy slips. I was too embarrassed to tell him that the second I got a permit I was the one taking kids to school. Sometimes neighbor kids too. Which made me late.

Anyway, the night before the midterm my mom freaked out. To this day I don't know what she was on, but it was probably some druggy booze combo that she's lucky didn't kill her. It took hours to calm her down. I practically had to peel her off the ceiling, all the while begging her to stop chattering, stop shrieking, because the kids were sleeping, and we had school in the morning. My textbook lay open on my bed all night, and I barely flipped it closed before I finally crashed. My phone alarm went off two hours later.

I had to pass. And I didn't cheat, I swear. When you don't get enough sleep, focus is out of the question. Your eyes wander. You blink a lot. Now combine that with a dead quiet room and a bunch of problems you don't know how to solve. And then there was the math.

Ha ha.

So halfway through the period, Jude gets it in her head that I'm trying to look off her paper. And because she's Jude and she never just let shit go, and she had to not let shit go in the biggest way possible, she got the dick teacher to come over. She interrupted everyone's test because I looked the wrong way.

And I got sent to Principal Murrell. I got suspended because I'm the kid who hangs out in the parking lot after school. Never mind I'm usually studying, and I'm killing time until my sister's kindergarten gets out across town. But Jude is the overachiever, the one with the power.

I'm not sure *I* would have believed me, to be honest.

That messed me up for a while. I started flunking the stuff that was so easy before. I couldn't concentrate. I started smoking up more, even tried coke once or twice. But I kept second-guessing my smarts. And at that point, my smarts were all I had.

I didn't really know her former friend. As you can guess we ran in very different crowds. I was bi too, though. Never a big joiner—as pretty much a parent, I didn't have time for that—but yeah, I kissed plenty of people who shared my gender and plenty who didn't. And more than that, I knew what it was like to have Jude-fucking-Cuthbert temporarily ruin your life.

So I said, yeah. Let's ruin hers.

CHAPTER TWENTY-TWO

Cass

"Is she even going to be there?" Porter asked, dealing me into Crazy Eights. A stupid game, I know, but my teammates and I had always played it while sitting around at comps. The game made me feel like a little kid again in the best possible way and I'd taught it to Porter and Bronwyn. It was our go-to stress reliever once the election was in full swing.

"Oh, she'll be there," Bronwyn replied, picking up her hand. "And so will the three of us." She smirked, smacking down two cards. "And it'll happen."

"*What* will happen?" Porter and I said at the same time, then grinned at each other. I wasn't attracted to him like that—lately, I'd been wondering if I was attracted to anyone or anything—but he was a great ally to have around when Bronwyn got like this. I raised a brow at him like, *here we go again.* Another party, but we'd be doing more than a scary tarot reading this time.

She put her hand down, fanned out the cards so we couldn't see them, and threw up her hands dramatically like the Thespians were always doing at lunch. "*Something!* I can't tell you what, but I have the feeling shit's gonna go down, and we have to be there when it does."

"As long as it doesn't involve blood," Porter said, pulling the long sleeves of his T-shirt over his hands. He looked down, face turning pink. What I always appreciated about Porter—and I think Bronwyn did too—was that he never tried to play it tough. The boy was all heart.

Sometimes I worried about him. And I wondered why I worried because I wasn't his girlfriend. Obviously.

Bronwyn and I exchanged a glance. She scooted closer and put her head on his shoulder. He murmured and kissed her hairline, and I felt safe. It was almost like watching my parents, if I had a dad. When

I watched them like this, I was no longer "cuz." I was the kid. I didn't mind.

He'd told us about the dream, Jude and the blood, vague, blurry images but disturbing all the same. Bronwyn brushed it off as nicely as she could: "it's just residual stress, Por. Dreams don't mean anything."

Me? I wasn't so sure.

I couldn't stop thinking about Jude's tarot reading, the one I was supposed to fake before the cards seemed to take over. Present betrayal, a future fall from grace. Big stuff. Even she'd been genuinely worried before she laughed it off. You can't fake that kind of reaction.

And then Porter had that dream.

Most likely, Bronwyn was right, and his subconscious was just stressed out. The tension was amping up at school and even the non-juniors like me were feeling it. Jude and Bronwyn practically snarled when they passed each other in the hallways, which they always seemed to do. Granted, our school wasn't huge, but you'd think they could at least try to avoid one another. I knew my cousin well enough by now, though, to be certain she didn't want to come off as weak. Being with Porter was already one strike against her.

People like Bronwyn were all logic where Porter was all heart.

I liked to think I was all intuition. Being on a team for so long, hoisting other girls above my head, trusting I could flip backwards in the air and not break my own neck, all required a certain amount of faith. Not to mention anticipation. Commitment. The slightest bit of foreknowledge.

And when Porter told me about seeing Jude, surrounded by blood, I got the same feeling I did before my flyer, Lex, a tiny girl who I usually supported during stunts, fell out of the pyramid. Even before she wobbled and then crashed, I could always sense it, before I clenched my jaw and braced for the impact of a ninety-pound flyer.

When Porter said "blood" that day at our kitchen table, my jaw clenched.

God, I just realized. It's clenching *now.*

Memory's strange, huh?

Chapter Twenty-Three

Bronwyn

Friday was the Party. The Day.

I knew had to be prepared. Be ready for any sign of weakness on Jude's part that I could exploit to ensure the presidency would be mine in the bag and I could sleep again at night. Any way to bring her down for good.

The plans, the phone, my coconspirators. All in place.

And that Wednesday, I called the whole thing off.

CHAPTER TWENTY-FOUR

Porter

She really did it. Two days before it was all supposed to go down.
Everything was going perfect. It felt like self-sabotage.
But Bronwyn was in charge. That never changed.

Cass

I pulled my left hamstring.
I was stretching on her floor when Bronwyn told me and Porter that she'd texted Jude, as "him" of course, saying he couldn't make it. Then blocked Jude's number.
I jerked up so fast. Should have known better. For the rest of the week, I'd hurt like hell and I thought my coach John was going to kill me.

Bronwyn

Yes, my cousin and my boyfriend both thought I was crazy. I saw them look at each other every time I mentioned Friday. I also knew Porter was still freaked out by his own dream and Cass by her tarot cards. Blood and downfalls and backstabbing, oh my!
Come on. This wasn't a Greek tragedy. It was high school.
I just wanted one minor thing to go wrong for Jude Cuthbert. One embarrassing slip of the tongue after too many of those alcoholic seltzers she loved so much and I thought tasted like flavored hairspray. One sloppy kiss with a girl who wasn't Karrie? Callie? Whoever that sophomore was, who was now Jude's flavor of the week but clearly

thought from the way she paraded around the hallways with Jude, nose in the air and short, flippy skirt, that she was the next First Lady.

If I was being honest with myself, I'd even welcome a truce. A conversation. An acknowledgment that hey, I could date the straightest guy in school and still be queer. That we could be friends again, and she'd let me have this one. Maybe she'd agree I deserved it more.

Because in my deepest, darkest moments—the seconds right before sleep, when you have the thoughts, you wouldn't share with even your closest confidantes—I missed Jude.

I'm no idiot. There's no way we could go back to before. Hell, I was living in a different *house* and my dad was God knows where, maybe eaten by a bear by now for all I knew. My pop didn't want me visiting him, and when he called to tell me, I pretended it didn't hurt even when I shut myself in the guest room for the rest of the night and Cass's mom left my dinner outside the door.

Speaking of Cass, I genuinely loved her. I was sad we'd missed out on all those years. I could even kind of understand why she was so obsessed with cheer. She wasn't going anywhere in my life, and neither was Porter.

But if I could talk some sense into Jude, if she was just liquored up enough to *listen* for once—it had been known to happen after two or three of those gross spiked seltzers, but no more than four—she'd understand. That sexuality was fluid, or at least mine was. That I really wasn't mad about her and Antonia. That I just needed this one win after a shitshow of a semester, and she could speak to me after that or not, I'd respect her decision. No muss, no fuss, no catfish.

Believe it or not, I was getting tired too.

A sit-down with Jude would be the best-case scenario. That said, I knew her. I couldn't let my guard down because God knows what she'd do, what she'd bring up. The thing about having a former best friend since childhood? Jude had *years* of shit on me.

I couldn't drink. I couldn't pick up any cup I hadn't personally poured or let out of my sight. I always needed Cass and/or Porter by me, preferably both, keeping watch. My own personal sentinels. Even if or when I got Jude alone, I'd dispatch them to stand outside the door.

No one wanted this to end peacefully, with me as student body president, more than I did.

If I could just get that through her head, we'd all be fine. But Jude was Jude, so I had to be ready.

For anything.

CHAPTER TWENTY-FIVE

Declan

In the end I was the one who got her to the party. Do you remember that?

Porter

Bronwyn dispatched Cass and me to reach out to Nasim, Declan, and Scarlett about the aborted plans. That Bronwyn thought it was maybe too harsh. That she realized a conversation with Jude was the way to go.

Looking back, of course I see her point. They should have talked from the beginning. I didn't give a shit what Jude thought about my relationship with Bronwyn, but I know Bronwyn missed her best friend. Maybe they could have patched things up, or at least gotten to the point where they could smile at each other in the hallway. No hard feelings.

Yeah. It didn't turn out that way.

Cass

We were supposed to text the others. We didn't. Porter and I, we barely had to talk about it. We'd made up our minds simpatico. He and I did that a lot, actually.

At this point no one knew Bronwyn better than us. We were her minions, after all. I was the mastermind behind the catfishing. We were proud of that.

She could change her mind at the last minute.

Why not leave everything in place?

CHAPTER TWENTY-SIX

Bronwyn

Here's why I called it. Or tried to.

I was on "him" duty that day. It had become downright enjoyable for all of us. First, Porter coached us how a guy like him would talk. No rambling. Let her take the lead.

I added that Jude liked complete sentences, even in texts. With periods. I knew her love language like no one else.

And it was working.

Have you ever read someone else's texts? Even an "*lol ok*" feels deeply personal. When it's just you and that tiny little keyboard, there's a freedom to be exactly who you are. No judgy glares. No anxiety over reading someone's tone of voice. In those small letters, you're laid bare.

Apparently, Jude felt that way too.

Or else why would she have texted someone whose first name she hadn't even confirmed…about her mother?

I can't remember the exact words. I know, I'm sorry. I've blocked them out.

I do know what they involved.

Cheating. Leaving.

Pregnancy.

Fuck.

Jude's mom was straight…or at least, she had been. But more than that, the woman was the definition of elite. Country club president. Not even my dads had belonged there. The place *said* they were okay with gay in a way you knew they really weren't. Jude's mom was also active in the local PFLAG. Definitely not cuddly, absolutely pushy, but always, always supportive. And, I thought, happily married.

Jude was an open book. And Augustus wasn't a big school, and at that point we were on extra Jude radar, our ears forever perked up for the slightest speck of dirt.

So where was this coming from?

Even after all we'd been through, I couldn't tell her secret. It was one step too far.

I deleted the texts so Cass and Porter wouldn't see. I canceled "his" appearance at the party, blocked Jude's number. Hid the phone under my mattress.

It was for everyone's own good.

The way I saw it, I could more or less corner Jude at the party. We could talk. Really talk. Maybe I'd open up to her about the catfishing. Maybe she'd tell me about her mom on her own.

Maybe we could actually work this out.

I was so naïve.

Chapter Twenty-Seven

Calpurnia

And here's where I come in.

Hi.

I feel weird talking to myself, so I'm just writing this down.

At this point, I'm a first-year. I established that at the beginning. What I *didn't* establish is that like Jude, I'm a lesbian.

It's not a word you hear a ton anymore among people our age, but it fit me then and it fits me now. Just who I am. Like Nasim, I came out in junior high, but unlike him I wasn't in Catholic school, so I didn't have to hide it. Augustus is pretty damn queer. Not a big deal if you follow those pesky unspoken rules established by one Jude Cuthbert.

I was a nonentity back then. A total dork. And not in the way that you hear a movie star or influencer say, before you find a picture of them in high school looking hotter than you ever will. I had braces, the metal kind. I'd begged my parents for contacts, but they took some getting used to, so I blinked a lot. My hair was limp, and as for style, I'm still learning what goes with what, so you can imagine back then I was a disaster. Let's just say I cannot pull off a tulle skirt, but I sure did try.

I loved Jude Cuthbert with every fiber of my being.

Not in *that* way, though if she'd asked me out, I would have dropped to my knees and praised a God I don't believe in. (Like that would have happened. See above for the description of how utterly unsexy I was first year.)

I think it's natural to crush on your upperclasspeople. She seemed so much older. Sophisticated. Sure of herself, secure in her identity, everything my baby gay, "What was I *thinking?*" tulle skirt-wearing, blinky self was not at fourteen.

As it was, she didn't know I existed.

Until that day in the parking lot when I invited her over.

CHAPTER TWENTY-EIGHT

Declan

I saw Jude Cuthbert talking to this geeky little first-year. Shit, sorry, you've just changed so much. I looked way different as a first-year too.

Anyway, I saw her talking to, um, you. And I knew I had to do something.

Because I was like, fully invested now. I didn't know about the canceled plans, the talk or whatever. None of us did.

We just wanted to take her down.

Calpurnia

She looked so crestfallen. I've never once used that word IRL, but writing it down brings back Jude Cuthbert's face. She looked down at her phone and sighed. Then she stopped in the middle of the parking lot, like she couldn't even muster the energy to make it to her cute, yellow vintage Beetle. I wanted a car exactly like that someday.

Looking back, I feel bad, being yet another person moving in while she was at her most vulnerable. But at fourteen you don't really think that way.

(This is a conversation, Ms. Strohm, that I am re-creating to the best of my ability. But that's almost not necessary here, as I remember it word for word. I played it in my mind every night for a long while after everything happened.)

"Are you okay?" I called from the spot under the flagpole where my mom usually picked me up.

I remember Jude glancing up from her phone. I'd walked by her a thousand times in the hallways, trying not to stare, but right then I knew she really *saw* me.

"Yeah," she said. "Just…" Shaking her head, she held up her phone, the black mirror winking in the late afternoon sunlight.

I assumed it was some girl. Some *idiot* girl. Of course I did. This was the day before the party.

"No plans tomorrow night, now." She was still rooted to her spot, and I to mine. I was afraid to move, like one step in the wrong direction would poof this magic moment away.

"Oh." And then, I called so boldly I still can't believe it three years later, "Do you want to come over?"

You knew me as a first-year, Ms. Strohm. Can you believe?

I wish I could say I'd had a premonition. That I somehow *knew* she'd be safe with me, eating white cheddar SkinnyPop and flipping through dumb old teen movies on demand. Of course I didn't, though.

I was a stupid kid with limp hair and braces and a striped shirt that didn't even fit me right.

Then I noticed the guy smoking by the old beater of a car. Watching us both.

Declan

I feel like shit now that I know that little first-year was you.

But you get it, right?

I had to laugh at you, insult you, ask Jude if she *really* wanted to hang with some little loser who didn't know how to party. I had to appeal to Jude's vanity, her cockiness. Her need to always look and feel in control.

I'm not a total monster. I swear I could see your heart sink when she snorted, like "What was I thinking?" and made her way to her car. Even then, stoned and leaning against my ride like an old-timey gangster, I felt bad for you.

I knew I had her, though. I'd done what had to be done, and the first-year with the shiny braces and the bad clothes would get over it.

Will any of us ever really get over what happened that night, though?

I wonder.

CHAPTER TWENTY-NINE

Cass

Parties like Annie's were decidedly not my jam.

Not just because I was socially awkward AF outside of cheer. Which I was. But at least in cheer, you know your enemies: the other team, easily recognizable because their faces were unfamiliar and their uniforms a different color. And at times, the people who have their eye on you because you out-tumbled them that one day, or lifted someone else higher so you got a better position in the big pyramid. Sure, I was the Killer, but I was a Killer who depended on her comfort zone.

At parties, everyone looked the same. Outfits, meticulously put together to look like they *weren't* meticulously put together, just picked randomly out of a closet with eyes shut. Hair, tousled within an inch of its life to look like you just fell out of bed, ideally with your biggest crush or three. Makeup that took dozens of YouTube tutorials to perfect.

The loopy curls, fake eyelashes, big bows in cheer comps? Felt way more honest. Noble, even: armor for battle.

Add in alcohol, pot, and God knows what else and everyone melded together into a multi-headed Hydra of conformism masquerading as being unique. I could tell myself how much stronger, smarter, *better* I was than my peers. Didn't make them any less terrifying, as Bronwyn opened the door of Annie's house and strode straight into the hellmouth. A woman with a purpose.

Sort of.

She wasn't sleeping, my cousin. I swore I could *hear* her kicking off the covers every night. Her cheekbones protruded like a model's, the dark smudges under her eyes like the heroin chic aesthetic of vintage Calvin Klein ads. The raggedy ends of the bob she gave herself two nights ago were mussed to perfection. She kept running her fingers through her hair, looking surprised when she hit air, like she'd forgotten she took scissors to her own locks, shaking off my help.

Bronwyn fit right in with the not trying too hard theme of high school parties, but only because she really wasn't trying. All she cared about was finding Jude Cuthbert.

"Come on," she murmured to Porter and me, leading us through the crowd of already smashed revelers. I didn't need to look at Porter to know he was also out of his element. Before hooking up with Bronwyn, Porter was a loner like me, playing video games on the weekends with his string of outsider girlfriends. In his threadbare tee and baggy jeans, he was just as out of his element as I was. Maybe even more so.

"I still don't get this," Porter muttered, and I rolled my eyes in agreement. Bronwyn clearly wasn't listening, so he glanced at me. "She couldn't text Jude?"

"She'd just block me," Bronwyn called over her shoulder. "This way she can't escape." She shot a glance at the two of us, flanking her like soldiers, and grinned. "Relax. It'll be fine. I just need to talk to her face-to-face, then we'll go back home and play cards like we used to."

Then Bronwyn turned to face us fully. Next to me, two girls I recognized from French were furiously making out against a wall. On the side of Porter, a dude whose locker was across from mine snorted a line of something white. I didn't want to know. And was that cigar smoke wafting through the air? So gross.

Suddenly, Bronwyn's face was next to mine. I could smell my own body wash, a peachy scent I'd picked up from the drugstore on a whim. I'd thought it was sweet, light, airy, but now the aroma was sickly. Artificial.

"Hey." She put a hand on my face. "I got this." She gestured between us. "*We* got this. We're gonna win."

And even though I knew she was manipulating me, warmth flooded through me. I didn't talk about this to anyone, but life before Bronwyn had been...lonely, almost overwhelmingly so. I was only fifteen, couldn't drive yet, so hanging out with my cheer friends was still relegated to texts and video chats, and awkward car rides with their parents when we could finagle IRL hangouts. Even then, my teammates had their own friends at the public school, where I was a jumping, yelling, tumbling fish out of water at Augustus. Plus, I wasn't dating anyone yet because I didn't know *who* to date.

Bronwyn changed all that. I had family now. Family who was

present, not to mention a new friend who liked fun card games. Family who let me into their brain, their heart, their room. I was *at* this party, wearing her socks because gradually our closets had merged into one. They had little cartoon monkeys on them. Of course I'd be the Killer for my family.

Now, my family kissed my cheek, and I was further assaulted by wafts of artificial peach. She tugged the shoulder of Porter's T-shirt sleeve, smooched him hard on the lips in view of everyone who'd followed Jude's lead and cast her out like an LGBTurncoat. Porter looked as stunned as I felt.

That was the power of Bronwyn St. James.

"Find her," was all she said, and then she was gone.

CHAPTER THIRTY

Porter

I had to find the right time to tell her.

This clearly was not it.

Cass was a deer caught in headlights, poor kid. Since Bronwyn and I hooked up, she'd become like a little sister. I wanted to take her back to her house and teach her how I played solitaire when my mind felt especially chaotic. Cass, with her ponytail and hoodie and nerves of steel under the shyness, when she wasn't yelling her head off for some invisible team—I still wasn't fully sure how competitive cheer worked—didn't belong here.

Not that I was one to talk.

Bronwyn kissed me, and I tasted the lip balm she'd just started using. Vanilla mint, sweet with a hint of sharp, just like her. I still couldn't believe someone like her picked me out from obscurity, for her first boyfriend no less. I had to live up to that, in every way possible. Which was related to what I had to tell her. Which was also why I was at this stupid party, looking for her former best friend so Bronwyn could do...something.

Talk to her. Or so she said.

I looked at Cass and said, "So do we split up, or what?"

We were here on a mission, after all.

Cass was gazing into the distance. For a second, I wondered if she'd gotten a contact high from the pot smoke, until she glanced back at me. Angled her head.

There she was.

Jude Cuthbert wasn't holding court like she did every day in the hallways, practically blessing the first-years and sophomores with her wisdom and (even I admit it) charisma. Instead, she was off in a corner, frantically texting and running a hand through her fresh haircut. Her button-down shirt looked a little askew.

"What do we do now?" I asked Cass. Next to me, some drunk chick shrieked and I jumped.

Just then, Jude grinned.

Shoving her phone in her back pocket, she hopped up the staircase to the lake house's second level.

Cass looked at me. Or I guess at this point, she was the Killer again. Wearing pink slip-on shoes. She had this little smile I'd never seen before. Or rather, I had seen it. On her cousin.

"Find Bronwyn," she ordered me through clenched teeth before following Jude. Like a wolf.

Chapter Thirty-One

Cass

That was the beginning of the end.

CHAPTER THIRTY-TWO

Porter

What if we'd just stayed home? Well, their home, but by then I considered it mine too.

Or what if Bronwyn and Jude *had* talked? Really talked, like Bronwyn wanted? Or at least said she did.

Even now, I ask myself all the time.

CHAPTER THIRTY-THREE

Bronwyn

I was eight years old and scared shitless the first time I saw Jude Cuthbert.

It was my first day at Montessori, after a few years at a neighborhood school that my dads had deemed "not challenging enough." Good enough for my older brothers, but not for me, who sneaked into their rooms and read their assigned books for fun. Who begged for extra allowance money so I could buy the entire Laura Ingalls Wilder box set. When everyone else was freaking out about Harry Potter, I was getting laughed out of second grade for wearing a bonnet to school. That I'd made myself.

Harry and company were fine, but witchcraft and wizardry were never my jam. I was more into the challenges of prairie life. You made do with what you had, from the scraps of fabric left over from sewing a dress, to animal bones and sugar you boiled and put on snow to make candy. (I got in very big trouble when I tried that myself and the kitchen was sticky for weeks.)

When I rode to ballet or violin in the back seat, I imagined my dad was Pa Ingalls, bearded and overall'd and true blue. I tuned him out as he yapped on his phone—Dad, not Pa. I wondered how my own family would deal with nothing but ourselves if we had to move from log cabin to lean-to to dugout every year. I wasn't sure how my parents and brothers would fare, so I figured I'd be prepared enough for all of us.

Anyway, the Montessori classroom was…overwhelming. Gone were the Pledge of Allegiance and ringing bells of my public school. Kids were allowed to work on whatever they wanted, whenever they wanted, basically. It was supposed to make us smarter, more self-driven, but at first, I just felt lost.

I wanted someone to tell me what to do.

Then I saw her.

Jude's hair was longer then, chestnut waves to her shoulders. When the other kids were in T-shirts (mostly Harry Potter-related) and jeans, she was in a little button-down and khakis. Seriously, *khakis*. Sitting in the corner of the classroom near the bookshelves, she was like a little teacher. More comforting, really, because Miss Melanie wore flowered hippie skirts and practically floated around the room, like she'd seen one Zooey Deschanel movie and run with it.

I set my denim backpack in the cubby labeled with my name. Then I tentatively headed toward the girl with the khakis, who had a circle of kids around her, hanging on to her every word.

"*Harry Potter* is fantasy," she said, little voice carrying a tone of ultimate authority. "The *Little House* books are reality."

I was hooked.

Later, we found out Laura Ingalls Wilder was a little bit unstable. That Pa probably had untreated mental illness, which could explain all the frantic moving around, switching homes and schools and fiddling tunes like it was his full-time job. One summer afternoon between sixth grade and seventh, we fell down an Internet rabbit hole debunking most of our favorite series. Finally, Jude turned off her laptop.

"I guess it was all fake," she said, and her voice broke. We cried, holding each other, until the sleeve of my green T-shirt was several shades darker, wet. Jude's mom came in at one point thinking something was seriously wrong.

We shook our heads. Asked if the housekeeper could bring us chocolate chip cookies, the kind from the premade roll. And immediately looked up our Harry Potter houses. I was Ravenclaw, thoughtful and smart, always in need of a concrete plan. Jude was Slytherin, devious but not necessarily in a bad way, more like goal-oriented and calculating.

Ha.

We never read Laura Ingalls Wilder again.

But Jude's influence over me remained, almost Svengali-like as the years wore on. If she told me a skirt made my knees look like doorknobs, I shoved it to the back of my closet. When she found a website with lesbian porn where the women looked like they were enjoying themselves, she taught me how to dismantle the parental controls on my laptop and phone. (In that way, I can credit my first orgasm to Jude Cuthbert.) There was no question of us testing at

Augustus in the fall of eighth grade, but our parents didn't push us. We wanted to be the best.

We knew we were unstoppable.

Jude had always had followers, but they came and went, where I stuck around. I got to see the inner sanctum of her room with its surprisingly white and frilly décor that she'd picked out herself. I knew when Eileen Ling broke her heart in seventh grade. She only cried in front of me.

I always thought Jude had all the power. In a way that's still true. She basically turned our whole friend group against me when I started dating Porter. Suddenly I, her second-in-command, was ghosted. I had my cousin and my first real love at this point, but it was still shocking. Lonely.

I think she forgot that I'd seen her undone.

I knew Jude's weakness. If you got to her heart, she was open and vulnerable. Just because that didn't happen very often didn't mean it didn't happen *ever*. I was living proof. I knew, even through her bluster, that by hooking up with Porter, I'd hurt her. Badly.

Laura Ingalls Wilder broke Jude's heart, even though she was long dead at the time, so Jude never read her again. Gave her books away. Glommed on to Harry Potter like the rest of our classmates and made it seem like she'd been doing the cool thing all along.

Knowing what we know now about Harry Potter's author...guess Jude was on to something.

I broke her heart too. So she got rid of me.

At least, she tried.

I wasn't lying when I said I wanted to talk to her at tonight's blowout. I thought maybe we really *could* have a conversation, work things out and end things to my advantage. I wanted to believe I could get through to her.

A bigger part of me knew better. Jude held on to things. Jude had to be the leader, the little teacher—she was still only five feet, you remember. The student body president, not just because she wanted it on her résumé, but she really believed she could get everyone to think the way she did.

If she weren't so exclusionary, I'd have been on board.

I had a lot of feelings going into this party: "take her down" crossed with "make her want to be my friend again." Now that I was *at* the party? I knew what we had to do.

The night before, I didn't toss and turn. I slept like a baby, waking up to find my covers neat and prim. When I got out of bed, there was barely an outline on my mattress. Like I hadn't been there at all.

I would get what I wanted. Be student body president. Hike my grades up and have my pick of colleges. Stay with Porter forever and ever, show everyone that queer could look however you wanted it to.

And when Porter found me, I knew my moment had come.

"She's upstairs," he whispered in my ear. His lips touched my earlobe the way they did when we were closer than close, and I shivered. Part of me wanted to find the nearest room with a door and have my way—maybe everything would *work* this time—but I knew we were in motion now. I had a mission.

"Cass is waiting," Porter added, before pulling away just enough to look me in the eye.

"Are you sure you want to do this?" he asked me, low and urgent. How many times had he checked in with me about this? A lot.

Instead of impatience, though, a wave of calm washed over me. This was my moment.

I smiled, kissed him full on the mouth, threading my fingers through the softest hair at the nape of his neck. "I got this," I said once we came up for air. "Trust me."

Without waiting for his reaction, I made my way up the stairs.

Slowly.

But surely.

It was time.

CHAPTER THIRTY-FOUR

Bronwyn

He came in through the window, Cass told me later that night.

I knew Jude Cuthbert. She thought it would be fun. Daring. Dangerous, in a way that nothing else felt anymore. She always did the right thing, but that night of the party, she wanted a little wrong.

No one was supposed to know.

Cass

The minute I got upstairs, I looked around for something. Anything.

I felt like a character in the video games I never played but my cheer friends loved, frantically thumbing at their devices in the van to comps, or between morning practice and afternoon during season. Standing in a hallway, frantically glancing around for the key, the emblem, the medallion that will level me up from random sophomore to potential savior. If only I could just find it.

Then I saw the cracked door.

Below me, the party raged: girls shrieking, guys daring each other to "chug chug chug," their low baritones scratchy, occasionally cracking. Someone daring someone else to make out, hysterical giggles before a brief awed hush. My senses felt sharpened up here in the quiet, as I crept toward the one room that was a little bit open. I knew, I just *knew*, I'd see what I needed to see, get the results that had been on my mind since Bronwyn told me she wanted to see Jude go down.

I hadn't had a drink or a smoke or anything. Not my scene. But in this moment, I swear Bronwyn—wherever she was—and I were one being, our wants and needs converging into a single, well-oiled unit.

We could do this. We could bring her down. We could *win*.

I slipped off my TOMS and set them silently by a closed door, where they waited patiently for my return, looking like a pair of hot pink mice. This open room could be a bathroom for all I knew. But something told me it wasn't.

The grunts and groans probably gave it away.

Flattening myself against the wall like a heroine in an action movie who knows her captor is just around the corner, I held my breath so as not to make a single sound and took a peek inside.

And immediately looked back down at my socks, light pink and green with monkeys, far too innocent to be in the vicinity with…that.

I had to look again, to confirm my suspicions.

Yup, that was her. Jude Cuthbert, in the flesh, half naked and getting fucked.

By a guy.

I was sure that the person I was seeing who wasn't Jude, was six-ish feet of pure cishet *dude.* The way he was standing, pants rumpled around his ankles, legs spread like he owned the bedroom that very likely wasn't his, since Annie didn't have siblings.

His wide shoulders. The deep *uh uh uh* he was uttering with every thrust. Even the bareness of his hairy ass. I couldn't see his face the way he was standing, back to me, but I didn't need to. Everything about the individual penetrating Jude Cuthbert said *guy.*

"Ohhhh, give me your—"

I can't even repeat what Jude was saying to you. Or even in my own head. But I sure remember.

By then, my face felt bloodless, cold. I was seeing our prospective student body president, an out and proud lesbian who insisted on using that label, noted hater of cis straight white men…having sex with someone who by all appearances was a cis, straight, white man.

I looked away again, this time bumping my head on the wall behind me. Rubbing the back of my head just under my ponytail, I glanced at my TOMS. It seemed like I'd put them there in another era.

His grunts were getting louder. She was whining, almost, a high-pitched sound. The whole sordid thing would be over soon from the sounds of it. I'd never had sex, but I knew that much.

And suddenly, something kicked into gear. The wheels in my head turned the way they did during cheer, when I could tell my top girl was going to fall and I had to decide in a millisecond how to catch her just the right way without killing us both.

If these two saw what I was about to do, I could easily run downstairs, put this disturbing visual behind me. If they didn't...

Victory.

I pulled my phone from my back pocket and reached out my arm just enough that it looked into the bedroom.

Set the photo app to video.

Hit Record.

CHAPTER THIRTY-FIVE

Bronwyn

I saw her shoes first. They were hard to miss, so bright they almost glowed in the dim light of the upstairs of Annie Murphy's parents' lake house. Positioned cutely and precisely, the way Cass did everything.

Then I heard the sounds. Unmistakable to anyone who's ever even *heard* of porn, let alone actually had sex. Two people were getting down.

And I was down the hall at this point, just at the top of the stairs, but I saw Cass filming.

Just then, she turned her head to me. I was glad because I didn't want to sneak up on my cousin and scare the shit out of her. Cass looked thirteen on a good day, but now, holding her phone discreetly while staring at me with wide eyes, she looked even younger.

Part of me wanted to hold out my hand, take her not only downstairs but out of this house once we found Porter, back to the safety of our tiny house and my tiny bedroom and our tiny lives playing silly card games.

The other part, the one who was gradually awakening to what exactly was going on, crept closer, stepping slowly so my Doc Martens didn't echo too loudly on the polished wood floor.

Holy shit, I whispered before clapping a hand over my mouth.

Coming into this party, looking for Jude at all costs, I didn't know what to expect.

Walking in on my cousin filming Jude Cuthbert having sex with someone who looked like a guy was definitely not it.

And they were being loud.

Not so much they drowned out the party below, that would have been impossible, but they were making noise. He was grunting like a frat boy hopped up on Miller Lite and toxic masculinity, Jude's noises were more of a high-pitched whine.

And it was definitely Jude.

I couldn't see the guy's face, but I could see hers, in the reflection of the window. And even if that didn't show up on the video, her haircut was unmistakable, as was the slope of her shoulders, her petite stature that was apparent even when on her hands and knees. On a bed.

First it was numbness, taking over my body to the point where I couldn't even move. If Cass had tried to drag me away, instead of standing silently filming in front of me, she wouldn't have been able to.

Then? Inertia was replaced by adrenaline.

I was going to win this election.

The guy—who still hadn't turned around, thank God—fucking *roared* out his finish. Someone had something to prove. I tapped Cass on the shoulder, inclined my head toward her shoes. Quietly but quickly now, we tiptoed back down the stairs and into a whole new reality.

A whole new reality where Porter was at the foot of the staircase, playing with his phone while trying to make it look like he wasn't standing guard.

The first thing I did was kiss him. Fast and hard. I hysterically giggled into his mouth before grabbing him by the hand and hustling him out to my Jeep, which thankfully wasn't blocked in.

"GO," I said once we were all in and I'd started the ignition. I peeled out, knowing I'd just talked to myself and not giving a shit how crazy that sounded. We needed to leave the scene and fast.

Behind me, I looked in the rearview mirror.

Cass, the Killer, held up her phone.

CHAPTER THIRTY-SIX

Cass

We never said it was a guy.

Genitals aren't gender. Everyone at Augustus knew this, even the shitty straights.

We also know that when presented with this kind of video, in this context, without any text to accompany it, people *will* fill in the gaps. They'll believe exactly what they want to believe. Especially when the video features someone people supposedly love, but fear way more. Who's already pissed off the ones who would spread whatever damning evidence we could give.

As the most recent prez race showed us: when a girl's on top, everyone wants to take her down.

Chapter Thirty-Seven

Bronwyn

"What do we do now?"

We were locked in my bedroom, my desk chair under the doorknob just in case Aunt Deb woke up and wandered in. Not that she ever did that.

Paranoia set in for the first time, but not the last.

The person asking was me.

We had a smoking gun in our hands, in the form of Cass's phone with its purple rubber cover and PopSocket with the tiger mascot of her cheer team. So innocuous, now containing a video that would ruin Jude Cuthbert forever, or at least for the upcoming elections.

I felt a hand on my arm. Porter.

"Think about this," he said, voice low. "Once it's out there, you can't walk it back, Bronwyn."

I saw him, those tired eyes, the hair that looked wilder than usual. I vaguely remembered the car ride back here, him running his hands through it like he did when the anxiety was taking hold.

"Will you still love me?" I asked. "No matter what?"

Without hesitation, he squeezed my hand. "You know I will."

It felt like a marriage vow. At any rate, it was the first time we'd said the L word.

I looked at Cass. "The online directory." I remembered Nasim, Scarlett, Declan. "Then we text the others, tell them to text *their* friends and say to check their school email. It'll all get out."

We were thinking on our feet, and it was so exciting I can't even put it into words. You just have to trust me.

It didn't take long to set up a random Gmail account. Sure, someone could probably trace it back, but they wouldn't. Despite what you saw on TV shows, cops weren't all that sophisticated, and this was a random sex tape from a party. It wasn't getting posted online. It was a girl and a guy. Nothing to see here.

Unless you went to Augustus High.

"Ready?" Cass said. The mouse hovered over Send.

I looked at Porter. *You can't walk this back.*

Will you still love me?

No matter what.

I thought back to the condoms spilling out of my locker, my backpack, the echoes of laughter. Jude's mean smile when she said "prom." The way she subtly went after me in her campaign speech. The way I really did want to talk to her tonight.

Her ultimate hypocrisy.

I didn't want it to be like this, but she'd left me no other choice.

"I want to do it," I said.

Cass scooted aside, and my fingers found the mouse of the laptop, a new MacBook that was a Christmas present and one of the last relics of my old life. The police hadn't confiscated it because I hadn't even known Pop was stealing, let alone collaborated. They felt bad, me getting kicked out of my own home. And I was, after all, just a dumb teenage girl.

Ha.

I clicked Send.

I couldn't help it, I squealed. Jumping up from my laptop, I grabbed Cass's hand and pulled her up too. "We won!" I screamed, before Cass shushed me and I remembered her mom was asleep. Grabbing her in a tight hug, I smelled artificial peach and shook off the chills that ran through me. She hugged back with a forceful squeeze, putting all her muscles into it. I'd never felt closer to my cousin.

Behind me, as we jumped and *eeeee*ed in our quietest voices, I felt two strong arms slide around my waist.

Porter's lips hit my ear.

"I stopped my meds."

I turned around, mouth dropping open. The word "hypocrite" flashed through my mind again. Only this time it wasn't about Jude.

Porter smiled.

In front of us, Cass happily danced.

ACT II

"Men willingly believe what they wish."
—Julius Caesar (the real one)

Author's Note

"Jude Cuthbert" initially declined to be interviewed for this project. However, she did grant me access to the audio files she kept from this time and gave me permission to use them as well as written documents in school records. She also provided additional information and verified facts as needed via text and FaceTime. I respect her need for privacy and consider her as much a part of this project as everyone else who spoke to me in real time. I hope her voice comes through as clearly as the others.

For what it's worth, she loves that she's the Caesar of the story.

CHAPTER ONE

Jude

I'm alone.

Tone, I'm alone.

Shitty poetry from a shitty human, I know. But there's not much else to do in exile.

As crazy as it sounds, Antonia—and I'm aware it sounds very crazy—I've started having imaginary conversations with you. Sometimes I write them down in the one notebook I was able to grab before they sent me away, blood still wet on the floor of my bedroom, while the video I didn't even know *was* a video made the rounds. During the fallout, I was on a plane, alone. And now I'm here, staring at four walls in a different state.

I hope someday I'll see you again and we can laugh at how stupid this all was. Not just that I'm talking to a person who isn't here, who stuck to me like glue after I dumped her, which was after my former best friend dumped her as well. A two-time dumpee. You're way too good for a title that sounds vaguely like bad porn.

Anyway.

How are you, Tone? I think about you a lot. Where I am, there's not much else to do but think, when I'm not scratching my undercut that's fast growing out or skimming through dog-eared romance novels for anything that sounds vaguely gay. Wondering if I'm qualified to do that last part anymore, or even think the word *gay*.

Can you tell how much I hate myself?

I realize I never asked you enough about *you*. Even when I did the whole cursory "How are you?" it was more of a springboard for how I was, how Bronwyn and her cronies had pissed me off today or how I had a new idea that would really crush her this time. And even that was on the surface. My real inner monologue was something I constantly shut up within myself. I trusted you most out of anyone in the world. I still do. Yet I couldn't bring myself to ask how you were.

Everything else seemed too essential. There *had* to be a campaign strategy we hadn't yet tried. After all, we knew jack about real politics, were learning as we went mostly from watching CNN and piecing things together. We figured if the idiots in the White House could do it, so could we. All along I constantly underestimated you, and I didn't want to know your inner monologue which was undoubtedly fascinating.

Now I'm here, and you're far away, and Bronwyn…I don't want to go there right now. It's three a.m. and I'm feeling lonely, like that dumb nineties song where the guy sounded like he was trying to take a dump. I told you that once and you laughed. Now I think that singer may have had a point. Three a.m. is the worst for loneliness.

Anyway, I should try to get some sleep. Got a whole lot of nothing going on tomorrow, completely the opposite from my former schedule, that I see now was jam-packed with bullshit. It's strange: now that I'm in a place I'm not allowed to leave unless I'm having a heart attack or something, I realize how much I never sat down and *thought* before. Always chasing that next idea I was certain was going to push me over the edge into genius-ville and make me feel less out of place. Part of me really was that confident, Tone, in my abilities and my ideas and my beliefs that I alone could change the world. The other part? Never knew what the fuck she was doing, and that's probably at least partly why I'm here.

I'm sure I'll talk to you later. Or whatever version of you my weird-ass brain has cooked up. Thank fuck I'm not hallucinating yet.

Ha.

CHAPTER TWO

Jude

Hey, Antonia, I'm back. I'm still not eating my own hair or scratching the days off in the wall. There's a free calendar from the local bank with a fawn for April, and my parents would kill me if I scratched the authentic seventies wood paneling.

I'm sure some people at school think I'm in a facility. Maybe I should be.

Did I fuck things up with Bronwyn? Of course I did, Tone. You know that better than anyone. I just have to keep saying it to myself, so I believe it. If I ever get out of here, I have to remember that.

I hated what she did to you.

You and I, Tone, have a...weird relationship. We tried dating after Bronny dumped you. After we broke up, we made that whole big show of how dating is passé anyway and the two of us were going to be exes turned friends. Real friends, not the kind with benefits who make out when they're drunk, or more. No loud fighting and storming off in the hallways, no angry texts, no rebounds with the other person's ex. Actually, I worried you liked Bronwyn better and I was the consolation prize. I was hurt, so I just made a big loud thing of my denial. Like always.

I miss you right now, Tone. More than I ever thought I would. More than I miss any other of our friends. Not that I had many, toward the end.

And I have to come to terms with why that is. I have nothing else to do here anyway.

Yes, I hated that Bronwyn didn't exactly cheat on you but almost. I think it bothered me more than it bothered you, who insisted you two had been over for a while anyway, this just made it official. I saw the hurt, though. The way you shut your locker door a little harder than normal when you saw them together in the hallways. Being left is one thing, being left for a straight guy is another.

The more I think about it, the more I know that what Bronwyn went through *wasn't* bullshit. She wasn't a turncoat or a traitor or any of the labels I hurled at her before ostracizing her completely, all the queer kids blindly following suit like I knew they would. Even the ones who didn't think bisexuality was a joke, identified that way even, had done the reverse of what Bronwyn did. Latch on to some dude so she could live out the prom queen fantasy like an old John Hughes movie? Marsha P. Johnson would *never*, we all agreed. Or really, I *decreed*, and we set about to make her wish she'd never been born.

You know that line "the lady doth protest too much, methinks"? Of course you do, your English grade was better than mine. I was a STEM girl, proclaimed that literature was borderline obsolete while secretly wishing I could unlock the puzzle of iambic pentameter, a foreign language in which you were fluent.

Are fluent, you're not dead like I'm presumed to be.

Anyway, that line has always stuck with me. Since the asshole with the tangerine face was unfairly chosen to run our country, with the most blatantly throwback of slogans on terrible square baseball caps, protest was my reason for living. I signed petitions. I called my local representatives. I decided to run for student body president and was pretty sure I could do so unopposed. And when Bronwyn dumped you to get with Porter, then almost immediately announced her candidacy, I vowed to bring her down. For me and for you.

What nobody knew is what I'm going to tell you now. It's what led to why I'm here, living in isolation while Bronwyn, no doubt, swans around Augustus High. The most protesting I did this spring was against myself.

It started out with a birthday text message right after the inauguration and Women's March weekend. I'd barely gotten home with my cleverly worded, now worn-out signs when my phone dinged, over and over. Reception downtown was crap because it was so crowded. Selfies from you, since we hadn't been able to meet up. You looked breathless with righteousness, your warm brown skin, tinged pink. Even then, I had to sit down because of how beautiful you looked holding your Planned Parenthood sign.

And one other, from someone I hadn't heard from in a long time.

Happy late birthday, dudette. What's up?

Six words that changed everything.

I'm not ready to tell you this, Tone. Even though you're only empty air. Maybe in the morning.

Good night.

CHAPTER THREE

PAGE FROM AUGUSTUS HIGH HANDBOOK, SECTION ON STUDENT ELECTIONS

Congratulations on running for Augustus High student government! No matter the politics of the outside world, YOU can help make a difference in your school community. Student government isn't just a line for your college applications: it's an opportunity to help your fellow students, and yourself, be better.

UPDATED FOR SPRING 2017 ELECTIONS: PRIMARIES

Due to the overwhelming amount of interest this semester, we will be holding primary elections for certain offices including Student Body President.

Before this election, each prospective candidate will be required to collect twenty-five (25) signatures from other students. If you are running for a class office, students must be in your year. Student Body President candidates must collect fifty (50) signatures that can be from anyone in the school. All of the abovementioned must be physical signatures delivered to Principal Olive Murrell's office by the appointed deadline.

CAMPAIGNING

1. No swag, physical, monetary, or digital. NO EXCEPTIONS. This will be strictly enforced.
2. Professional posters are for professional politicians. If the candidate chooses to have posters, they must be handmade

or designed on their own computer. All posters must be approved by the principal's office. No social media ads.

3. All speeches for the campaign assembly must be approved by the principal's office by the appointed deadline.

Speeches

1. Must be written by the candidate, though they can receive help from other students such as campaign managers.
2. Must be previously approved (see above for guidelines).
3. No mudslinging (picking apart other candidates. Think of the ads you see before every major election, and don't do that!).
4. No mentioning other candidates by name.

General note: "Ask not what your country can do for you, but what you can do for your country."—John F. Kennedy. Try to think of what's unique that YOU and only YOU can bring to the office for which you are running!

CHAPTER FOUR

Jude Cuthbert: Final Speech for Student Body President—
APPROVED

You already know who I am.

And by the time I'm done, you won't stop thinking about me, and why I'm the exact right choice for next year's student body president.

As a reminder, I'm Jude Cuthbert. I'm a junior, and currently ranked second in my class. Not only am I on the executive student committee of the LGBTQ+ Alliance, but I served as class representative as a first-year and as a sophomore. I took this year off from student government to concentrate on campaigning for the woman who many of us hoped would be our next president, serving as a communications intern in the local office. To many of us, that election was a crushing blow. However, armed with this practical, political experience as well as my own strong convictions, I am ready to serve this school with every strong conviction I have.

And I have many.

Mudslinging gets us nowhere unless you're a bully. Any of us who watched the presidential candidate debates bore unfortunate witness to that disgusting behavior. I'm not here to personally trash any student who serves our school, particularly my opponent. That said, I'd like to restate that I have principles. I have beliefs. I have detailed plans for everything from revamping the cafeteria menu to include more vegan options, to increasing opportunities for tutoring and extra study halls, to liaising with faculty to maximize our academic and extracurricular offerings. At Augustus High, we value excellence, and we are resolute in taking that excellence to the next level.

I assure you, I will follow through on these plans, and more, to the best of my ability. I will not abandon my convictions to chase what I feel are the best personal options for me and me alone. In short, I'm your candidate. The one who doesn't forget. The one who won't change her mind.

I'm Jude Cuthbert, and I don't flip-flop. I will take your disappointment in our world and turn it into something better, and I will let nothing distract me. Nothing.

Thank you for your time, and I'll see you at the polls.

CHAPTER FIVE

Jude

Okay, I lied. I guess I really am a politician. Telling untruths to the empty air. Aaaaand now I'm a bad pop song. Sorry, Tone.

Really, everything started the day after the presidential election—the real one, not the stupid school one—when my mom told my dad and me that she was leaving us.

And it gets worse. She left us for a *couple.*

Doesn't exactly go down well with instant oatmeal.

This is the first time I've said the words out loud. I'm counting it as telling somebody, even though you're not here and I might just destroy this whole damn tape. In case you're wondering, I'm recording all of these on an old tape player I found in the attic my first night here when I couldn't sleep and visions of Bronwyn crowing about her victory and…other things I don't want to think about were dancing through my head like angry sugarplums, the kind of faeries that want to steal your soul. I don't know who left it here, the house has been in our family for over a hundred years. But there it was under a thick layer of dust, gray and ugly and with a whole bunch of blank tapes. Waiting.

Oh yeah. My mom.

She *wanted* me to tell my friends. To *process.* Honestly, I think she wanted me to do her dirty work, spread the suburban gossip to the girls and their moms, even though Bronwyn's lives in Florida, I think, and her aunt works all the time. And your mom is above all that crap.

But I kept it all inside this whole time. Yes, even when you and I were dating. I'm sorry, Tone. Besides the whole spiting-my-mom factor…I didn't want to acknowledge it myself.

My family split up because my mother isn't straight and can't pick a side, or person.

From the way my dad dropped his bowl in the sink—I can still hear the *clatter* of pottery on stainless steel—I knew he was just as blindsided.

She laid out the facts, like the journalist she was before I came along, an oops baby if there ever was one. Just like she taught me to do. Just like I can't, because I have a tendency to ramble, which I know has always disappointed her.

They met on an app. She'd been seeing *them* for six months. *They* were buying a farm downstate. One, big happy throuple, Old McDonald not included.

She moved out that day but comes back a lot when she knows my dad will be working late. Which is always. Obviously, she's not that bright.

She wants me to meet *them*. To see *their* apartment downtown, where they're camped out before the farm. To be a part of *their* life.

Yes, *they* have names, but I don't want to know them.

Okay, I guess she *did* make up her mind. She made up her mind to abandon me and our family for a sexier option. She gets to be all hippie earth mom and have lots of sex with more than one person. Good for her, but I hate it.

Tone, can you blame me? If I'm gonna be really shallow about it, this is *embarrassing*. Emphasis intended. My mom used to lunch at the country club. I hated that she did it, but seeing as she grew up Jewish and wasn't allowed in the tony places she longed to frequent, even in the friggin' 1980s, I sort of understood. I wasn't the only person at Augustus descended from a lady who lunches.

And now she's growing out her hair and flashing cleave in hippie dresses.

I could maybe handle it, maybe, if she'd left us for *one* other person. But no. She left us for *two*. Can't get enough, I guess. My mom, the helmet-haired head of every committee, who gets regular highlights and ask me way too many probing questions because, again, former journalist...is having threesomes regularly.

Where exactly do I fit in?

When she showed up to drive me to the airport, with my dad, I was almost relieved to see the resting bitch face I'd grown up with instead of the dippy smile that looks like she's high.

And now that I'm away from it, I see things way more clearly. This is why I leaned so hard into the lesbian identity. *This* is why Bronwyn's new dating life offended me so personally, when it probably shouldn't have.

Not that it excuses any of the bullshit she did pull. Or at least, I think she did with her stupid boyfriend and her cheerleader cousin with those weird tarot cards. That reading or whatever it's called *was* strange, though. Like she could see everything I wasn't dealing with.

But yeah. Here in exile, with no one to talk to but myself, I can finally pull my head out of my ass. Start to piece things together a bit. My home life that had been almost blindly boring suddenly became weird and humiliating with the drop of an oatmeal bowl. My mom exploring her own sexuality—ew, sorry, I still can't with those words in the same sentence—at the same time as my best friend? I couldn't handle it.

And instead of talking about it like Mom wanted me to do so badly, instead of *processing*, instead of even shutting myself off and figuring out how I felt, I puffed up like a peacock. I waved that pink-and-orange-striped flag, a one-woman Pride parade. I strutted around shaming everyone who was a little bit different from what I thought was my own elevated state of being.

Eventually, I trusted the exact wrong person and I paid for it.

I'm sorry I never told you. But where would I start?

Chapter Six

Jude

Power is a funny thing, isn't it, Tone?

I don't want to compare where I am to prison or anything. I mean, I don't have to go to the bathroom in full view of anyone else. I get groceries and meals delivered, and they're good. Healthy. I can take walks on the beach even though it's too cold for swimming. It's not like there's anyone else around at this time of year anyway. I used to always want the run of this house, all to myself, until I actually had it.

Sorry. Lost my train of thought.

I didn't set out to be the queer alpha bitch of Augustus High, no matter what Bronwyn says or thinks. It just...happened. The grade school Bronny and I went to had way more straight people than Augustus, but even so, that's where I started to notice how everyone— not just kids, but teachers and parents and even the principal—really listened when I talked.

When I was younger, I was just another kid who got all As and never had a growth spurt. But around sixth grade, the situation started to shift without my having to do much of anything. Maybe it's *because* I was short and stayed that way even when people were shooting up all around me. I was never quiet, but I figured I had to be even louder to make myself heard. At the same time, I'd been dragged to my parents' work functions and country club crap since before I could walk.

I knew what adults wanted to hear, but I wasn't one of those weird kids who could only talk like a grown-up. I paid attention to what my classmates liked and wore, until they started paying attention to what *I* liked and wore. My dad would incorrectly call this "street cred."

You called me a "born politician."

I like that better, and not just because it's coming from you.

I've seen the really old *Spider-Man*, though, and I know that with great power comes great responsibility. I even have a T-shirt with that saying from fourth grade, that I've never outgrown. Until Bronny…did what she did, I always took that seriously. Sure, I had influence, but I couldn't use it to hurt people.

When Bronwyn started dating Porter, though, I did exactly that.

The condoms in her locker went too far, I admit. Now that I'm miles away from normal, I know that I should have told the first-years and sophomores to cool it. Bronny and I were already not as close, so I really don't know whether she was serious about that guy or just freaking out because her world had fallen apart.

I do know that I was so wrapped up in my own loneliness, I wasn't really fair. And I'd been judgmental of queer girls who date guys before. That hot soccer player, Scarlett, comes to mind. She wasn't my best friend, though.

I won't compare my shit to yours, Tone. You've called me out enough that sadness over one's circumstances is a whole different thing than being deathly afraid to leave your house, and I appreciate that. And you. But I was wrestling with a lot that spring, and if I'd opened up to you, or Bronwyn, or anyone, I would have lost my power. And I felt like I was already losing enough.

The election, the candidacy, was your idea, and it was a fantastic one. Spreading that good old queer influence. Really educate everyone about queer history, something Augustus wasn't great about. They postured as progressive but rarely delivered.

It could be a whole extension of my lavender menace project, I told Mr. Roman excitedly after school shortly after I won the primary. I could bring meaning back to all of us, the way we truly were, the way we were born. I wouldn't let people like Bronwyn play around with queerness, discard it like a coffee cup she was finished drinking from. Cardboard, stained and useless, taking residence among the crumpled-up papers and rotting food.

On the inside, I knew it was a way to own my power *and* be responsible. And after Bronwyn lost, she'd fall in line just like she always had, stop hanging out with her weird cousin and a straight guy who could offer her nothing.

Senior year would be back to normal. Only better.

In the meantime, while you and I hammered out campaign strategies over bags of those cheese Sun Chips you loved and I pretended to like—sorry, Tone, but in my defense, you're just so cute when you're plowing through them and offering me the bag when you remember—I was thinking up even more independent study projects for history. Earning smiles from Mr. Roman, the memory of which kept me warm when I got home from school or your house—with your happy, loving, always present parents—to a cold, empty foyer with a plate in the refrigerator and instructions for heating from our housekeeper. Poor little rich girl, I know. I know.

I also know why I was clinging to the word *lesbian*, even though a lot of people our age think it's dated. Why I wanted to take my own queerness one step further. Why I was shaming Bronwyn so hard, looking away in the halls when she tried to catch my eye, confused and pleading without saying a word. I may not be in prison, but I've had a lot of time to think.

I was a lesbian in every sense of the word. I was sure. So why not reclaim it?

Except maybe I *was* attracted to a guy. But he didn't count. He couldn't.

Those text messages kept me going. I just liked having a fun little secret. Stress relief.

I was allowed that, right?

CHAPTER SEVEN

Jude

What can I say about you, Tone? You took me by surprise. In the best possible way.

I'm having a lot of revelations while in exile. Exile sounds way more romantic than "my dad doesn't want to look at me." Turns out Augustus took up my whole life. Who knew?

Also, you are way more intimidating than you realize.

Looking back, you should have been the candidate, not the campaign manager. Not that there's anything we can do about it now. Hindsight twenty-twenty, right?

Even now when we can't talk, I feel connected to you. Until we briefly dated, I didn't know we had so much in common, even though we've been hanging out in the same group for two years. We both watch CNN for fun. We both love our parents more than we'll ever admit, not in an affectionate way like you see on old sitcoms but a deeper respect that borders on reverence, because they may not be warm and fuzzy, but they will damn well make sure we make our own way in the world, and successfully. Well. That used to be true, in my case.

We both believe that "lesbian" is a highly underrated identity among our generation, who embraces "queer" as a catch-all, but it's also kind of lazy. You may be born this way, but your choices of how to express yourself, who to love, should be strong. That was my whole platform, your very excellent idea, until it all went wrong in such a spectacular way.

I like to think it would have worked, Tone, that we would have won.

I think of you, not just physically, though your face is flawless and your hair majestic as a monarch's. More than anything, I miss your company. Your solid presence. Your wicked sense of humor that I got to see more than anyone else before everything imploded.

It was you, Tone, I told about Mr. Roman.

It started out as sheer admiration. I used to think history class was bullshit, a fluffy way to waste a class period that could have been devoted to STEM. Coding. Meal prep, even. Real skills that would see us through life in a way that learning about old straight white guys who dictated the way the world was for far too long. Fuck history. Let's make our own.

The funny thing was, Mr. Roman agreed when I challenged him. He didn't use the textbooks that biased everything in favor of dudes who looked like him. He let us do our own independent projects. No topic was too controversial, whether it was poor Henrietta Lacks who suffered for everyone else's benefit, or what really went down on plantations. I spent a whole quarter working on my "lavender menace" research paper and ensuing oral presentation and got an A for my efforts. His approving smile meant more than any grade ever could.

I didn't make the connection then, the way I do now. This past year, my parents have been out of the house more than ever. Work is demanding, I'm old enough to fend for myself now, blah blah blah. I know all of it. Proving oneself doesn't end once you get into Harvard or Dartmouth, it just gets more intense. I understood that, of course I did. They'd both been poor, lived in small towns, with none of the advantages I had. My mom's Jewish and got anti-Semitic rhetoric thrown at her at her school, and this was in the *1980s*. I loved them for giving me everything they'd lacked, and I appreciated the constant work it took to keep us privileged.

Of course, I eventually *learned* why my mom was out of the house so much.

But I missed them.

Custom-prepared dinners and endless takeout are fun for a while, but not when you're constantly eating on your own. I suppose I could have invited myself over to our friends' houses, but that felt sad and pathetic. I'm Jude Cuthbert, for fuck's sake, and I'm supposed to be better than that.

So I clung to my identity, the various facets of it, the way a smaller kid would have held on to a teddy bear. The more I dove into my project, the less lonely I was. And my determination to reclaim "lesbian," and spread the gospel of owning one's sexuality, only increased. Our foremothers had worked so hard, after all, and honoring what they'd gone through was only right.

Mr. Roman, a straight white guy, saw this in me. Recognized my drive. Appreciated and rewarded it. Not my first choice for a mentor. But at this point with my mom going crazy and my dad checked out, I'd take all the guidance I could get.

Of course I ended up sticking around after class, then after school. Once we even sat in the teacher's lounge, sipping coffee and arguing political theory, like real adults.

I thought I'd found my equal.

Finally.

CHAPTER EIGHT

Jude

I knew, Tone, that Bronwyn wanted to Talk.

Bronwyn always wanted to Talk, with a capital T, about everything. I was the doer, she was the fixer. Her whole life was discourse. Well, I guess it was till her father got arrested. I'd get it more if she was raised by therapists, but one of her dads was a CEO and the other stayed home most of the time. I know some people need to process every single thing out loud, but God, it got annoying sometimes.

One thing I didn't miss when our friendship ended, and our rivalry began.

I hit my limit when she tried to explain Porter to me. You do you, Bronny. But did you have to do you in such an aggressively hetero manner? If he were bi, or trans, or anything other than Basic Straight White Dude, I might have understood a little. As it was, it felt like she was kicking me in the teeth.

Have some empathy, you told me later. You and I, Tone, we were still dating then. I vented *hard* that night, sitting in my car after we'd fogged the windows up getting out our respective frustrations. Me with Bronwyn, you with the unexpected C minus on a pre-calc quiz.

I remember laying my head on your lap in the parking lot of the playground on the edge of town. Outside, a breeze blew the swings, so they looked like ghost-kids were riding. She's lost her whole life, you reminded me, a gentle sway to your voice, just like those abandoned swings. Did little kids even play outside anymore, or were they all about their screens like us?

Just then, my phone buzzed. I knew who it was, but he'd have to wait for now. You kept going, running your fingers over my undercut the way you always did, stroking just right until I wanted to purr. As it was, I just listened to you talk. I never told you, Tone, but that was my favorite thing to do.

Or maybe she really loves him, you said.

That did it. I lifted my head up and cracked open the door. I could practically see our collective heat whooshing out as I huffed my way to the driver's seat.

You didn't join me right away. Just sat there in the back, studying me with that intense gaze of yours. Our eyes met in the rearview mirror. I looked away, started the ignition.

My phone buzzed again.

You joined me in the front seat, and I drove you home in chilly, awkward silence. Just as you got out, you walked around the car, motioned for me to roll the window down with an elegant gesture. I obeyed.

Think about it, you said in that quiet but commanding tone I loved. You leaned down until our faces were close enough to kiss. My face flushed and I wanted to take my hands off the wheel and pull you toward me.

Instead, you stood up and walked to your front door, leaving me alone with my thoughts.

Buzz.

It was him. We'd been talking more and more around that time. Tone, as much as I loved confiding in you, just being in your presence really, you were right there in it with me. You were not only Bronwyn's classmate but also her ex. Even though you'd established you were clearly and firmly on my side—I knew for a fact you and Bronwyn hadn't spoken since your breakup—there were certain things…things I couldn't tell you. I knew that just like tonight, you'd give me advice I knew was the right call, but in no way wanted to hear at this point in time.

Like how these texts were seriously messing me up.

But in a good way, maybe?

I could open up to him. Talk about what kept me up at night. About why this election had suddenly become priority number one. About how I wanted to really send a message to all the young queer girls at Augustus—some of whom weren't even out yet—that they could do, could be, anything, no matter what President Dickhead of the Disunited States said or did.

He was a neutral party. More importantly, he got it. Got me.

At least that's what I thought then, Tone.

He was such a good liar.

Chapter Nine

Jude

I don't know what I was thinking, Tone.

I wanted an escape from reality. Bronwyn was so sure I just danced through life, collecting amazing grades, hot girlfriends, and loyal followers along the way. She never said it out loud, but I know her, okay?

The stress I'd been feeling all semester—stuff I couldn't even tell you, my most recent ex and current closest confidante—came to a head at that party, in that bedroom, with that…person.

Not Mr. Roman. I don't know if that's a rumor, but I hope not. He was just doing his job as a teacher, encouraging me to be my best, to ask questions, to dig harder and further than a basic Wikipedia search. We're talking actual books in the town library. Augustus loves to gossip, but we never texted. He didn't have my number. We never hung outside of the building, and even inside, all we did was talk about my project—and how I could keep the momentum going even after the inevitable A plus. You know my feelings about straight dudes—at least, what I projected to the world—but he's a good one.

Also, not the guy from first-year debate tournaments that I texted with for a while.

Did I tell you about that? No. Of course I didn't. I was a Lesbian with a capital L, after all. At least, I wanted to be. No one was pressuring me to do this, but I am one hell of a persuasive self-talker. As you know, Tone.

So, Debate Guy. I hadn't seen him in so long, but I remembered those dark curls, that pearly grin. He may have been queer, but I never asked, and I sort of pretended he wasn't? Felt more dangerous that way. A fun little secret.

All the while I was texting with two different dudes, Debate Guy and…him. And Debate Guy was fun. Flirty. We just texted, but I always felt like he was really listening. Probably why I told him about Mom.

I feel so guilty about that now, Tone. I should have told you. Debate Guy had the advantage of being far away. I think he told me he lives in New York now. He didn't say much to the Mom thing, just that he understood it was a difficult and humiliating situation. Probably tough to figure out on my own. He was honored I confided in him.

That's the word he used. *Honored.*

By the time he canceled on the party invite, I figured out it was a lie. And I could have done that way earlier—I mean, social media exists for a reason. I liked that cocoon, though. That intimacy. Even when I realized it wasn't really coming from Debate Guy…I dunno, it's stupid, but I was grateful to whomever was on the other end of that phone.

Yes, I suspected Bronwyn and her cronies for a while, but once he backed off, I waited for the fallout at school.

Nothing. And I knew Bronwyn, and how our rivalry was at its peak. Why wouldn't she have wanted to air my threesome mom's dirty laundry to everyone in the middle of our race for president?

Probably someone from a random school, I thought. Or even someone at Augustus who hated me. Wanting to make trouble. I wouldn't give them the satisfaction.

So I leaned into…him. Even more than I had before. Once that parking lot burnout who copied my test answers talked me into the party after all, I invited him. I think I'd just been waiting for an opportunity.

And it's why I'm here now, in hiding and in isolation. My recent project has been watching *The L Word* and taking notes on how problematic it is. And I have a *lot* of notes.

Sorry for the tangent. It's easier than thinking about what brought me to this place, not just physically but emotionally too.

Anyway.

You weren't there that night and I'm still a little mad at you for it.

I'm sorry. It's not rational, I know. You're not my keeper, and you had a valid excuse. Your family's important to you, not just your parents but the whole Marcus clan, who've always accepted you as exactly who you are, not only that but *celebrated* your every milestone.

My parents, and Bronwyn's, took it for granted that we were queer, which of course is fine and preferable than the alternative, but your mom and dad baked you a goddamn cake with your pronouns in rainbow icing. Of course you wanted to be with them that night. Annie Murphy would no doubt throw other parties at her stupid lake house.

I still missed you. As long as I'm playing true confessions with your invisible presence, I always missed you when you weren't around. You had the true confidence that, more often than not, I faked. And you were reassuring, not like a parent, but you were above all the petty high school bullshit that I relished. Quiet and fully evolved. You were everything I wanted to be. Still are.

It's why I was too ashamed to tell you about the texts, the plan. I knew you'd disapprove, and that would have been enough for me to cut it out completely, erase him from my life. And here's the thing, Tone: I wanted this.

Annie's parents' lake house was intimidating, sitting there all stately and proud on the dark water that gave off a horror-movie shimmer. Like ghosts were going to rise out of it and wreak havoc, or a serial killer would pop out of the manicured bushes. And when you got inside, she had a full fucking bar setup. No bartender because we were underage, but all the other accoutrements. Not only every kind of alcohol known to humanity, but accessories. Ice buckets with dainty little cubes, shiny silver shakers, little red cocktail straws. Even, I shit you not, cut-up fruit, lemons and limes and strawberries of all things.

I bet most of it rotted.

And people had put on the style, more so than the usual jeans and T-shirts of Friday night gatherings. We're talking high heels, short and tight skirts, snappy button-downs. Even the straight dudes had ironed their shirts for once. Or had their housekeepers do the honors.

But I barely noticed any of this because I was glued to my phone.

Tonight was the night.

We wanted to hook up, even though it was sort of wrong, but that's what made it fun. We wanted a place more civil than the back seats of our cars, because…uncivilized. Not to mention basic. A hotel was too much, though, and even under fake names there was too high a risk of getting caught by someone who mattered.

Speaking of risk, though, we wanted a little—because otherwise, where was the fun?

This place, this time, was the perfect opportunity for a tryst. It was a given people were going to hook up in bedrooms, because no matter how much Annie tried to fancy it up with a "cocktail hour" dress code and real martini glasses that would likely get broken, this was a high school party. Because this was a lake house, there weren't streetlamps and you could easily park your car out of sight. I'd never been there but we were able to look up the listing on Zillow, find the room where he could scale the wall like a demented Romeo wannabe. Slip in undetected to everyone but me.

For me, planning has always been a turn-on.

And I was craving this shock to my system. I was well aware that if…this, any of it, got out I would be ruined. Not even just the class presidency, but my whole reputation. My resolution to reclaim the L word, paying homage to our queer elders who paved the way, would go straight out the window. Ha. Straight.

It wouldn't get out, though, I was sure of it. After all, people sneaked around all the time and got away with far worse than what we were planning. I would experience all the sheer *fun* and suffer none of the consequences.

God, I was so naïve.

"I'll make it good for you," he promised, and I believed him like the stupid girl in the Garbage song from a million years ago.

All our texts, the inside jokes we'd developed, the sweet words he said to me when no one else would, would come to a head and then never be spoken of again.

I didn't even see Bronwyn and her crew walk into the party.

I only had eyes for my phone. I went in a corner and waited, turning on the camera to inspect myself, my carefully chosen outfit and fresh haircut. Finally, the phone came alive, generating the buzz I'd been waiting for since I walked in the door.

Go upstairs, he texted. *Open the window. You know which one.*

And I went.

ACT III

"He was my friend, faithful and just to me. But Brutus says he was ambitious, And Brutus is an honourable man…"
—Marc Antony, *Julius Caesar*

Author's Note

"Antonia Marcus" was in the middle of a particularly grueling semester when I reached out to them, but graciously shared the journal they kept during this time period. With one exception, all Antonia chapters are taken from said journal.

Chapter One

Antonia

Jude Cuthbert brings out my mess.

I am a lot of things in one taller-than-average package. Kenyan. Greek. Gemini. Trans. Demigirl. She. They. Lesbian. Depressed. OCD. Loyal.

That last thing, above all.

I handle things. That's what I do. I wasn't surprised when Jude asked me to be her campaign manager. In fact, I would have been shocked if she'd gone with anyone else, even if Bronwyn and I were still together, even if Bronwyn were still in our circle at all.

I like the idea of being a handler. Not a wrangler per se: that word suggests wild animals and possibly missing limbs if you make one wrong move. But my whole life, I've handled everything. Even my brain, which can be really shitty if I let it, telling me I'm not good enough, that the world wasn't made for someone like me, whatever *that* means on any given day. My dad will tell you, when I started sleeping a lot, losing interest in reading and writing and watching CNN, when my grades dropped, I found him and asked to see a psychiatrist.

I was eleven.

Maybe I'd heard about depression symptoms on a commercial for some supposed wonder drug, but I like to think I just have good instincts. And now I'm in therapy and on meds that work. Even before I hit puberty, I knew how to handle it. When I was diagnosed with OCD, I was already well equipped to handle that too.

Besides my ability as a handler, I am bar none the best public speaker Augustus High has ever seen. As my parents love to remind me, it's not bragging if it's fact. I can find the right words for whatever situation, spin like a champ, and when needed, put those perfectly spun words into someone else's mouth like custom-made cotton candy. I aspire to speechwriting glory, and what better way to start than with the highest-stakes election our school has ever seen?

The new president of the Not Really Ever United States is an affront to everything I am. Everything. As much as I want to help Jude, she'll never fully comprehend that level of fear I had when the results were finally called. I stayed up until three a.m., fighting the demons in my own head while also acknowledging they were there for a reason. I still don't know what "visibly" queer means. I do know I am visibly Black, and that's a problem for assholes like the one currently running our country. As if worrying about cops wasn't bad enough, now I have to worry even more about laws, and I'm sure that stupid bathroom debate will rear its ugly head again before too long.

I know, however, that the biggest changes are built from the ground up. And people like Jude, who can command a room like nobody's business, are the ones who can effect that change. Until everything happened and Jude disappeared to a location I don't even know, I was happy to stay in the background.

Make them think I'm dead was all she texted before her parents whisked her away to parts unknown. I tried to text back a couple of times, but I don't think she's using her phone anymore. I didn't question her then, and I don't now, even before I'm about to declare her martyrdom to the whole school. I don't know the circumstances behind the video, and honestly? I don't need to.

I hope wherever Jude is, she's okay.

We dated, briefly, Jude and I, before deciding we were better off as best friends. I don't think of it in terms of filling the gap Bronwyn left. I think our relationship, Jude's and mine, was meant to be in that exact time and place. I'm not sure what I think about fate, but this relationship with Jude feels pretty damn close.

Bronwyn and I, we never felt *right* together. Even before she decided she liked a straight cis guy better than she liked me. We weren't in love: in another time and if we were heterosexual, we would be referred to as a *marriage of convenience.* Our hooking up, then dating, felt premeditated but in a way that wasn't fate of the romantic sort. We were in the same group of high-achieving, proudly queer friends, had known each other since first year at Augustus.

As juniors, people were pairing off. Even Jude, who couldn't stay with anyone longer than two weeks (that "anyone" included me), was always part of a twosome. But I wasn't a player, and neither was Bronwyn. So we were together until we weren't, until Porter got her attention with his performative allyship. Or maybe it was real allyship, I don't know. It's hard for me to tell what's real anymore.

Do I wish Bronwyn hadn't dumped me over text? Sure, I guess I'm supposed to. Or maybe not really. If she wants to embrace even more privilege than she already has, that's her funeral. If I'm feeling more generous, I can admit that she *has* been through a lot and sometimes extreme change makes people behave in crazy ways. Jude basically faked her own death.

About Jude.

I'm not a blind follower, no matter what anyone else thinks. Not like Cass, who trails after cousin Bronwyn like a lost little puppy who's finally found someone who kind of, sort of, resembles their mother. I could say the same for Porter. In the end, Bronwyn got everything she wanted. I *know* she was the one who hit Send on the video, like anyone at Augustus with a working brain. No one seems to care, though, except me. If I were a blind follower, I'd immediately fall in line with whatever Bronwyn wants as student body president, leader by default.

Instead, I'm going to make sure no one forgets Jude Cuthbert.

No one.

CHAPTER TWO

Nasim

I love Shakespeare, but after Jude disappeared, "blood on my hands" felt like an understatement.

Chapter Three

Cass

I couldn't get it out of my head.

Why did I even look? After the quick glance that confirmed what was going on, that the girl was Jude and the guy was…most likely a guy, I could have just hit Record and put my phone in the right spot. I didn't have to keep looking, and yet I did, and now I see it all the time.

Once we sent the video, I started doing push-ups. Like, constant push-ups.

I used to bitch about push-ups. We weren't allowed to do the ones on our knees unless we had some sort of injury. I was yelled at—not in an abusive way, but in a tough way—about my form since my first official day of cheer in my little purple leotard and miniature black shorts. I can, and have, out push-up-ed every classmate in every school PE class…ever.

I understand why we do them, of course. Upper body strength is a must when you're responsible for literally throwing another human. And the best way to build that strength? You guessed it.

After the video was sent, I grunted through push-ups every morning and night in my room. Sometimes in PE at Augustus, I dropped and gave twenty to an invisible drill sergeant, or I imagined I was in trouble with my cheer coach John for talking back (which never occurred in real life). When actually at practice, I added fifteen more to whatever John had us do for warm-up. Sometimes twenty.

Were the push-ups penance, for my part in humiliating someone so much that she…disappeared? Leaving a broken window and a puddle of her own blood in her bedroom, or so the story goes. Rumors were flying with the speed of light.

Or was I trying to get the sex out of my head?

Sophomore year, when I was still figuring it all out, I didn't really know what sex looked like. Most everyone in cheer, most everyone I *knew*, had done it by then, or at least watched enough online porn to know what they *wanted* to do once given the opportunity. I knew the mechanics of different bodies. My mom's a nurse, after all, and that was never privileged information.

But what I saw that night, Jude and the mystery guy, was just strange.

Disturbing, even.

He was just rough, going in and out of her in a way that couldn't be comfortable. And the sounds he made, so deep and raw. I'm sure people are into that.

Something tells me, though, that Jude wasn't.

What did I know, though? I was a dumb sophomore who was undecided about her sexuality. Who'd barely touched herself. Who had muscles but almost no boobs, and had more in common with the little kids doing their first stunting than even the first-years at Augustus, who seemed decades more evolved.

Maybe if I pushed myself physically, I'd find the answer.

Or at least stop hearing the sounds.

CHAPTER FOUR

Antonia

Before we go any further, there's something you should know about who I am.

Or I guess, who I was.

And by "you," I mean this weird diary I've started to get through all of this. It's not one of those journals you buy, write in for one page and then abandon forever. (Or is that just me?) It's *definitely* not anything you can find online. After what happened with Jude, I'm shocked more people at our school didn't swear off social media forever.

My dad loves that old show *The Office*. I kind of get and kind of don't, and why is almost everyone straight? I do, however, love the character Creed. I guess that's the actor's real name and he was in a band that's older than my parents, and you get the feeling they just let him wander around on set and do what he wanted, saying lines when it suited him. Anyway, Creed keeps what he thinks is a blog but is really a Word doc that a temp set up for him and titled "Creed Thoughts."

And that gave me this idea.

I even titled this doc "Antonia Thoughts." So silly, like that show, but it makes me smile. Which isn't happening much lately. But my therapist and my parents love the idea, so with three therapists behind me, I'm forging ahead.

Where was I, Word doc? Oh yeah.

I was a child model. My mom is the complete opposite of what you'd think when you think of...moms of child models. And I can see the picture you've already got in your head, Word doc.

We were at a department store in the city, looking at argyle socks, of all things and an agent gave us her card. The fact that Becky is female and butch went a long way. We still get Christmas cards from her and her wife.

It was never anything major. Kids don't do runways or editorial. Just some catalog stuff, a few Gap ads back when holiday sweaters were their thing. Nothing out of state, that was my parents' rule. Because I did it long enough, it pays surprisingly well, and my parents aren't sleazebags, I can pay for any college I want out of my own pocket. Which was a huge selling point even for me, only five and already a big fucking nerd. When I was twelve and started growing for real, I told my parents and Becky I was done and that was that. I already knew I didn't want an eating disorder or even just general insecurity about whether I was petite enough, pretty enough, enough enough.

You learn more on go-sees and sets than the obvious: one, sets are hot and boring, and two, pile on enough of even the best makeup and it feels like concrete on your baby skin. Those things, anyone who's seen reality TV knows by now. What I didn't realize I'd absorbed until Jude disappeared was this: I've been sizing up my peers since I was five. I could make it a party trick if I were into that, but I can tell your height, weight, and even your heritage, and I'm not just talking about biological parents. Porter Kendrick has a Canadian grandma he sees twice a year and I could hear it in his voice. I'm that good.

So, I knew something was up with Jude. In the weeks before she was gone, she was unnaturally glued to her phone. Like, even for us, a generation who are notorious for our techno-dependence. But it wasn't just that the phone became an extension of Jude, barely concealed from our teachers even though that was Augustus protocol, her thumbs beating on loose-leaf paper during class until she could text away once the bell had barely trilled.

She had this little smile. This crinkle between her perfect brows. Like she was getting away with something.

And more than that, like she was *relaxed.* Genuinely chill. And if there's one thing Jude wasn't known for, it was having even an ounce of chill.

I should have asked. I know that now. Not an excuse, but prying wasn't my style. Still isn't. I hadn't yet learned that sometimes you should absolutely pry.

I wonder if I had pried, and I'd seen even *one* text, what would have happened.

I never had any…problems as a kid model. My mom is usually the one who went with me, not because of any gender role bullshit but because she could come with me into dressing rooms and stuff without anyone giving it a second look. Easier access, more protection.

And you don't mess with her. That classic mom look also works on photographers, lighting people, stylists with their fingers on tiny bodies. She scared them all.

We knew, though. Model parents talk. About whom not to work with because of everything from gut feelings to murmured experiences that led to more than one mini-model leaving the industry forever and hopefully careening headfirst into therapy.

All this to say, I was primed to suss out perverts and listen hard to whisper networks, because they're almost never wrong, years before my classmates. I learned to listen to my little gut very early on. And maybe that could have helped Jude, which is still hard to think about.

Anyway.

The second thing I learned in my brief, unspectacular, largely trauma-free modeling career was how to have a *look.*

I'm not talking about the look on your face. I'm talking about the way you put yourself together. People act like it's not important, it's shallow and silly, but have you *seen* a good pantsuit? Which, by the way, I told Jude she should wear. The pantsuits I will fully take credit for because they were brilliant and she looked stunning, yet totally in control. You've seen photos, right?

You can't be around racks of clothing and see yourself rendered on a two-dimensional page for seven of your most formative years and *not* learn about the power of clothes. And hair. And strategically applied makeup, though not enough that it feels like concrete. Doesn't read well under harsh fluorescent high-school lighting anyway.

So even before I finished my speech, what I was going to say to all of Augustus so that everyone but mostly the right people would hear…I was thinking about my look.

First, I shaved my head. I've been all cheekbones since I was a kid, and now, they were fully on display. Big light brown eyes. Smooth skull. No one would be able to look away.

Then I took out the boots. And by boots, I'm talking *boots.* They would hear me coming.

I can still remember doing final touches in the mirror that morning. What I said to myself, a mantra I came up with on the spot and still kinda love:

"Mesmerize. Then surprise."

CHAPTER FIVE

Declan

After Jude left school, I started smoking my mom's pot.

Like a lot of it.

I'd been a casual stoner before, but the rest of that year, we're talking wake and bake. Toking in my car during free period. And homework after school? Forget it.

My junior year grades were so shit I'm surprised I got in any school at all, let alone a scholarship to a really good place.

Why'd I get involved in this conspiracy? Because of a stupid pre-calc test? Yeah, that sucked on Jude's part. I'm not saying she was a great person back then.

But even just texting people that Saturday night, telling them to check their school email because there was a sex tape of Jude Cuthbert and a guy? Maybe I was just the messenger, but that night I was the kind of lowlife my mom would bring home, that would scare my brother and sister, that was the kind of person I swore I'd never be. And I have to live with it even now.

I'm sorry, Jude. I don't know where you are now. I'm just sorry.

Chapter Six

Bronwyn

At this point we still weren't sure what happened.

I hit Send on a Saturday night. By the time we woke up Sunday, it had spread like wildfire. You can't post a sex video on social media anymore, and no one was stupid enough to do it, but social media was ablaze with insinuations, comments, questions. So many questions.

After a while, the three of us stopped keeping track. Cass even went to the gym like she usually did Sunday afternoons. No one else on her cheer team went to Augustus, so the undoing of the iconic Jude Cuthbert would mean nothing to them.

Porter, whose last doses were still wearing off, slept over an extra night. Told his parents we had a test the next morning and would be up late studying. He knew I wanted to curl around him, my mind whirring with the possibilities of what would happen now, what our future would look like now that she was ruined.

Monday morning, Jude was gone.

Like, *gone* gone.

She wasn't in school. She'd deleted all her social accounts. You couldn't really blame her because she'd been tagged a thousand times on Sunday, everything from the benign "*u ok?*" to long screeds asking her to explain her hypocrisy.

Augustus was full of vultures. We *prided* ourselves on our cutthroat abilities to knock one another down for grading curves, college essays, and early decision acceptances. It's why our parents insisted we test in eighth grade—and in some cases, like mine and Jude's, why we wanted to for ourselves. It was well-known the school took more first-years than it could handle, because so many were weeded out in the first semester. If you made it to first year, second semester, it was almost like getting into Harvard.

This is a long way of saying that even the concern trolls were full of shit.

They smiled in your face only to stab you in the back with words. They didn't care if Jude was okay.

Jude answered none of their queries.

I wasn't surprised she was out on Monday. Who wouldn't take a mental health day after what we'd done to her? But I also knew Jude would come back and explain herself, in a big way. If I was right, though, people wouldn't listen.

That's when we heard what happened.

This wasn't a mental health day. There had been blood on Jude's bedroom floor—someone who had ties to the hospital emailed around a photo, and sure enough, that was Jude's room, rust stains amid polished hardwood and white frills. Like a scene from one of those shoddy PG-13 horror movies that aren't really scary, except this? Definitely was.

The enigma of Jude's disappearance didn't stop there. Mark Cuthbert was *not* talking. He wasn't even in town anymore, having escaped to the family beach house in Florida, where Jude was definitely not. Either that or he was hiding from the obvious "everything's okay" Instagram photos where Mark was clad in all white and clutching colored cocktails with umbrellas on a sandy beach. His knuckles were white in a way that suggested he was the opposite of relaxed.

As for Jude's mom…I'd *never* planned to sell her out that way, not ever. At the time I liked to think I had scruples. She couldn't help what happened with her family. She *could* help who she slept with, as she was so fond of telling me once I got with Porter.

Still, the rumors started flying. It doesn't happen at Augustus, people said, but we weren't the smartest in this suburb for nothing. We *knew* queer kids kill themselves all the time, even if we didn't know any personally. Especially when they're humiliated in the worst possible way. Only in this situation it was the reverse: Jude the lesbian was caught with a dude. And for sure he was a dude, otherwise why the blood on the floor, the vanishing?

At what point do you go from a good person doing bad things, to a straight-up bad person?

And if you've gone past that point, is there any coming back from it?

This is when I stopped sleeping.

My brain wouldn't stop asking questions. *Did* she deserve for us to take this opportunity, even though basically she'd asked for it by not shutting the door completely? I mean, even in the throes of passion, you'd think Jude Cuthbert of all people would lock herself and her secret boyfriend in a room of a house that wasn't theirs.

It was like she wanted to get caught.

So what we, Cass and Porter and I, did wasn't so terrible, right? Anyone could have, would have, done the same. Jude...rubbed a lot of people the wrong way. Which is why it wasn't hard to get coconspirators. She wasn't popular because she was *nice*. Or *tolerant*. That girl had clawed her way up the ladder since Montessori. I know. I was there.

Still, I had to concentrate. The election was so close I could taste it. And now, I was running unopposed. It was almost comical how we were keeping up appearances, considering how unlikely it was that Jude, alive or dead, was going to pop back in, all *"hey lol jk"* and walk away with the win.

Or maybe she would. That's why I had to stay vigilant, till the very end. And try to unsee that photo: the rusty pool, the white frills.

With that video, I'd gotten what I wanted. Way more, really. And I was so close to having it all.

I couldn't let guilt fuck it up.

Did I mention though, or maybe you remember? After all that, there *was* no election for student body president.

Principal Olive Murrell announced over the PA on Tuesday morning. I'd won. By default.

Not the stunning victory I'd imagined. What I'd wanted is the alternate reality of the outside world if *she* had won instead of the titty grabber. What I got was a lukewarm "congratulations" from above, before reiterating that it was Tater Tot Bar Day in the cafeteria. I haven't heard "tater tot" the same way since.

And of course, everyone was talking about Jude. Not me.

My pop loved this Hole song about getting what you want, then you never want it again.

No matter how gradually it had started to creep in in at three a.m., slithering around Cass's house's guest room like the bogeyman. First a flicker, then three, steadily growing into a full-on flame.

I saw *her*. Jude. As fully formed as you sitting on the other side of this phone screen right now. Wearing that stupid She-Hulk T-shirt and hissing at me, four words over and over, a terrifying mantra as Porter snored beside me and Cass finished her nighttime push-ups in the other room. Four words only I could hear.

What have you done?

CHAPTER SEVEN

Jude

I couldn't take it anymore.

Listen, Dad, this break has been nice and all. Yes, I'm aware of how privileged we are. Your precious youngest gets to go off the grid to lick her wounds after a reputation-destroying video went email-viral. Mom gets to have three-ways, a kid she actually wants, and a whole new sister-wife lifestyle. You, my dad, get to escape to beachfront property in the non-tacky part of Florida—it exists, really, you tell your country club friends—to lick the wounds your child inflicted not only by being a slut but also a giant fucking hypocrite.

This way you won't have to look at her. Ask her what went wrong. What led to the events behind the video, which aren't exactly how they're being portrayed. How she's feeling. We may be Jewish by heritage, but we're WASPy everywhere else. Why talk when you can drink your emotions, right? If you plan for food delivery, tell her to turn the lights in the cottage on. Have a neighbor check in periodically to make sure your daughter hasn't run away or *actually* killed herself this time. That's infinitely more preferable than having to deal.

This whole "vacation"—which, if you'll recall, is how it was pitched to me—has reminded me how lucky I thought I was.

My parents, Tone. Maybe now you'll believe me when I say they're *definitely* not like yours. At all.

I'm under strict instructions *not* to contact anyone from Augustus. I can't go online, not that I'd really want to. Maybe the fervor's died down in favor of a new scandal, but more likely Bronwyn is reveling in her triumph that someone, I don't know who, finally caught me in the worst possible act of all. I'll be fine if I never see any of those assholes again.

Except you, Tone.

Which is why today, I walked to the next town over.

I waved at Mrs. Sinon, the year-rounder who's supposed to be keeping an eye on me. Had my parka on because it's cold near the ocean right now, and with my bright smile I could tell she was reassured. Knowing how many noisy parties my parents throw here in the summers, I very much doubt she gives two shits anyway.

Pulling down the brim of my dad's baseball cap like I was hiding from invisible paparazzi, I quickly found a gas station that had exactly what I needed. I paid and headed back to the house.

I never thought I'd say this, Tone, but it's kind of nice not being glued to my phone for once. The birds are starting to come back, chirping and twittering and singing like idiots. Plus, I don't have to be paranoid about endless buzzing and beeping and crap.

I don't need to wonder whether or not *he's* texted me.

Even though I do wonder. All the time. Sick, right?

Got back to the house and locked the door behind me. I don't know why—it's not like anyone's going to burst in with a phone pointed in my face—but guess what, I'm paranoid now. Afraid of feeling as violated as I did when I got the email, late Saturday night after I came home in a daze, and my world was rocked forever. Not in a good way.

I flipped open the burner, thanking whoever is above that I'd memorized your phone number long ago. I didn't know why at the time, considering I barely knew my own. Now I'm getting slapped in the face with that truth, which I'm not quite ready to deal with yet if that's okay. You understand.

Then I texted you the first message since that night.

Only a few words, but with proper grammar, spelling, and punctuation so you'd know it was me. Augustus may have turned against me, but it ran deep in my blood. Fragments of words were beneath me.

Us.

It's me. I'm okay. Hiding out for a while. Will call soon. Don't tell anyone yet.

A dispatch from an untraceable phone and location. You didn't know where this house was, that we had this house at all. A total disregard for the rules my parents had imposed, ostensibly to keep me safe. I was breaking all the rules today.

But I wanted you to know, Tone. Just you. No one else. Not just because I knew you were the only person who'd be genuinely worried about me, but for my own sake as well. I needed to prove I still existed. That I mattered.

Send.

CHAPTER EIGHT

Antonia

It was like any other spam at first.

I was in my room like I'd been almost constantly since all this happened. My parents, almost *too* perfect as Jude used to say, were giving me the space I needed to "process" that my ex-girlfriend and current closest confidante disappeared from her home, leaving only shattered glass and a pool of blood in her wake. They'd called the school, who was sending me assignments until I felt well enough to return. They'd made their own conclusions, and it's not like Jude's mom and dad were talking either.

The thing about the suburbs is that if you're white and rich—but especially white—nobody asks questions, even when your overachieving daughter disappears with a bloody trace. People take you unequivocally at your word.

If I disappeared, the cops would be all over my parents. Just a fact.

My own mother was making me healthy smoothies that I immediately poured down the drain because they tasted like very well-intentioned lawn mulch. Mostly I sat on the floor, ate the Doritos I'd stashed under my bed long ago and forgotten about until now, and held on to hope. And my phone. Just in case.

At any rate, I nearly hit Delete on the unrecognizable area code without even reading the message, just like I always did. A slip of the finger, maybe? Or that stupid hope that Jude wasn't dead seeped from my brain to my hand.

Then I saw the text and I knew, Jude, it was you.

The first thing I did was throw the phone across the room, because how fucking dare you.

We used to talk every day, Jude. Not even every day, every hour. I knew your inner workings to the point where I could picture your brain, your intestines, working and whirring and lighting up like one of those exhibits at a children's science museum. Before everything happened, when I couldn't sleep at night, I pictured you, but not your lips or your eyes or your soft hair (though those were lovely). Even when we were dating, Jude, I pictured your insides, and I would relax enough to give into sleep almost immediately.

When you left me, I didn't know what to picture. Who to have those conversations with that I told no one about. When I didn't know what to do, Jude, whether it was study those extra ten minutes for a quiz I already knew I was going to ace or take one last Dorito, I would ask you, or that version of you with the fantastic inner workings. When you disappeared, you took all that away from me, and I didn't realize until my phone *thwacked* against my bedroom wall how much I hated you for it.

As I flopped facedown on my bed so I wouldn't have to look at the phone, at the text, I knew how irrational I was being. Me, Antonia Marcus, the coolest and most levelheaded junior at Augustus. Known for being sure in my identity, my goals, my plans, but a few words from you and I was a goddamn mess.

I wanted to be more empathetic, really I did. I got the video just like everyone else, watched about three seconds before I went to the bathroom to throw up. I've been out sick from school the past few days, no questions asked from my parents, who likely know everything if the lawn mulch smoothies are any indication.

The thing about my OCD is that leaving my house is my biggest trigger. I have to make sure I have my keys, wallet, lipstick if it's that kind of day, my lunch, the list goes on. If I blank on one thing, I gaslight myself, calling myself a stupid bitch in my head. Goes nice with depression, when I don't want to leave the house at all! Ha ha.

But hearing from you? I knew I'd have to leave the house again. And I would be prepared.

I know what this means for you, the proud misandrist, not only to be caught in such an intimate act, but with a person who looks like everything and everyone you claim to hate. No one knows who took the video, who sent it, if they're the same person or a group of conspirators. Who even gives a shit at this point? The damage is done, the glass is broken, the blood is spilled. And I have no proof, but I have my suspicions of who's behind it. Never mind tracing emails or whatever; I have the feeling that this person's going to show their ass(es) sooner rather than later.

The phone is beeping.

The text showed up on my lock screen: a selfie of you and me I took when you were unaware, Jude, but it's just so beautiful. You're looking off in the distance, laughing with your mouth open. I'm doing one of those basic bitch duck-faces at the camera, with a big theatrical wink. I don't even remember who or what we were laughing at or about, but it's so…genuine. Even though now I feel sick for capturing you on my phone without your permission—because, well, look at what just happened—I can't bring myself to delete it off my phone.

Ding. There it is again, the reminder I have a text. I breathe in a mouthful of cashmere blanket, raise my head to cough, and see my phone, still kicking even when it's bounced off a wall and is lying facedown on the floor.

I don't know what possesses me to do this, but I roll off my bed, army-crawling to the little square that now connects me to you. I reach out one hand for the blue rubber cover and flip over the phone.

Read the message again, for real this time, a bubble of letters situated right under our grins, from that day that seems like another lifetime.

It's me. I'm okay. Hiding out for a while. Will call soon. Don't tell anyone yet.

It's definitely you, Jude.

You're staccato through and through. It's why you and Bronwyn were such a power duo for so long, almost impenetrable until you let me and a few others found worthy into your inner sanctum. Bronwyn is much bubblier than she pretends to be, her thoughts crowding her head and then her mouth when she tries to verbalize them. She rambles; you state. She skirts the point; you get right to it.

Like you're doing here, with proper punctuation and capitalization because you wouldn't do a disservice to yourself. Or me. And just like that, anger is replaced by pure elation, flowing through me so potently I scramble to my feet and bounce on my bed so hard, for a second, I'm suspended in the air. These words, this possibility of you, are *here*. I'm not alone after all.

Flopping on my back and holding the phone over my head, I read your words until I've committed them to memory. Then the analysis begins because it's how I work.

You, Jude, are alive. That's the biggest takeaway.

You're hiding…somewhere. I could google the area code and eventually I will, but your exact location is almost beside the point at the moment. Wherever you are, it's likely your parents know, and they too want you to stay hidden. Besides, it's not like I'm going to fly to wherever and surprise you.

Unless you ask.

You'll call soon. I create a new contact in my phone for this one, likely a burner you got at some random gas station or Walmart if they have them where you are. (For some reason I am picturing a Walmart, which I know is very classist of me.)

At this point it occurs to me that maybe, just maybe, someone's pranking me. That said, this is just vague enough and no Nigerian prince asked for my bank details, so I think it's actually you. And when you call—because I know you will, Jude, you may have been a player, but you *always* got in touch when you said you would—I will know for sure.

Don't tell anyone. Don't worry. I could shock you with what I know about people at Augustus. I barely know Bronwyn's cousin Cass, but I would bet my college fund she's the same. It's always the quiet ones.

Speaking of Augustus…I think it's time I went back to school, Jude.

These past few weeks I've lolled around, worrying the shit out of my parents and projecting pure inertia.

Now, I have a purpose.

Chapter Nine

Scarlett

After Jude, I didn't quit soccer. Exactly.

What I did do was stop showing up to practice, enough that Coach Amarin called my parents. She basically looks like a Thai Soccer Barbie, with this gorgeous long ponytail and smooth, round calves ideal for kicking. And her voice is so cute and poppy, even when her words of concern meant my parents were going to yell at me, then apologize, then ask if I needed or wanted therapy, which no.

They asked if I wanted to tell them what was going on. Also no.

So Coach Amarin, because she is a saint as well as beautiful, put me on hiatus for the rest of the semester and gave me a training program that I ignored.

Instead of going to practice, I drove around aimlessly blasting podcasts that forecasted the end of the world thanks to our shitty new president, who now made me even more afraid to be a Black girl in America. If I really wanted to punish myself, I'd play clips of his disgusting, triggering voice. The sound bites where you could *hear* him leering.

I know it sounds bizarre, but if I didn't have my car and those doomsday warnings, I might have done something worse to myself. My guilt was that strong.

Still is.

ACT IV

"Did not great Julius bleed for justice's sake?
…You have done that you should be sorry for!"
—Brutus, *Julius Caesar*

CHAPTER ONE

Bronwyn

Three weeks after we sent the video, Antonia Marcus marched back into Augustus High.

March is the only word I can use to describe it. They had a goal, a purpose. Even if no one knew yet what it was, I suspected we'd soon find out.

"Why do I get the feeling I'm on trial?" Porter murmured to me as we stood by his locker and Antonia sailed by. They'd chosen high-heeled boots today, the buttery brown leather pair I'd always joked I was going to steal, and from the way they *click-clacked* on the linoleum I knew the choice was deliberate. Suddenly, he squeezed his eyes shut, pinched the bridge of his nose. "Sorry."

I took his hand in mine. "Brain zaps?"

"Again." He opened his eyes. "That one's gone." Porter smiled, but I could tell he was still in pain.

Worry flooded over me. "Don't you think you should talk to your mom, at least? I don't think you're supposed to cut yourself off like that." I took his hand. "I love your brain. I just want it to be okay."

Porter smacked a kiss on my cheek. "You and me both, but I'll be fine. My body's adjusting. Besides," he said, leaning in so his lips brushed my ear, "it's been pretty great so far, yeah?"

I shivered. *Great* was an understatement. Certain…parts of Porter were working now, and last night I'd had to bite my pillow so I didn't wake Cass and Aunt Deb. Thank goodness Porter's parents let him sleep over whenever he wanted.

"Can you come over tonight?" I whispered back. Porter leaned in and I was rewarded by the most intense kiss I'd ever received, from anyone. I was still catching my breath when the bell rang.

Three minutes later, I was in complete and total shock.

"Emergency student government meeting?" I whispered to Cass, who'd immediately shown up at my locker. I could *feel* everyone looking at me. From the way she was pulling her Tigers hoodie around her, I knew Cass could too. "What the hell is that for?"

"Maybe…to welcome you as student body president?" Cass offered tentatively, but the way she looked down at her sneakers, I knew she was grasping at straws. "Welcome" and "emergency" didn't really go together. She didn't look like the Killer much these days.

Just then my phone—technically forbidden during school hours, but teachers didn't enforce the rule as long as you weren't in class—dinged. My lovely Porter. *I heard, I love you, be strong. See you after school.* I showed the message to Cass, and she winced. We were on the same wavelength: as well intentioned as Porter was, which I genuinely appreciated, the fact that he'd told me to "be strong" didn't exactly inspire confidence.

"Bronwyn."

Antonia. My ex-girlfriend and knowing their loyalty to Jude, wherever she was, likely now my ex-friend. Staring at me from on high, the boots made her just taller enough to be intimidating. They glanced at Cass, giving a nod of acknowledgment that looked almost regal.

My heart dropped to my toes.

"Are you coming to the meeting?"

And I knew, I just *knew*, Antonia was behind this somehow. What the fuck? They weren't even *on* student government.

Jude.

I gritted my teeth. Like Cass, Antonia was the kind of quiet that fooled you into complacency at first, until you realized how insanely perceptive they were. I couldn't let them see me nervous. Too much.

Silently and subtly, Cass reached for my hand. Grateful, I squeezed it before saying to Antonia, "Well…yeah. I'm president now by default, right?"

Antonia arched their eyebrows and smoothed their crisp pinstriped pants. "See you there," they murmured before *click-clacking* away.

I turned to Cass and said, "We're fucked."

Chapter Two

Calpurnia

Jude Cuthbert was dead.

Okay. We know now she really wasn't. She was hiding out at her parents' vacation home and there was this whole situation with her family that she hadn't even told Bronwyn, back when Bronwyn was still in her life. As for what really happened at the party? Well, there are still a lot of pages left in this report, so.

But it *felt* like she was dead. Her locker had one of those weird shrines like you see on highways in true crime shows, right where the cheerleader was pulverized, her future cut short by a stalker with an agenda, or a drunk who wouldn't come forward until way later. More likely the stalker, because it's a true crime show. Anyway, there were stuffed penguins in front of the locker. Silk flowers in light pink and purple. A random debate trophy from her first year. How did any of this represent her? I'd had exactly one conversation with Jude Cuthbert, and even I knew how wrong these tokens were.

More than the shrine, which everyone had to step around until finally someone cleared it away, were the general vibes around Augustus.

People were afraid of Bronwyn St. James.

You're always on us to be clear, Ms. Strohm, so I'll do my best. I think Bronwyn wanted that fear, to an extent. She missed how it was when she was Jude's closest confidante and there were first-years literally following them around, practically begging to buy them bottled water from the closest vending machine. Baking them cupcakes with the Pride flag. Staying a respectful three feet away.

Then Bronwyn was an outcast. Her cousin didn't stay three feet away. Her new boyfriend sure as hell didn't. But I remember seeing them in the hallway one time pre-election. Jude was nowhere to be found. Porter was showing Cass and Bronwyn this deck of cards with unicorns on them. And Bronwyn looked…content. Her jaw wasn't set in the usual way like she was going to kick everyone's ass and you would beg her to do it again. Even though we all knew by then where her dads were, she seemed happy. Almost approachable if it weren't for her history as Queen B.

After Jude disappeared, though, Queen B was back. And no one baked her cupcakes or bought her beverages. She still stuck with her two-person crew, but they were more like hostages by this point. Dragging, not walking. Cass looked thinner. And at times it was like they were physically holding up Porter. Whispers circulated that he was off his meds and his parents didn't know.

The school days went on, like they do. Lockers slammed. Chimes rang signaling the beginning and end of classes because Augustus High was too good for clangy school bells. That one bathroom still smelled like chili, always.

My braces came off and I bought my first hair straightener. I realized I hated polo shirts and started my flannel phase, accessorizing with my mom's hemp necklaces from the nineties. I started keeping a journal, toting that purple mottled composition book with me everywhere I went in case of inspiration, even though it was mostly really bad poetry. It all happened pretty fast.

And I thought about Jude. Every day. If she was really dead. If not, where the hell she was and what happened the night of the party I wasn't invited to. What would have happened if she'd watched Netflix with me instead.

I wondered if *she'd* be the subject of a true crime documentary someday, then scolded myself for being so Goth. Macabre. I meant macabre.

I was so fascinated by Bronwyn and her pals death-marching through the hallways every day. I wrote a poem about them and immediately burned it in our backyard fire pit, which we only used for the annual Fourth of July barbecue.

And then, Antonia Marcus came back to school.

CHAPTER THREE

Antonia

You would have been proud.

I channeled you, Jude: everything I've admired about you since day one and then some. The way you stand like you're the giant in a room of Lilliputians, even though in reality you're practically, adorably miniature. (Sorry. I know you hate when people comment on your size. But it really is cute—not in a little kid way, just genuinely *you*, Jude. Anyway.) How you wear your tallest shoes when you want to feel the most confident—oldest trick in the book, you once confided to me, but it's amazing how many people don't use it, and how just as many fall for it. Even the pinstriped pants I dug out of my mom's closet this morning, looking for something appropriately…official, to make up for the way I was shaking inside, knowing what I was about to do.

It wasn't hard to convince Principal Murrell how much we needed this meeting. First of all, she loves me: not only because of the straight As, but because I check so many diversity boxes. I know people like you and Bronwyn, so supposedly woke, don't like to think about that, but it's true: I'm a mixed-race demigirl who photographs great. There's a reason I'm all over the Augustus website.

Plus, this was a situation without precedent. Never before had a candidate vanished into thin air on a random Saturday night, after a sex tape of her with the unlikeliest of partners went viral. We weren't a scandal type of school, especially when it came to school elections. Until now.

I brought this up to her, and she listened, expression focused and spine straight. And I didn't intend for it to happen, really, but I got a little teary. I mean, *I don't know where you are.* Granted, she probably wouldn't be able to tell me for legal reasons, but from the confusion on her face when she said your name, I don't think Murrell even knows.

Things are that dire.

"Do you want me to make an announcement?" she asked, moving one manicured hand toward me on the desk. (I think it was supposed to be comforting but she didn't want to touch me because, you know. Lawsuits.) I tried not to smile because that was *precisely* what I wanted.

For certain people to hear and get nervous.

Did I mention it's in the auditorium and the whole school is welcome to attend, not just student government? Everyone's seen the video. I'm anticipating a big crowd and trying not to piss my pants in the next six hours because I hate public speaking so very much, Jude. Feeling on display, like the worst catalog shoots of my childhood, that photographer whose breath smelled like last night's spaghetti sauce left out to rot. You know that.

But this is for you, so I'll hold it in.

Next stop, Bronwyn's locker. Looking at my ex who was clearly freaking out, and her cousin, who's really an innocent bystander in all of this and if anything, she's *too* loyal. I know that life—I felt a tinge of regret. I used to date this girl, sleep with her in that giant bedroom of hers, had a toothbrush in her private bathroom because if I have a kink, it's dental hygiene. As much as I wanted to fight for you, I couldn't deny that Bronwyn St. James and I had a history.

Also…

"She's been through hell," I could hear you say, in the weeks before you disappeared. "I know she's a total hypocrite because of the boyfriend thing, but I'm picking my battles with Bronwyn and we all should, Tone. We're not going to shame her for losing her *parents*."

Despite the bluster, you are way more rational than you give yourself credit for.

Watching her face fall and her cousin reach for her hand in a way she thought I couldn't see, I thought about going back to Murrell's office, asking for a private meeting instead.

Then I remembered the three seconds of the video I could stomach. The brutality of it. The inkling I had about your participation in the act, which was growing every day, to the point where I worried it would overtake me, blur my focus. I didn't want to ask you yet. We only had that one text message, and it was your story to tell. Or not.

I knew Bronwyn was behind your humiliation. And because of that, she didn't deserve my mercy.

"See you there," I told her before gliding away on my tallest boots, the ones I knew she loved and yes, that's part of the reason I wore them.

They hurt my feet, but as adrenaline took over, followed by the anxiety that I really could not pull this off, aching arches were the least of my worries.

I won't let you down, Jude.

I promise.

CHAPTER FOUR

Bronwyn

Spontaneous speech. Okay.

After French, I was physically holding Porter up again. I could smell the pine of his deodorant mixed in with a little sweat. It wasn't unusual for him to run hot in those days. Cass came running up to us. Her sneakers slapped against the linoleum, and I remember thinking even before I saw her face, that I wasn't going to like what she said.

"Murrell wants to see you."

Yeah. I was right.

That whole encounter was a very brief blur. Porter and Cass waited outside while I entered Principal Olive Murrell's inner sanctum and was informed of the following.

One. Antonia Marcus was back in school—which I knew already and was still recovering from.

Two, they had requested a special assembly after school, which had just been announced over the PA.

Three, they wanted to give a speech at said assembly.

Four, as student body president by default—I had to fight not to roll my eyes at the "default" and ended up snorting Pine-Sol through my nose, because the custodian had gone above and beyond that morning—I was entitled to give a speech before theirs.

Five, even though this wasn't a campaign, because it did have to do with the recent elections, campaign rules still applied.

No profanity.

No personal attacks. Against other candidates. This includes Jude Cuthbert.

Principal Olive Murrell peered over her unassailably cool reading glasses when she said Jude's name. Which I hadn't uttered since the night of the party.

Six. Because of the quick turnaround, and because the principal had a full day of calls and meetings, my speech didn't need to be preapproved.

But.

At this point she looked at me over her glasses again. I swear, and this is not hyperbole, her gaze penetrated my *soul.*

But she went on. As student body president—this time there was no "default"—she was *trusting* me to keep it classy.

She didn't say keep it classy. At this point, though, I was the one who was sweating.

I floated out the door, where Porter and Cass were waiting. Cass started peppering me with questions. I know she said "campaign manager" more than once. The Pine-Sol was still stuck in my nose.

Porter took my hand. He was standing up straight now. Even his curls were standing up now. Alert.

All I could say was, "Does she know?"

She couldn't, right?

She couldn't.

Cass

I skipped practice.

I should want to be there for Bronwyn, right? As her campaign manager, it's literally my job.

But for once I wished Porter could take over, that he'd stayed on his medication so he wouldn't get brain zaps so bad he could barely hold his head up, that he could do *something* besides limply hold Bronwyn's hand.

Even more, I wanted to call my mom. Have her get me out of this stupid meeting. Tell her how even push-ups aren't working anymore to erase my guilt, my part in this. I didn't hit Send, true, but I was the one who found Jude. I was the one who turned on my phone.

But what would I say? "Thanks for all the time and energy and money you've put into supporting my dream while you watch children die of cancer every day! I've decided to repay you by helping my cousin ruin her ex-bestie's reputation, so she'll win an election that really means nothing in the end, oh yeah and I took a video of people having sex"?

Yeah, no. My mother didn't even know I went to parties with

alcohol, let alone witness debauchery before broadcasting it on a student email network.

The final bell rang, and people streamed into the auditorium with way more fervor than they did for any assembly. We had everyone from straight boy slackers to parking lot stoners finding seats while whispering to one another. Some of them were really loud, too, speculating what happened to Jude Cuthbert and who was the mystery guy on the tape who got her to throw over her lesbian agenda.

I guess sex really does sell.

A podium sat in the center of the empty stage. It looked dignified, tall and proud and waiting for someone with authority to bless us all. We had no idea who would stand at it, what was happening, what that meeting would bring.

I had the feeling it wasn't a pro-Bronwyn rally, though.

Speaking of my cousin, she sat on my right, clutching one of my hands and one of poor Porter's, who looked zombified. I wanted to hug him, but that would require climbing over Bronwyn and shoving my ass in her face, and the way she gripped my hand, so tightly I worried I'd bruise, I didn't dare move.

She bumped my shoulder and I glanced over.

"I'm scared," she whispered.

Suddenly, we were little again, hiding in her dads' bedroom closet where we're convinced a ghost lives and we want to see if he'll talk to us.

I wanted to whisper, "It'll be okay." But I didn't believe it, so instead I bumped her shoulder back. Much as I hated what we did, Bronwyn was all I had.

Just then, the lights dimmed.

CHAPTER FIVE

Transcription of Principal Olive Murrell's introduction to the Augustus High student body, taken from audio and video files:

Good afternoon, Augustus High student body. Thank you for taking part in this optional, after-school assembly.

As you are likely aware, our most recent election was particularly contentious. One of our candidates, in fact, is no longer a student here.

(At this point, a voice can be heard saying "Where is Jude Cuthbert?" In the video, Principal Murrell holds up a hand, and there is silence.)

I'm not at liberty to discuss the student's whereabouts. However, two of her classmates would like to speak today.

First, we will hear from junior and next year's student body president, Bronwyn St. James. Second, fellow junior Antonia Marcus.

I am asking, no, I am *instructing* all of you to stay civil and respectful. Anyone who does not will be escorted out and will face further consequences. This includes our speakers.

I'm watching.

CHAPTER SIX

Transcription of Bronwyn St. James's first address as student body president, to the Augustus High student body, taken from audio and video files:

Uh. Hello. I'm Bronwyn St. James, and I am next year's Augustus student body president. I apologize if this speech is less than prepared, as I was just informed of the assembly this morning, shortly before the announcement. I was expecting to take a French quiz today, not address what appears to be all of my fellow students.

(Pauses for laughter. There are a few weak chuckles.)

I'll get right into it. Things are different now than they were even one month ago, when Jude Cuthbert was still a student here. She was my friend for a long time. And then she wasn't. And then we were running against each other for student body president. And then she disappeared.

("Where is Jude?" from the audience. A different voice this time. Principal Murrell stands up from where she has been sitting behind Bronwyn. Shoots a lethal, warning gaze at the entire student body. Quiet.)

I don't know any more than anyone else sitting here about where Jude is. I hope she is well. I also hope you will respect her and her family's need for privacy at this time.

Augustus High, I invite you to reflect on the past school year. Though we pride ourselves on enlightenment and open-mindedness, unfortunately the outside world does not have the same priorities. I know I'm not alone in saying, this most recent presidential election was a shock to our systems. Everything is different now than it was a year ago. With all due respect to our principal, I don't think it goes against campaign rules to say that most of us would *not* have voted for the current Chump in Chief.

(Real laughter this time. Murmurs of agreement. Principal Murrell can be seen covering her mouth with a flawlessly manicured hand. Wait, does she have dimples? Anyway...)

I think you can also remember how in the days after the election, reports of harassment at Augustus were at an all-time high. Suddenly, the open minds appeared to close. People felt powerless and instead of reaching out, they closed ranks. I am probably guilty of this myself.

As student body president, I want to focus on unity. On... reeducating those who may have seemed the most open on the surface, but not so secretly had their own biases. Who turned against their closest friends when they made decisions perceived as unexpected. Who resorted to cruel, sophomoric pranks instead of having a dialogue, trying to understand, or just plain practicing the acceptance they were so fond of preaching.

I ran for the highest office at Augustus High because I wanted to eradicate this behavior before it got truly ugly. Before that hypocritical and divisive spirit descended into all-out mutiny. Friend against friend. Simple but hurtful goofs morphing into violent hate crimes. Good intentions resulting in the ultimate damage.

I didn't want to win this way. I really didn't. But Augustus High, I invite you to consider the alternative. This election was only going to get worse, much like what we saw on television this fall. People would have gone to extremes to get what they wanted. And what would that do for Augustus?

I love this school. I have ever since I came from my small, sheltered Montessori elementary to take the placement tests. I remember crossing my fingers *and* toes, wishing with all my might that I could be part of the best and brightest in the state. I know I'm not alone.

How this election has shaken out is unfortunate, to be sure. But I know that together, we can all reunite, be good to one another, and try to understand our friends and classmates, even when they make decisions that confuse us. Whatever sacrifices I—*we*, I mean we—have made to get to where we are today, I don't regret. Sometimes, you have to do what needs to be done.

Augustus High, forget the past and those who were part of it. Let's make a new plan and move forward together.

Thank you for your time and attention.

CHAPTER SEVEN

Transcription of Antonia Marcus's speech to Augustus High student body, from several audio and video files, below:

Jude Cuthbert was my friend.

Today, when I asked for an emergency meeting of student government, I also asked for two other things. First, I wanted to speak. I'm not on student government, have never been interested, but now I'm rethinking things.

I'll get to that.

Anyway, Principal Murrell said yes, if student government said it was okay. I'm grateful they took an emergency vote at lunch, and it was unanimous. I'm not going to waste my time, or yours, today.

Second, I wanted the meeting to be open to the whole school, which I'm told isn't typical of student government. Not to go off on a tangent, but shouldn't it be, though? We're literally your representatives, are making decisions that ideally benefit you. I think the recent election has shown us that we need *more* voices in every room, not less. And voices of every kind. Even the straight, white, cis male ones.

Ha.

I'm glad you're all here. I really am. That means you're open to what I have to say today.

It also means you probably saw the video that went out to all our school emails late Saturday night a few weeks ago.

Look, I'm not going to get into who might or might not have taken the video and shared it. Could have been one person, could have been fifteen. I know we're all talking about it, that we have our theories. I know I have mine.

But really, who cares?

This isn't a eulogy for Jude Cuthbert. As far as anyone knows, she isn't dead. And wherever she is, she's not in this auditorium to defend herself.

I'm also not here to put her on a pedestal. Honestly, I think she'd hate that, and I feel like—and if you think I'm wrong, feel free to correct me now—I knew Jude Cuthbert better than anyone.

And I know she had, *has*, her faults.

Not just the little things, like how she chewed with her mouth open. That wasn't a secret or anything. If you've eaten in the Augustus High cafeteria, you've been in the splash zone once or twice. Or if you're me, every day of junior year.

Jude was practically brought up in her parents' country club, took years of etiquette classes, the whole shebang. But she could never quite kick that one bad habit. It horrified her mom, which made Jude laugh. I always thought to myself that she had so much to say, not even chewing her food for three seconds could keep her quiet.

She really had a lot to say. We all know that too. And more often than not, it got her in trouble.

Jude Cuthbert didn't listen. She talked over anyone, anytime, anywhere. No holds barred. And that could be great. If you were her friend, she'd protect you to the ends of the earth. Unless you made her angry. In that case you were worse than her very worst enemy.

Some of you sitting in the auditorium know exactly of which I speak. You've felt the wrath of Jude Cuthbert. Maybe she took you down in class for an opinion she considered wrong. Maybe she didn't agree with choices you'd made in your wardrobe, or who you spent your time with, or what activity you did after school. Maybe you deserved it. Maybe you didn't.

Anyone sitting in this auditorium right now would likely agree that Jude Cuthbert knew, *knows,* exactly who she is.

I'm standing here telling all of you this:

You're wrong.

I don't know who the other person in the video is, and I don't really care. It's like the people who took the video. Whoever sent it out, that doesn't matter to me. All that matters is that you know that Jude Cuthbert was just as scared as the rest of us.

Because we're all scared.

Not just scared about the SATs and college essays and padding our résumés in a way that looks well-rounded but authentic, and not like our parents paid a sleazebag to get us an athletic scholarship when really, we can't even make one lap around the track. Of course the whole college application process is why we're here at Augustus, and it is very, very scary. But I'm talking about something deeper. More fundamental.

We're afraid of who we really are. What we're capable of. I don't think anyone went to that party and said, "I'm going to catch Jude Cuthbert in a sex act and ruin her life." Probably, that person's just as normal as the rest of us. Just as scared. And convinced they're a good, honorable person.

We all like to think we're honorable. We're not.

We're afraid of what will happen to our country now that someone who openly hates women and people of color, who has no regard for anyone but himself, who prefers Twitter rants to real conversation, is in charge. We're afraid of the people who put him there, some of whom might be our own parents. We're afraid of what our lives will become.

We should be.

We should also be afraid of what we do to others, in the name of being "honorable."

We love to talk about how progressive Augustus is. How supportive. How accepting we are of anyone and everyone. How here, you can be whatever you want to be, which isn't always the case in the outside world. This isn't just marketing speak on the website and Facebook page. It's something we all feel in our bones. Why we were drawn to this school, even if initially, our parents made us test in. Why we find comfort here, at a student government meeting, when our real government is in shambles.

Jude loved this school like no one else. Augustus fueled her identity and her ambition. It's why she was running for student body president. Even if some of her ideals were misguided, she *had* ideals. She genuinely wanted to make Augustus a better place for everyone sitting here this afternoon, giving their time to listening to me ramble when they could have been doing anything else.

When Jude was scared, these walls gave her comfort. She wasn't perfect, and none of us are. Clearly. But in the end, she wasn't supported.

I don't care who made the video and sent it. But it's likely they're one of us. And whoever they are, they must live with that. With turning on one of their own, someone who's just as confused and vulnerable as they must have felt to do an act so heinous.

And we're all guilty. All of us who watched it, who gossiped about it. I count myself among the guilty, one hundred percent.

There is a way, however, we can turn things around.

We can reopen the student body president election. I know we could take the easy way out by letting Jude's opponent win by default. But where's the honor in that? The pride? The *active* choice?

I can't say when Jude will be back, or if she'll be back at all. I can only hope so because…sorry. I really didn't want to cry in front of everybody, like I've been doing in my room since she disappeared. I'm so worried about her. My mom says I'm actively grieving, and I don't know about you, but I really hate it when my mom is right.

(Laughter)

If I could run as a placeholder for Jude, I would. But I'll say this: I knew her well enough to know what she stood for. That she was active. That while she could be difficult and frustrating and sometimes even nasty, she would have *never* done to another person what someone, or *someones*, did to her last weekend.

I'm not on student government, so this isn't up to me. But I plead with them, and all of you, to open up the election again. Where any rising senior who wants to, can run.

And if they approve, of all of it, I will here and now announce my candidacy.

CHAPTER EIGHT

Declan

What. The fuck. Was *that?*

All I remember was after that shitshow of an assembly, I went outside and smoked a bowl. Then another. Then another, until my car smelled like my mom's boyfriend's apartment that was basically a shrine to the Dead.

If you could do pot like shots of alcohol, I would have been slamming pipes like whoa.

I didn't know Antonia Marcus. Hell, I barely knew *Bronwyn St. James.*

But after their speeches, I knew that if anyone found out about my part in all of this, I was well and truly fuuuuuuuuuucked.

Nasim

If I'm being honest? All I really remember about that whole thing was the drama club president—a really gorgeous guy named Ash—putting his hand on my knee.

He did it right when the lights went down and Principal Murrell walked out onstage. His hand was big and warm, and I was wearing shorts that day. If kneecaps were capable of orgasms, mine would have been coming multiple times, really loudly like the bad porn I used to watch before my first secret boyfriend turned me on to the good stuff.

Ash never touched me again. He barely looked my way in the halls.

But that's what I mostly remember. Isn't that pathetic? Not the guilt I should have been feeling over spreading that awful video like a contagion, infecting all of Augustus High and especially Jude Cuthbert who'd always been an asshole to me for reasons I still don't really get, but my own horniness.

In my defense, we were in high school.

I think that's what people forgot when the speeches went viral. We were *kids*.

Scarlett

I had a cold that day and was sneezing the entire freaking assembly. You can even hear it on some of the videos, though not the big one that went viral. Maybe whoever it was edited out my mucus explosions. Probably a good idea because there were like thirty of them.

Why did I stay if I was sick that day? Um, how could I *not*? At first, people thought Antonia and Jude ran away together. They'd gone out before. Did that whole thing where they decided to be friends, which always struck me as super performative. Why can't you just *be friends*? Why does everything have to be some huge announcement?

Then Antonia just came back, which shot that rumor to hell, but damn they looked fierce. One of my teammates saw Antonia go into Principal Murrell's office, then Bronwyn. And the announcement happened, and you knew shit was going down after school. I know the theater kids were hoping for a dance off, *West Side Story*–style.

My own guilt didn't come till later, honestly. At this point I was still officially on the soccer team. I could distance myself from the damning words in Antonia's speech, the hypocrisy in Bronwyn's declaration of hypocrisy. We all knew who she was talking about. She might as well have told her whole sob story.

Oh. I'm just now realizing, how many years later? That damn assembly is probably what did it. Really got me thinking about the honeypot thing. Nothing wrong with acting sexy, but the reason I did it...just wasn't okay. Why was it so important to me, showing some girl who I should have forgotten about the second she rejected me?

But most of all, I regretted hitting Send on those texts. A stupid action you don't even think about because you do it every day, posting on social, letting your teacher know you have a question about the homework, texting with your friends, taking a pic. Maybe that's the problem. I didn't think. That night after two wine coolers, it was just another Send.

Except it ruined a girl's life.

Yeah, that assembly is when it really hit for me.

I should have just gone home.

Chapter Nine

Cass

That night, the speech went viral.

Of course, we weren't expecting the sex tape to go beyond Augustus. It got taken down so quickly some people never even saw it. They just heard the details, and the exaggerations of the details, which is what we were counting on.

Speaking of viral…that sex tape was probably a felony. Came close at least. But it never went public. No lawyers involved, even. Augustus and the people who run their email servers would rather just pretend it never happened.

We were not expecting the rest of it, though. Antonia had always stayed behind the scenes, writing the golden words, not speaking them aloud. Since when were they the next Obama?

And Bronwyn. Oh Bronwyn. She tried. And to be fair, she had very little preparation time, when for all we knew Antonia had been working on that speech the whole time they were out of school. But my cousin couldn't have come across worse if she tried.

Everyone knew. She might as well have worn a T-shirt that said *I DID IT.*

AND SO DID CASS.

CHAPTER TEN

Bronwyn

Antonia knows.

Those words burned into my brain, like branding, as I sat there, one of maybe five people in the auditorium who weren't standing and fucking cheering like they were at the final game of the World Series, or if they weren't into sports, the closing performance of *Wicked.* Two of the others who weren't standing were Porter—who, even if he weren't my boyfriend, was looking so bad he probably *couldn't* stand—and Cass. My ever-loyal cousin. Whose smooth pale skin looked decidedly green.

They know.

Porter laced his fingers through mine, squeezed my hand. We were united in sheer worry. Paranoia we could laugh off in the privacy of my bedroom, now steadily becoming real in the midst of our whole school.

I had to give Antonia credit, even in the moment. That was a whopper of a speech. I always knew they wanted to do that kind of thing when they grew up, but writing words down is one thing and delivering them in a way that suggested Barack Obama *and* Hillary Clinton was quite another.

It was all there: the short sentences, the punchy delivery. The folksy demeanor and hand gestures of Obama with the take-no-shit attitude of Clinton, together in one pinstriped powerhouse of a package that was Antonia Marcus. Tall and stunning, those pinstriped pants and high boots making their legs look a mile long. A fantastically crisp white button-down, bringing to mind Jude Cuthbert's signature look without directly copying it like a hanger-on. Smooth shaved head where there had once been long braids I played with after we fooled around, emphasizing Antonia's enviable cheekbones. The entire look was flawless, the words even more so, the delivery so on point it put the phrase "on point" to complete and utter shame.

Even the three-week absence I knew was probably OCD-related, but in the moment, it felt *strategic.*

I know we'd been on debate together, but that was first year before I threw myself into AP classes, not wanting to admit that it took me way more hard work to get As than naturally brilliant people like Jude. Antonia had always been an ace speech writer, but during first year, she was not nearly this kind of a speaker.

People had their phones out, recording. I wouldn't be surprised if this speech went viral in a way Jude's sex tape never would. No nudity, for one. But Antonia was just so goddamn *genuine.*

She didn't turn Jude into some paragon of virtue, which was smart. Enough people at Augustus had had run-ins with Jude Cuthbert, so elevating her too much would have lost the audience immediately. She acknowledged Jude's many faults. She even broke down at the end, which was just fucking brilliant. If it were anyone else, I would have accused them of faking those tears. Not Antonia. There's a human that's incapable of fakery.

But as people continued to clap and scream, I continued to sit. And freak out.

Because during the speech, Antonia would periodically glance at me.

Not in any way that would put a spotlight on me, sitting in the auditorium and trying to be as unobtrusive as possible. I wanted to skip this, I really did, but Cass and Porter, in a lucid moment, convinced me that my absence would be even *more* noticeable. Best to try to blend in whenever I could. I agreed, and I thought it was the right thing—until Antonia kept consistently, but unmistakably, looking at me.

They know what you did, Bronwyn. Now I was hearing Jude's voice in my head. Fab.

These past few weeks had been great, when I wasn't racked with guilt, but the party was officially over.

Antonia absolutely, positively, unequivocally knew I was involved in the making and disbursing of the Video that drove Jude...someplace that wasn't here and should have won me the election.

And from that, and her heartfelt eulogy turned into a call to action, I was now sure of it:

Antonia Marcus, my ex, was going to take me down.

CHAPTER ELEVEN

Jude

Hearing your voice was like that first sip of latte.

Tone, I'm feeling *poetic* after that phone call. I guess that's the upside of isolation: any kind of contact whatsoever at this point feels like magic. But you. Talking to you felt on another level.

Just like I said I would, I called you. I waited until ten at night your time, an hour I knew you'd be home and awake, reading before you went to sleep as was your habit. I didn't want to rouse you out of slumber and worry you (and probably, your parents if you got loud enough). I also wanted to catch you at a time I knew you could listen. Whether you *would* listen was a given, but I wanted your full attention.

I hope you can understand why, Tone.

Anyway, that first sip of latte. I'm addicted enough at this point in my life that I wake up with a headache that, I shit you not, is soothed as soon as I put a drop of coffee in my face hole. Ideally, a maple latte from Starbucks, the special kind the barista who thinks I'm cute only makes for me, the one I'd pick up on the way to school after downing a shot of espresso that still didn't quite keep the headache at bay. Hearing you, a little gravelly from the epic speech it turns out you gave that very day, but still smooth and calm the way I always loved. Yeah, I'm saying it. *Loved.*

Love.

At first it was awkward, and that's entirely my fault, Tone. Keep in mind I've barely interacted with humans since I got shipped here. Those skills really do atrophy—now I can kind of understand why Jodie Foster could only speak gibberish in that old movie where she'd mainly raised herself in the woods. Definitely not my situation, but still. I was awkward. I'm not used to being that way.

But oh God. You. All of you. A whole hour of just hearing you talk to me, your sheer and honest support coming through this cheap ass burner phone.

I miss you so much.

I didn't know you'd take up my cause so passionately. Honestly, I didn't think I was a "cause" at all. But when you told me about the speech you gave, taking me through the entire day starting when you marched into the principal's office with pinstriped pants and high-heeled boots like a freaking *boss*, I had to sit down to keep from swooning. And then you basically, single-handedly gathered the entire school to tell them that even though I wasn't perfect I deserved respect. And Augustus deserved way better.

Fuck.

I didn't think anyone cared about me that much.

For just a second, I wondered if you were using me to win student body president. To push your own ideas, where I'm just the conduit. But I know you better than that, Tone. You've always had that quiet power. And, hey, if I'm the reason you're starting to realize just how *magnificent* you are? I'll take it.

We also talked about Bronwyn. A lot.

I'm still figuring out how I feel about Bronwyn, Tone, I'm not gonna lie. Not like romantically because I've never felt that way about her and vice versa. But I know I didn't treat her right. She didn't deserve to be shamed and cast out of our friend group for who she chose to date. Whether or not she was going through personal shit, which she was.

I was wrong.

But as you pointed out, I also didn't deserve to have something so personal broadcast to the entire school.

Even if the sex was consensual.

Which it was not.

I can't unpack that now. I couldn't get into that on the phone with you, though. Not yet.

I'm still processing it myself, and when my lovely parents shipped me off, they didn't think to connect me to a therapist.

But yeah. It wouldn't have been okay for a video to be taken of me, without my permission, if I were having *consensual* sex. No matter who my partner was.

For me to know a video of my rape is out there? And I was *punished* for it, while he gets off (ugh) scot-free? When I can't even bring myself to *think* his name, let alone say it to an empty house where I'm currently living all alone, because again, I was caught on camera?

It tortures me, Tone.

And you and I both know, even without any concrete proof, that Bronwyn was behind it.

I'll call again soon.

CHAPTER TWELVE

Bronwyn

I didn't anticipate how hard this was going to get.

I'm talking about remembering the worst, scariest, guiltiest part of my life.

No, no, it's okay. I want to help. I owe…you? Jude? Karma? Someone or something.

Here's what Porter and I did while waiting for Antonia Marcus to ruin me:

We drank. A lot.

And fucked. A lot.

Neither of which we'd done before the video.

Porter said drinking quieted the brain zaps, and who was I to argue with that? He was suffering, I knew. Liberated, or so he said, but suffering. I could sympathize, but not empathize with what he was going through, then or now. Thanks, PSAT prep, for helping me learn that difference. I loved Porter, but I hadn't struggled with the contents of my own head since before I could read.

"I just don't want to *depend* so much," he'd told me before the shit hit the fan with the video, right after he dropped the bomb he was dropping his meds. "I hate side effects, and they always exist. I hate setting my alarm, so I remember to take what, when. Sometimes I'm so foggy I can't fucking take it." We were lying on my bed, fully clothed and on top of the covers, too wired to sleep as we'd just sent off the video. He slid his arms around my waist. "You know?"

"Totally," I said, even though I didn't. I buried my face in his neck, inhaled the Porter scents of coffee beans, dryer sheets, and something spicy and uniquely him. I wished I could bottle that scent for when he wasn't around, so I settled for stealing his T-shirts. Cliché but true.

"Still though," I said when I finally had to come up for air. "You sure you don't want to talk to your mom about this?"

He touched his forehead to mine. "Positive. I love her, but do you know what it's like for your parent to choose their *career* based on your fucked-up brain?"

I pulled him close again. "Touché." I knew about his mom but hadn't thought about it that way. Of course, it was a lot of pressure, way different from academic pressure most of us got from our families. More…fundamental. Consistent. Bone-deep.

Still. I worried. But who was I to judge, really? I'd just sent out a sex tape of my ex-best friend so I could win a school election.

For the good of Augustus, and Bronwyn St. James, of course.

Anyway, Porter, who never drank before this, became a drinker. Just at night. Just a gulp or two before bed. Or so he said. Though he was spending more time in my room, I couldn't watch him twenty-four seven. Besides, I trusted him.

Even though I wrestled with the idea of telling his mom, who was blissfully unaware he was flushing his prescription pills down the toilet. It's one of the many things that started keeping me up at night. One of the many things that woke me up at the exact same time in the wee hours, punching the air and twisting the covers with my feet. Trying to escape the hell of my own making, that was supposed to be utopia.

Speaking of, I wish I'd never wished we could do more than we were doing. Oof. Awkward sentence but very genuine thought.

I never told him, but it bothered me that Porter couldn't…fire on all cylinders or whatever euphemism straight people use. I loved him, all of him. And I wanted to experience him. All of him.

Once we *were* doing everything, though, at first it was amazing. Porter was attentive and sweet and up on his consent ethics. If he was a little rougher than I'd like sometimes, if occasionally I wondered if he was using my body to get out of his frustration, well, what was I supposed to say?

I knew we should talk.

But after we started having sex, we didn't talk nearly as much. Once Porter went off his meds, it was tough for him to follow long conversations. He swore me to secrecy, but I would have bet my government-seized trust fund our teachers noticed too.

Also? I felt like I deserved it.

Sex shouldn't feel like a punishment, or penance. I had this drilled into me since I was old enough to pronounce the word *sex*. As many faults as they had, my dads did that part right.

I just always thought issues like that were black and white, instead of murky gray.

He was always my sweet, loving Porter afterward. He started spending extra time at my house, extra vigilant of my every mood and feeling. If anything it was a little annoying, but it made him feel useful, so again, what could I say?

Cass couldn't stay out of the house enough, while Porter became codependent.

My reward was watching him sleep. It wasn't adorable: the guy drooled, for one. Snuffle-snorted like a hippo at the zoo. And his mouth dropped open and stayed there, the way Jude's used to be when she was eating lunch and making a point at the same time.

The biggest upside of Porter going off his meds, the way I saw it, was the deep, pure sleep he never got to enjoy because one of his prescriptions had a side effect of frequent insomnia. I hoped he had nice dreams, though I never asked. I wanted him to have one thing for himself that didn't involve me.

I loved him so much it hurt.

I knew I could be a fixer again. Make sure Antonia never leaked the truth about the video. Convince Porter to put his pills in his mouth instead of down the toilet, without having to tell his mom and embarrass the shit out of him. (At that point, I was willing to go full *Lysistrata* if that was what it took.) Persuade Cass that what we did was right—because I knew she doubted that. Otherwise why was she avoiding me like I had the plague, spending all her free time at cheer, and avoiding me when I passed her in our hallway at home?

Also, a good night's sleep wouldn't hurt either.

I didn't think Porter or Cass dreamed about the video. I didn't either. Though Jude's ghost or whatever kept coming back in that She-Hulk T-shirt, hissing *What have you done?* I can't tell either of them, they'd think I was insane.

I couldn't rationalize away my own guilt. And believe me, I tried.

I thought what I did was for good. A way to represent my own identity the way Jude wanted to push hers. A line on the college transcript I desperately needed to spruce up after the bottom dropped out.

When I woke up with my fists punching the air, I wasn't fighting with Jude, or wrestling an imaginary person or sentient being.

I was trying to punch away my own guilt.

And failing miserably, night by night.

Chapter Thirteen

Cass

I hadn't touched my cards since that night.

I missed them. As corny as it sounds, I missed feeling *seen.* Those days after we did…what we did, felt more like the really tense moments of a comp before we went out on the mat. Only without the fun nerves, the potential to dazzle, the general kickass energy. And with way more "we're gonna lose" type dread.

What was worse, I could swear they were judging me.

I know how crazy this sounds. Cards are inanimate objects. But when I say it felt like judgment was edging in from everywhere, I mean it. I was a sophomore, and you know how it is. You blame everything around you to avoid the chaos of guilt in yourself.

One day before *that* cheer practice, as I've now come to think of it, I gave in.

The second my hands touched my favorite deck, my first deck, they instantly relaxed and I realized how they'd been hurting. Clenched into fists at practice, gripped around pens or door handles. Classic white knuckling, right? If hands could let out a breath, mine did when I started to shuffle, infusing my energy into worn cardstock and ink.

For the first time since I took the video, I felt free.

I checked my phone: enough time for a three-card spread. The most basic, the same spread I'd done for Jude. Past. Present. Future. All I needed, really.

When I put down the three cards, I wasn't surprised.

Remember how I told Jude that the cards don't really tell the future? They're more about what's already going on?

Yeah. In those three cards, I saw it all. My actions. My fate. My punishment.

The first card was past. Seven of swords. Swords are hella dramatic, and the seven of swords signifies deviousness, deception, and betrayal. Touché, tarot. Touché.

My present: even more swords. Like I said, drama. And not the stupid high school kind I would have killed for in that moment. Oh, to worry about my sexuality and stupid dates at Applebee's and not fitting in at Augustus.

Instead, I had the five of swords. The no-win situation. I'd won my cousin's respect, she'd won the election, Porter had won…sex, I guess?

And the three of us had lost our minds.

The future card was so spot-on, I actually looked around to make sure Jude hadn't come back from wherever she was, to literally stack the deck.

No Jude. Just justice. The card that symbolizes righting of wrongs. Comeuppance.

Like I've said so many times, the tarot isn't a crystal ball.

I shivered anyway.

Chapter Fourteen

Jude

I can't tell you all this over the phone. I just can't. Talking into a relic of technology is...well. It isn't easier. But I can get through this way.

Tone, he made me feel so special.

Oh God, I hate myself for even *thinking* that. No matter the gender of human, it's such a crappy cliché. I thought I was smarter than that, Tone, I really did.

Maybe my hubris is what got me here in the first place. When you think you're unstoppable, the universe lies in wait to knock your ass down. Especially when you're a girl.

The more I hang out up here with nothing but my thoughts, the more I realize what my mindset was at the time. Not that I'm blaming myself for the...incident. I know none of that is my fault. But without blaming myself, I see how much of a target I was to a sicko like him.

I do want to clarify that I'm not talking about Mr. Roman. Or Debate Guy. I'm talking about *him.*

He's going to stay *him.* I don't want to say his name ever again.

Anyway. What led to me texting him back. Over and over and over.

I felt like people only liked me because of what I could do for them.

You, perhaps, were the only exception.

Anyway.

I was always busy, even before I decided to run for president. Running around since I had the physical capacity to do so. I could take the easy route and blame my parents—and believe me, I blame them for plenty—but I *liked* being busy. Kicking ass in the summer reading program. Speaking out for gay rights once I found out gay people didn't *have* rights outside of our little suburban haven. Academics were easy, so I made it my business to excel at every activity I could.

Except sports. I really didn't give a shit about them.

I knew the influence I had over people, and I took advantage of that more often than I should. But it was the price I paid for being popular—and not popular in the ditzy, big-titty way you see in old John Hughes movies, but popular in a politician way. Looking back, I'm shocked I didn't run for office until after the stupid real presidential election. I craved the approval of my peers, so much that though the public Jude was a large and important part of me, I was afraid to show people the private Jude.

I was too busy.

And I see now how much that cost me. I don't apologize for being smart, accomplished, and passionate, and I never will. But letting one's guard down is also a sign of strength, and I missed the memo there. I wasn't vulnerable, just tough tough tough twenty-four seven. Like the Marvel superheroes I loved: one hundred percent badass all the time.

When you're not a superhero, though, that gets exhausting. Lonely. Sad.

He sniffed out that weakness in me and exploited it. Like predators do, in a way that's so insidious in its smoothness, you have no idea what's happening until there's a sex tape of you two going around your school.

Tone, I'm still terrified he's going to find this number somehow. The burner phone that no one but you know I have. Every time it lights up with a text, I freeze for about ten seconds, before I can look over and let all the breath out of my body when I see it's you.

Because you see, that's how he got to me. The texts.

They started out innocuously enough: a *"hey what's up"* here, a toilet emoji there. The latter was an inside joke because it had made us laugh since we were kids. Sounds pathetic to say that seeing a tiny toilet was the highlight of my day, but I'm trying to be more vulnerable here, Tone. When I tell you about this, I know you won't laugh.

I know now I was vulnerable with the wrong person.

Then we got to talking about the good old days, before his family moved three hours away—not a super long distance, but when you're six years old and your cousin is your whole world, feels positively catastrophic. Life-ruining. I wouldn't come out of my room the day he moved away. When I saw him at family gatherings after that, I felt like

I'd won a prize: not a shitty carnival panda full of Styrofoam, but a real Gund, soft and cuddly and all mine.

Two whole years older but he always paid the most attention to me.

Now, that's sickening to think about. But not so long ago, we started texting again—extended family gatherings had become a thing of the past because everyone was older and busier. Tone, I needed someone outside of our siloed environment who would listen and understand. He was my family. We had a history unmarred by drama over who was dating whom and who was running for what.

And okay, the texts got flirtatious.

Just silly things, joking about what we'd do to each other if we weren't related. More of that came from him than from me. But even when I tried to steer the conversation back to stuffed animals and toilet emojis, I liked the attention.

I was afraid of how much I liked it.

Weirdly, not because he was my cousin. At that point I still trusted the guy. But because he *was* a guy.

I know now that's why I was so hard on Bronwyn. So insistent on reclaiming "lesbian," on trying to push the word on every girl who loved girls. There's nothing wrong with being a lesbian, of only loving women, of course. It may or may not be a choice, or how we're born, no one really knows even though they pretend to. Maybe if I'd been more honest with myself about exploring my options, my own identity, I wouldn't have liked his attention so much. Started egging him on.

Him coming through the window? All my idea. It seemed fun, daring.

Bad.

I know I'm not supposed to blame myself, Tone.

But sometimes, it's really hard not to.

CHAPTER FIFTEEN

Antonia

Every time she calls, my resolve strengthens. My drive to get out of bed returns.

My love grows.

Originally, I just wanted to help Jude. I wasn't mooning away, wishing for a past brief relationship to come whooshing back to the present like some kind of rose-scented wind. I wanted to right the wrongs that had been done to my friend. Because she *is* my friend.

Now, though, I realize how much I admire Jude. How we'll both always be in the process of kicking our demons' asses, and how it might be kind of great to do that together. How wild physical attraction to one another was never the problem.

I can't tell her I love her. Not yet. Not when we've just hung up the phone, this time after two whole hours of talking. When I came out of my bedroom to brush my teeth, my dad was standing in the hallway, trying to act like he wasn't waiting for me.

"There's a smile I haven't seen in a while," he said. "Not going to ask. I'm just happy they made *you* happy, Antonia."

I couldn't help it—I gave my father a hug. We're a touchy-feely family of three, but I hadn't done that since the night Jude disappeared. I could feel him stiffen a bit in surprise before relaxing into it.

He kissed me on the forehead before releasing me. "That's my kid. G'night." The guy practically skipped to his and my mom's bedroom. I knew he would tell her everything and my heart filled with gladness.

All because of Jude Cuthbert, calling me from a distance.

She was thrilled about the emergency student government meeting, about the unintentional eulogy I gave followed by a call to action. "That's badass, Tone," she kept saying, using the nickname she has for me in a way that gives me goose bumps every time.

Then I told her about my bid for student body president, how the election was open again. How kids who'd never talked to me before were coming up to me in the hallways, saying they were Team Antonia. How it had become a hashtag on social media, how a sophomore named Tara who was also ace at art and design volunteered to make me posters. Stunning, people coming out of the woodwork to support me.

Us.

Jude was thrilled by all of it.

She didn't tell me where she is, and I didn't ask. I figure she'll get to it when she gets to it, or she'll just come back, and we can pretend none of this ever happened. Except...

Jude wanted to hear how I was doing. She really did. I knew the flat tone, the monosyllables she gave off when she was bored, which used to happen very easily, and she was genuinely excited about the new developments. Plus, she asked me how I was holding up and really listened when I told her, honestly, that her being gone was hard on me, much more so than I would have expected.

I didn't add how I think that's telling me something, that maybe my feelings for her extend beyond friendship. That no matter how much we blustered about how stupid high school relationships were, how above it we'd be by breaking up and staying platonic, feeling superior the whole time, I was starting to think differently. Like maybe, we could give it another shot. Anyway, this was neither the time nor the place. Not when everything was so up in the air.

When Jude started opening up about the video, I knew this was *definitely* not the time or place to declare my non-platonic love.

She didn't tell me the whole story. That's going to take more than one phone call. But she started giving details about what happened, who the guy was.

Because he *was* a guy. Is.

He's her cousin.

And it wasn't consensual.

It's a damn good thing I was sitting down, not in the range of any weapons, with no knowledge of this rapist asshole's address.

I'm also grateful this wasn't a video chat, so Jude couldn't see my face when she described the texts, how they'd elevated from silly chitchat, something about a toilet emoji, to more flirtatious. She started babbling, words overlapping until I asked her to slow down, to take a breath, that I could call her back if she was worried about running out of juice on her cheap burner phone, knowing full well that wasn't the case but not wanting to freak her out any more than she, clearly, already was.

Jude stated to me over and over in a way that meant she was trying to justify it to *herself*, that she knew how wrong it was to like her very own cousin and that's probably why she doubled down on the lesbian thing and ousted Bronwyn from our group and how horrible she feels about it, all of it, and at this point tears of sadness and flat-out rage were running down my face, and I was swallowing my sobs so she wouldn't hear them, because at the heart of it, this wasn't about me.

Until this call, I didn't know about her mom situation. I didn't know about Mr. Roman, or Debate Guy. Mr. Roman always seemed solid, and I'm glad we don't have a teacher situation here. As for Debate Guy, I'm almost certain that was Bronwyn and Company, but I want to stay focused on Jude.

I didn't push her to tell me more. She will, or won't, when she's ready. Instead, I made sure she was in a calmer place before we hung up. I told her to call me every hour if she needed to, that I'd sleep with my ringer on. I thought about calling the police to do a well-being check like they always do on *Dateline* before I remembered I didn't know where she was.

Jude promised she wouldn't hurt herself, that she'd watch *The IT Crowd* on Netflix until she fell asleep, just like she always did when she was the most stressed. She thanked me over and over, until I made her stop. We traded "I love you, buddy" endearments—our habit since the breakup—before disconnecting.

So why was I smiling when I saw my dad in the hallway?

Because as sick as it sounds, Jude has chosen *me.*

I'm not only happy to share her burden, I'm grateful. I know she's alive and she's okay. I really don't think she'll hurt herself—if she's gotten through this much already, she can get through another night. I know at least part of what happened that night I *couldn't* be there for her. Bottom line, I *know*. The murky amorphous blob has started to fill in with lines and shapes and colors, and those are all things I can work with.

I also know this:

I *will* take Bronwyn down.

For Jude.

Chapter Sixteen

Ms. Strohm,

Here's where we have a PLOT TWIST, as you would yell during class when we were talking *The Great Gatsby* or *Native Son*, or when it was two thirty-three on a Monday afternoon and you just wanted us to wake the eff up.

I was in the midst of putting this project together, adding the finishing touches, getting ready to print it out even, when I got a phone call.

"Jude Cuthbert" changed her mind.

She wanted to talk to me.

ASAP.

She was in the area: didn't say why, and I didn't ask. For most of the call, I couldn't believe I was actually hearing her voice. I'd grown familiar with it, of course, listening to the old-school tapes she FedExed over on the still-dusty recorder she'd thoughtfully included in the package, carefully protected in bubble wrap.

The way she sounds, it's…wispy. Like a little girl who got into her great-uncle's cigarettes while visiting his Depression-era farm. Still young, but she's seen some shit. Jude sounded that way at Augustus, and she does years later.

We met at a coffee shop in the next town over. Jude's choice, so she wouldn't run into anyone she knew. The reasons would become very clear when she started talking, why she didn't want to be disturbed.

See, Ms. Strohm, Jude hadn't told me over the phone exactly what she wanted to share. I had my suspicions, though. And I was right.

As she sat across from me, nursing her vanilla soy latte, those icy eyes darting around the room as she joked about the band setting up and how she hoped they were nu metal, I could tell she was uncomfortable. Part of me wanted to touch her hand, to reassure her that I wouldn't share anything she didn't want me to. To remind her that I was changing almost everyone's names, that the only person who would read this besides me was a teacher who students regularly confided in, who was known for her soft reassurances that aside from extreme stuff she was legally mandated to report, what was discussed in her office stayed exactly there.

But Jude knew all this, because I'd told her initially, when I really wanted the whole story from her perspective.

Besides, I was too busy trying to be cool. To not regress back into that first-year with a mouthful of metal braces—everyone else had the clear kind but my orthodontist was stuck in 1985—and stringy hair and shirts that didn't fit right. To be the more self-assured lesbian with a better smile and fuller hair that was still a work in progress, but the great Jude Cuthbert didn't need to know that.

It got easier and easier as she talked. As her eyes focused on me, her hands occasionally gestured but mostly fiddled with the handle of her comically oversized mug that made her fingers look so small. Occasionally she looked away, scratched the back of her neck, especially when the story got really tough.

She was hard to listen to, but I knew I had to. Not just because it would positively make this project—and I'm ashamed that popped into my mind, but I am an Augustus student, after all, driven to the end— but…well, you'll see.

I'm sure you've put it together by now, Ms. Strohm, what Jude wanted to talk about.

And somehow, it was worse than I'd imagined.

CHAPTER SEVENTEEN

Jude

At first, it felt good.

That's what I keep coming back to. It's a recurring theme with me and my therapist. How something so awful can start out…lovely.

I'd never had to hide anything before. No secrets. This wasn't, like, Nebraska where kids could still get beat up or worse, just for being who they were. Even the smaller, dumber things, like drinking at parties, weren't a big deal. Everyone knew, even the cops. As long as no one was getting into fights or jumping off roofs, you didn't have to worry.

I now realize a lot of that safety was my own white, rich privilege, but hey. That's a rant for another time.

Anyway, before my mom, I'd never felt I had to keep a secret. Which should be good, right? A sign that the world is moving in the right direction. And the secret about my mom felt like shit.

No one ever told me that secrets can also feel *great.*

Every text I got from him was like a pot of gold. My body grew primed for the "good morning, beautifuls" and the silly stories about his day, like when his jockiest classmate fainted at the sight of the fetal pigs they had to dissect in biology. While I was proudly asserting my lesbianism and pranking Bronwyn, the texts fueled me. I smiled more, my confidence soared. If anything, it reinforced who I was. I could carry on a flirtation that was forbidden, not only because he was a guy but because we were *related*, and still crush it at Augustus.

Talk about a superhero.

You already know the basic details. Everyone does. He came in through a window, like that old Beatles song my dad used to play when I was five, before he was a total workaholic. We'd dance around the living room, him and me and my mom before *she* became a country club bitch with helmet hair. People I barely recognized anymore.

I probably even brought this up to *him*—sorry, I can't say his name. We're gonna have to go with pronouns here. Okay?

Okay.

CHAPTER EIGHTEEN

Porter

I don't remember much about that episode I had. The one that almost killed me.

I do remember calling Bronwyn at some point.

I wish I didn't.

CHAPTER NINETEEN

Jude

It's still kinda fucked how they teach us about rape.

Sure, statistics exist. The ones that warn us most of the time, the attacker isn't jumping out of a bush wearing a ski mask and wielding a knife. That we're the most vulnerable to those we already know.

But who takes them seriously? Even the phrase "date rape" brings to mind the 1950s or something. Sharing a milkshake with two straws before getting it in his car. A lot of grabbing, maybe even ripping open a soft sweater, a poodle skirt. *Grease* gone bad.

They still don't talk about how at first, you can really want it.

Even then, I was naïve but I wasn't stupid, and there's a difference. I knew about the Kinsey scale, how sexuality is fluid and just because you're gay doesn't necessarily mean you've *never* felt anything for another gender. And why should you have to tell everyone? I'd been taught since Montessori that actions speak louder than words. And I believed it. I thought I knew everything and believed what was important.

He came in through the window.

What my dad especially wanted to keep quiet was how I'd been drinking. Like, a lot. Even by junior year, I was one of those drunks who didn't appear to be. I could debate the failures of the Democratic Party when most of my peers would have their heads in a toilet. So by the time *he* came in through the window, I was way further gone than I looked.

I was nervous. About being caught. About what we'd implicitly agreed to—again, this was what I believed, which is different than what was true, I know that now. About how freaking excited I was, weeks of texts made real. And in a more pathetic way, just to see my favorite cousin again.

This wouldn't ruin me if I was careful.

He looked different from his pictures. Harder. His voice was deeper than I remembered, which makes sense, considering we'd barely seen each other as teenagers. He said my name as he walked toward where I was sitting on the bed. I could smell the beer on his breath but that comforted me, like he was nervous too and had to use liquid courage. In my case it was vodka because there wasn't a smell.

He whispered in my ear, asked me if the door was locked.

Here's the part that felt good.

It'd been a while since I *felt* this much. I made fun of Bronwyn for the goo-goo way she looked at Porter. The truth was, I recognized it: that's how I tried not to look at Antonia. I know you remember, though, girls weren't supposed to be vulnerable then. To have feelings at all. We were conditioned to be these little powerhouses, knocking down our enemies left and right. To act obviously in love? To cry? That invited the bad stuff in. It wasn't in the plan.

I know part of it was the alcohol, but during that first kiss, we got right to it. I was happy to just let myself feel everything. Nervousness. Happiness. And I'll be honest, all that buildup and making of plans left me really horny.

I think I need a break. Can we talk about something else for five minutes? I'll come back to it, I promise.

CHAPTER TWENTY

Bronwyn

Oh, that phone call. From Porter. Do I have to talk about it?

It'll help you, right? It'll go in the paper and illustrate what shitheads we *both* were at this point?

God, I feel terrible saying that about Porter, who was clearly suffering.

Didn't make the things he said easier to hear.

Chapter Twenty-One

Jude

We used to take baths together!

It was funny at first! When we took our shirts off, I had this random flashback of us in the tub at our grandma's house on Christmas Eve. We'd gotten into the plum pudding, and when you're four and six that means sticky purple stuff everywhere. Which then means you get to splash around together and throw around her ancient rubber ducky. And now we're getting naked but for entirely different reasons. Funny!

I tried to tell him. I even joked, saying things like "ohhhh" and "give it to me," thinking he'd pick up on how this was getting intense and I needed to joke as a coping mechanism. Because he knew me so well!

But by that time the vodka was really hitting, and he was touching me everywhere and I wanted to stay in the moment anyway. I don't think the words made it out of my mouth. He ran his fingers up and down my body. More clothes came off. I liked it all and I didn't even hate myself yet. Because the door was locked.

I hate to even admit this to you. I've only ever told my therapists. At this point, though, when it still felt good...I sort of let myself fantasize. I *knew* what it was like in other places. Not cities, but smaller towns. Even if you were on a road trip, stopping at a gas station to pee or get a Coke, people like me were at risk. Horror stories all over the Internet.

I'm going somewhere with this. I swear.

What Bronwyn didn't get at the time, and maybe she does now, is how she would have an advantage *everywhere.* She could hold hands with her boy toy at those gas stations. Kiss him. Practically have sex with him against a wall if she wanted. If he looked male and she looked female, and I'm aware that's problematic but whatever, she could do anything, anywhere.

I, however, would always have to be on alert. To know where was okay and where wasn't. To look up those horror stories on the Internet if I ever wanted to take a road trip, so I'd know exactly where to avoid—there were whole websites out there with dos and don'ts. I was privileged in all the ways but this one.

And because we had a new president who was encouraging hate crimes, I knew it would only get worse. More sad and scary testimonials on the websites. More places to avoid.

So I indulged my curiosity. And I let myself float into dreamland. Maybe we could go where no one could find us. Hide out in a small town. Rent a trailer or one of those tiny houses on the home and garden channel our housekeeper liked. And because I looked like a girl and he looked like a boy, we could take baths together in the backyard. Like we used to before everything got so complicated.

That's when I realized his fingers were inside me.

Chapter Twenty-Two

Bronwyn

I tried to reassure him, I did. I offered to come over. Talk to his mom.

Anything to stop the screaming:

"Was it about winning? Or proving? Or fixing?"

"Was it ever just about *me*, Bron?"

…I have to stop for today, Calpurnia. I'm sorry. This is just too hard.

CHAPTER TWENTY-THREE

Jude

I still ask myself why I didn't stick around. Talk about this. Scream out to the world that I'd been raped, by a family member no less. In another time, maybe I would have.

Maybe.

The fingers in me. That alone was a violation.

But it didn't stop there.

At one point he got up to put a condom on.

I don't know if he unlocked the door at that moment or if it was already unlocked or what. Thanks to the water bottle I'd brought in that didn't have water in it, I was full-on drunk at that point. In a daze. Already hurting a little bit.

And already blaming myself.

CHAPTER TWENTY-FOUR

Calpurnia

Sorry, Ms. Strohm. I keep interfering with the narrative. I hope it doesn't cost me points.

I do think it's important to ground you in the moment here. You always say that's important. By "moment" I'm not referring to the coffee shop, which has cleared out at this point except for one barista who's wiping down the espresso machine and the four band members, setting up and chatting on the opposite end of the room. We're talking quietly enough that Jude feels comfortable. She's hunching over my phone, where I've been recording our conversation with her permission. Focusing more on it than on me, like she has to get all of this down before she forgets, even though of course she never will.

That moment is important.

More important, however, is the moment we were in the night of the party. We were still months away from those viral Tweets that became a movement. When women, and people of all genders, started really talking about what had happened to them over the years. Hurtful words and brutal actions. The behaviors that seemed innocent at the time, or even invited. Often inflicted upon them, us, by people they, we, were told to trust.

Can you blame Jude for not talking? I can't presume what was in her head. All I know is what she bravely chose to share with me.

But I want you to remember. This was when the gray areas weren't discussed as much. Everything was a whole lot grayer.

CHAPTER TWENTY-FIVE

Jude

I wasn't a superhero anymore.

Through the fog, I was split open. His face had changed. The roundness I loved so much, that was so familiar to me, had sharpened into edges. If I touched them, I'd get hurt.

He pushed and pushed into me. I felt myself regress and I was four years old again, covered in plum pudding. Feeling dirty.

He wasn't that huge of a guy. Not like a quarterback or anything. I'm small, though. And my fake water bottle was almost empty. If we'd been among other people, I would have cut myself off a long time ago.

But it was just us and an open door I didn't know was open, and I was pinned to a bed that wasn't mine, and he was hurting me a lot.

Somewhere along the line I changed my mind. I know this now. At first I laughed, and pushed at him a little. Joked "give it to me." Tried to bring him back to the round-faced kid I once knew. I've gone over and over it in my mind, whether I said no or not. I know that doesn't matter. And yet it bothers me still.

I did try to punch him in the arm, but my hand was more like a wet fish.

I've read a lot of stories since then. Experiences like the one I had. You can find them everywhere now, which is both a blessing and a curse, I guess. The words "enthusiastic consent" are way more prevalent. Maybe not everyone knows them, or listens, but people like me now know it's possible to change your mind mid-act. Even if you thought you wanted…whatever this turned out to be.

Anyway, the stories. Often more horrific than the road trip warnings. A lot of survivors talk about how they left their bodies. Like benevolent spirits, they floated above it all. Watched themselves get violated from the ceiling.

That's not me.

I felt every thrust I didn't say yes to. I stopped fighting. What was the point: he was going to do what he was going to do.

I'm still ashamed of what was going through my head at the time. No matter how many therapists reassure me that it wasn't my fault, the tiniest part of me still wonders. Did I ask for this?

They tell you, right, that rape isn't just a scary guy in a dark alley. That it happens more with people you know. I *knew* this. But in Annie Murphy's guest bed, piss drunk and just fucking tired, all I could think of was the stranger in the alley.

And he wasn't that. He was my friend. And he was a horny teenage guy and I hadn't discouraged him. So of course, he's going ahead with it.

I wanted it at first. I was curious. I liked having a secret made up of silly texts and childhood memories and a person who validated my existence, who I didn't feel I had to constantly prove myself to.

This should have stayed funny. Before he finally grunted in my ear, pulled out of me, got up to get rid of the condom and close that fucking door, I realized he'd flipped me onto my knees. I was that out of it. So out of it I even said some stuff I didn't mean, before he finished. And the memory of that Christmas Eve bath, plum pudding, and little kid slippery skin, had all but faded away.

I watched him pull his pants up and I still loved him a little.

So why did I feel like hammered shit? Why did it hurt? And I'm not just talking about my parts, though those would ache for days after. I even bled some, which had never happened. I thought it was my period at first until I remembered I'd had it the week before.

Why was I so, so stupid?

I'm sorry, Calpurnia. I...I have to stop now. I hope you got what you needed.

CHAPTER TWENTY-SIX

Porter

You know about the phone call, right? You asked Bronwyn too?

Okay. I guess I'll tell you the rest. Give you context. Ms. Strohm loves context, I remember.

I didn't know how much more I could take.

I missed Exploding Kittens.

I thought going off my meds was the right thing to do. I honestly didn't remember what it was like *not* to be on meds. Not to be dependent, not to be under the control of doctors, not to mention my mom who hinged her entire career on my mental illness. No pressure or anything.

Besides, I wanted to have sex with my girlfriend without it being a whole thing. Conceptually, I know what we were doing was technically sex, and I know how ridiculous it sounds, but I wanted to do everything. Like, everything you're thinking of that I was unable to do before because my parts didn't work—one in particular—because my brain has never worked like it should.

Once I went off meds, my thoughts were a constant run-on sentence.

I loved the sex. I'll say that. All rough and sweaty, the way I always dreamed it would be. Sure, I was drunk most of the times we did it, but it was nice to finally put the condoms I bought the year before to use.

That was the other thing: the drinking. Normal for a red-blooded high school guy, but not great for a high school guy like me.

I thought it would feel so much better.

I knew what I *should* do: first, talk to my mom, eight months pregnant at this point and trusting me to take care of myself. Fess up that I've been flushing everything down the toilet, in case she checked my medicine cabinet. Then maybe, actually, go back to my doctor. Talk about changing things up so I could get a boner and get rid of the brain zaps that were still plaguing me.

But the further away from meds I got, the harder it was to string together a complete sentence, let alone have these tough conversations that would likely result in screaming (my mom) and talking about my dick (doctor). Plus, what if something happened to my baby sister? When I was at home, not at Bronwyn's, we were all so excited for a new Kendrick.

On the plus side, I could finally understand, better than ever, why Bronwyn wanted to be student body president. Even though it was mostly a title, no one could take it away from her. She'd technically rule over *something*, even just a class full of nerds. A ruler, of any scale, is more than most of us can ever be.

At that point I just wanted to rule over my own mind. Bend it to my will. Make all of my own decisions and stop diluting the scrambled thoughts and mumbled words with alcohol and fucking.

I wasn't eighteen, though, so I had to sneak around like a douchebag and fool everyone. And hope things in my head came to some sort of stasis that was livable, so I could have sex *and* imbibe responsibly *and* play Exploding Kittens with my girlfriend and her cousin.

I wasn't asking for much, really.

We tried to play cards, Bronwyn and I. But I kept getting foggy. I didn't want to worry her anyway. She wasn't sleeping, and she thought I didn't know, but I did.

She grasped on to every straw, while slowly losing herself. So we drank. And we had sex. And we didn't talk the way we used to.

Straight dudes are supposed to...not worry about that, I think? But hey, I wasn't normal and never had been. I missed hearing everything that popped up in her head, whether it was about how Marvel didn't respect women or LGBTQ people as much as they pretended to, or how she was sad her dad didn't send her more than postcards. Or just silly stuff about college and our futures. I missed her voice, and her words, and being able to follow her trains of thought.

I wanted us to go back to before.

CHAPTER TWENTY-SEVEN

Cass

Before that party, I followed my cousin around like a lost puppy, just asking to be kicked.

After, I resented the hell out of the enclosed space we shared.

Used to be, no one gave a shit about school elections. After we did what we did, *everyone* gave a shit and I found myself involved because a) I was too stupidly enamored with my overly ambitious, borderline estranged until she became my roommate family member, and b) I was the one who found Jude with some guy who had yet to be identified.

If the right person had been elected president of the United States, none of this bullshit would have happened.

I had to grow up overnight, and I was already too old for my age. Forget the bows and pleated skirts that make us all look like the teenagers we were, if not younger. I'd disciplined the hell out of myself since I was three years old, teaching myself how to do back handsprings in the courtyard. I was alone most of the time, physically and in my head. Even my classes at school just felt like background noise.

Maybe it's something about adopted kids, in my case displaced before I could form my first word. You're never really *of* the place that you currently are.

Not that I could explain any of this to Bronwyn.

On this day, my ride fell through, and that day was a really important practice I couldn't miss. Our biggest round of competitions for the year would start next week. My mom was working a double.

So Bronwyn was dispatched to haul me to the gym in her big Jeep that was too much for a seventeen-year-old girl, but that's who her parents are. Were, I guess. I got in the car knowing for the next twenty minutes because traffic was an absolute asshole, it was me, Bronwyn, and an invisible fog of resentful anger that grew thicker by the second.

"You got pom-poms in that thing?" She stopped at a red light and jerked her chin toward my overstuffed gym bag.

I thought, further evidence that though she'd lived with us for two months now, Bronwyn had no idea what's going on outside her own little fantasy world where she's president and queen of everything. "No." I practically spit out the word, staring straight ahead at the windshield wipers doing their best to control the downpour.

Then for some reason, I immediately felt guilty. Force of habit, I guess. "Um, these days poms are really small. Maybe the size of two fists? And for now they're all at the gym." I still didn't look at her but my tone was considerably softer.

"Oh." Her voice was soft. She knew I was angry. Perceptive, for once. As we inched down the road, a gray Mercedes Benz in front of us, Bronwyn took a deep breath. "Cass, I—"

"Don't." The snapping was back. Deep breaths only meant serious heart-to-hearts, like right before my coach John told me my sprained ankle was so bad, I was out for the first round of comps in eighth grade. I cried for a week.

I focused on the Benz, the rain, the gray surrounding us. "No one caught us. Yet. I did what I was supposed to. It's not my fault Antonia gave an Oscar speech to almost the whole school and Porter's freaking out more every day."

"Wooooooooow." The Benz braked hard, and so did Bronwyn, so we both lurched forward. Temporary panic assuaged, I sat back and sneaked a glance at her.

Fabulous—my cousin was full-on staring at me, having just drawled out her answer. "Last I checked, *Cass,* you were the one who got out your phone. Who had the bright idea to give Jude the tarot reading to throw her off. Who agreed to be my campaign manager even though your experience with anything *not* involving pyramids or whatever is for shit." A little smile grew on her face, before disappearing. "Little late to act all innocent."

"I never said I was innocent." My ponytail brushed my cheek as I shook my head. "I will say that you, cuz, are manipulative as fuck."

"That's crap," she murmured, turning away from me to inch forward some more before laying on her horn at the Benz so long and hard I covered my ears. I could see it though: her tell. That slight little blush. She knew I was right.

"Do you care about me at allllll?" I mimicked. "We *took you in*, Bronwyn. Not just me and Mom—who doesn't really need another mouth to feed—but Porter." I thought of my card-loving friend. "He wasn't hurting for some…" I remember searching for words that would hurt. "*Ex-lesbian* to make him her bitch."

Bronwyn inhaled sharply. Achievement unlocked.

I focused on my lap, the black drawstring of my sweatpants so threadbare it'd practically disintegrated. But the floodgates had opened. "Do you know what you've *done* to him, Bronwyn? Have you ever thought about it?" I thought back to that first night, when I was so scared to approach them both. "He didn't *have* to be nice to his new girlfriend's baby cousin." I swallowed hard. "Much less become my friend."

Now we were at another red light, and I could feel Bronwyn's eyes on me. "Holy shit. Are you in love with Porter?"

"No!" I threw up my hands. "You're all…so obsessed with that stuff. Is it an our-age thing or an Augustus thing, because either way I feel like I can't fucking breathe anymore. No one ever shuts up about hooking up and parading around who they like to sleep with and not that there's anything wrong with any of it, but I have *no space* to figure out who I am, what I want, what I don't want, because none of you fucking listen!"

Silence. By now I'd wrapped my drawstring around my pointer finger so tightly it was bright red and starting to fall asleep. And I realized how wet my face was.

"So no," I barked before Bronwyn could say anything patronizing. "I'm not in love with your boyfriend. I'm not in love with anyone. I don't *want* anyone that way, and maybe I never will. But you manipulated both of us and now he's off his meds and…"

"I haven't slept since we hit Send, Cass."

We were in the parking lot of the gym, notoriously unpaved. Usually, I waited for the big bump and the inevitable spray of gravel, but I must have missed them while I was screaming and crying.

I looked over at Bronwyn, slumped back in her seat, staring at the steering wheel like she'd have a test on it. Defensive and tense when she started up the car back in my—our driveway, now she was quiet.

Defeated.

"I worry about Porter every minute of every day," she said, not to me but to the steering wheel. "I want him to talk to his mom, and I've asked him to so many times, but even when he's lucid enough to hear me, he won't listen." She took a long, shuddering breath. I could so easily reach over, put my hand on her shoulder to comfort her, but the twelve inches of air between us might as well have been a brick wall.

Then I noticed her hair. When she first came to live with us, it was so artfully messy in a way that looked effortless. Now it was stringy. Like straw. When she looked at me earlier, I saw purple smudges under her eyes.

I knew then she wasn't lying.

"I don't want to stop," she said slowly. "I think I really *do* have something to offer everyone at Augustus." She glanced at me. "The ones like you, who aren't really sure who or what they want. And the ones like me, who thought they had everything figured out, until one day they realized they didn't."

She clenched her hands on the steering wheel, even though we were parked. "And Cass? I think you *do* know who you are. In a lot of ways. You're amazing at cheer and tarot. You're so intuitive. I wish I knew myself, what I love, that well."

My phone dinged with the alarm I always set for practice. I knew I should get out. Instead, I sat, and Bronwyn kept talking.

"I know we went too far. I don't think Porter going off his meds is my fault, but I *know* everything else is. I shouldn't have gotten you involved, and I'm sorry. Antonia's made it clear they're onto me, and who knows if they're bluffing or telling the truth. And shit, Jude's not even *here* anymore…" She trailed off, as the windows beaded up with the rain that was coming in sheets just a few minutes ago, now reduced to a sad, slow drizzle. "It's all my fault."

She was right.

But what was I supposed to say? Did she want comfort from me, the pathetic little sophomore who did her bidding, who no one took seriously? Was this just more manipulation from someone who's just way too good at it?

I was so young.

I needed to refocus, like I did every night with my push-ups till my arms hurt, every time I pushed open that gym door and smelled sweat and hot lights and hope. I couldn't let *anyone* control my thoughts, take my focus away from my goals. *Humans can let you down*, John told me once, *but cheer never will.*

"I gotta go," I muttered, then threw open the door and scrambled

out before slamming it so hard I half-hoped it would break off the stupid Jeep. I looked over my shoulder at her and said those last words:
　　"I'll call an Uber when I'm done here."

An hour later, I'm sweating my ass off and completely stoked.
　　Everything was on point that day. Our choreography was tight. Our stunting was awesome. We were even blowing John's mind and he's notoriously picky. This is our year, he kept saying as Lexi or Morgan threw another flawless tumbling pass or Ken and I successfully caught our flyer again, depositing her on the floor so she practically bounced back up off the ground again. This would be our year.
　　"One more time?" John yelled, a question that's not really a question because he was our coach, and we all cheered our approval. We were strong. We were hungry. Our collective cry was less of an affirmation and more of a primal scream.
　　I was ready.
　　It's like the universe knew things were going to shit at home and gave me this beautiful, perfect moment, doing what I loved most with my favorite people in the world. People who would never dream of talking me into sharing a sex tape of a girl who's so *not here* she may as well be dead. People who had my back, whether I get sentenced to extra sit-ups for being late (which happened that day, and I welcomed the extra pain) or finally nail my full-full (which *would* happen sooner rather than later if I had my way).
　　At first, I felt like I was in a movie, my childhood favorite *Bring It On* or a much better, fiercer remake. I'm not the best dancer, but as I chaîné turned and kicked, I felt like a Rockette, that crisp and precise and one tiny person of a multi-headed Hydra of a cheerleader. The spangled shiny orange poms slid with sweat under my hands as I grasped them for dear life, clapping in front of my chest before thrusting my arms overhead and screaming "Go Tigers!" until my already-scratchy throat stung even more. I barely noticed, so high was my adrenaline as we got into the final pyramid, the most ambitious collective formation we'd ever done as a squad. Before today, we were about fifty-fifty in nailing it. That day? We'd hit it every. Single. Time.
　　What happened next isn't a blur, but one I can still experience with a simple and perfect clarity.
　　I knew we shouldn't have tried a double down.
　　To be fair, we *all* knew this. The stunt's been banned from high

school comps since 2012 for a reason. A lot of reasons, all of which have to do with traumatic brain injuries, spinal fractures, and other major injuries that even sound scary.

Essentially, a double down involves the flyer making two twists in the air, before the bases catch them in a cradle. When done right it's gorgeous, a stunt that makes even the most anti-cheerleader person whistle in awe. When not done right? It's a disaster, and not just for the flyer. If you don't anticipate just right, don't balance your weight and brace for impact, synchronized with your other base like fucking clockwork? Your flyer can kick you in the head, can even land on your head with a force like you wouldn't believe. Impenetrable. Even if said flyer is ninety pounds soaking wet.

The thing about cheer, which anyone who's even watched one YouTube video or read a cheerlebrity article knows, is that we get hurt all the time. I've sprained both ankles so much that twisty pain doesn't even register anymore. I dislocated my shoulder for the first time when I was nine and popped it back in before my coach knew there was a problem. For the most part, you tape up, pop ibuprofen, and march onto the mat like a good little soldier in a tiny skirt.

And concussions? Those happen too. I never told my mom, but I powered through more than one practice after a bonk to the head. I'd lie that my head wasn't spinning when all I wanted to do was lie down.

You don't become the Killer by crying on the sidelines.

That day, though, we tempted fate in a big way. And I lost.

But you have to understand. At this point I had nothing *to* lose. I'd gotten away with ruining another human being, and that feeling was amazing until one day it wasn't and then I couldn't stop doing jumping jacks. I wanted something that was dangerous and not tied to my cousin for once. I wanted to embrace my Killer status and rise above it, all at once.

Our coaches weren't paying attention because there was a little kids' class on the other side of the gym. And anyway, practice was over. We hung around and goofed off all the time. We were champions. Untouchable.

And anyway, the double down was my idea. My reckless, stupid, *stupid* idea.

We throw our flyer in the air. By this time, I'm up on Ken's shoulders, and she's supposed to land on mine, each of her sneakers planting on either side of my head, a period on a sentence, a promise. Now, we've gotten this wrong before, many times, our side of the pyramid collapsing as we tumble down like dominoes. Or the other side of the pyramid does the same thing as we stay frozen in time, secretly smug we got it right and they didn't. I'm sure the reverse is true too.

Now, though, everything falls apart.

All ninety-eight pounds of my flyer lands squarely on my head.

The collective weight is too much for Ken, who collapses as well, landing on his left shoulder and screaming in raw pain.

The flyer falls to the side of me. She had the farthest to go, from up in the air to *smack* on the ground. And yet, I get the worst of it.

Both my neck and my back are thrown out of whack, and I fall and land on my right foot.

Hard.

Landing on one's feet is an excellent metaphor, but in practice, can be devastating.

As I hear more screaming mixed with John's deep baritone ordering me not to move and the front desk to call nine-one-one, see the dirtied white shoes rush toward my collapsed figure and realize I can't move my fingers, I shut my eyes and replay what just happened over and over and over.

Unconsciousness would be an improvement.

Chapter Twenty-Eight

Porter

At this point I was just tired. Sleeping at night, so Bronwyn thought I was okay, but really my brain was zappier than ever. I couldn't focus on cards or homework or anything except sex and I couldn't use Bronwyn any more than I already was.

Might as well light the match.

This is hypomania. What I used to call "squirrelly" in private. People with bipolar one have what you know as manic episodes, but my people have a prefix. Best way I can describe a hypomanic episode is…ever ridden a roller coaster? Okay. You know that feeling you get when you're going up and up and up? Yeah. Your stomach's kind of a mess, your adrenaline is shooting way the fuck high, and the best part is the anticipation. Where you get to scream it all out as you barrel down, and then you get to hop off the ride and eat a corn dog or whatever. Go on with your really fun day.

Hypomania is the up and up and up, with no hope of the screaming release.

The shit of it is, these episodes happen even when you're doing what you're supposed to, taking meds and breathing and using your coping mechanisms. When you're racked with guilt over ruining a girl's life and you somehow thought flushing your meds down the toilet would make everything a-okay?

You go to Augustus. You're smart. You can figure it out.

I don't remember getting on the train. I do remember taking a Lyft two suburbs over because I thought it was an amazing idea to just… get away for a bit. Take the edge off. Essentially, escape my own brain.

They later found my phone in a trash can outside another train station. Not the one where I barreled onto the train and handed over whatever was left in my wallet for a ticket before stepping off in another state—geographical and mental—entirely. Didn't take long for voice mail to fill up. And police to get called.

And somewhere in there, I called Bronwyn.

Chapter Twenty-Nine

Jude

I just hung up with you, Tone.

Now you know everything. I'm recording this for posterity. Not sure what I'm going to do with these tapes. Shove them in a shoebox and store them in this attic? Or bring them home with me? Keep them out on my dresser, as a reminder?

I'm not sure how to feel yet. I know I'm supposed to be relieved, that I finally shared my burden with a willing soul who cares about me. Maybe I'll get there. But first, I'm going to lie down on this crappy couch and talk to you in my head. For some reason, that's what I need to do in this moment, and it's not like I have a therapist here to tell me if this coping mechanism is the right one or the wrong one.

I don't know if I know what's right or wrong anymore.

Wait. That's not quite true. You reinforced what I believed but couldn't bring myself to articulate. What my cousin did to me was wrong. All of it. From the silly texts of childish emoji and supportive phrases that slowly became more sinister, as was his plan, to the act at the party, to what happened after that led me to cutting myself in my bedroom before my mom walked in and we all disappeared, our return dates currently open-ended.

You told me none of this was my fault. It may take a while for me to fully believe that—as you reminded me, patriarchy is an asshole that affects us all and the desire for victims to blame themselves is deep-seated—but after tonight's call, I feel like I've taken one small step toward a state of mind that's not completely self-loathing.

Progress.

I've seen *Law & Order* and even if I don't press charges, I'll likely be recalling what happened to me in some form or another for the rest of my life. I might as well start now with simple and plain sentences. Like I just told you, Tone.

Deep breath. Here goes.

My cousin raped me at a party. I consented at first, I changed my mind, he kept going. Doesn't matter that I was drunk and initially into it. He raped me.

Afterward, we sneaked out the window and he drove me home. During the drive, he didn't talk to me or even look at me. He dropped me off at my cold, dark, empty house without another word.

The last phrase he uttered to me, during the act itself, was "C'mon, you can do better than that."

I'll never hear that sentence the same way again. Yay, I now legitimately have a trigger. Do I get a trophy for that? Ha ha. I now understand gallows humor too.

What my Augustus classmates—and until tonight, you—don't know is that I wasn't aware of the tape until the next morning, when I was on my way to the airport.

I thought my parents knew about my cousin and were taking me somewhere safe and far away from him. Maybe my dad was going to confront him. Maybe they'd go to the police on my behalf.

I didn't realize until I asked them what was going on, how vastly I'd overestimated my parents' love.

"Where are we going?" I asked, cradling my hastily bandaged wrist and trying to blink the crust out of my eyes. In the wee hours, I'd managed to cry myself to sleep when I wasn't gasping with pain.

The cut went deeper than I intended. Scratch that, I don't *know* what I intended, except that I was getting ready for bed and ended up staring down at the pack of razor blades I kept in my bathroom.

Until then, I'd been fine. *Just bad sex*, I'd told myself during the drive of deafening silence not full of awkwardness as much as shame. *Just a mistake I'll never make again.* Until what must have been trauma-induced adrenaline wore off, I wasn't even that bothered that said "bad sex" had been with a blood relative.

Then it all wore off at once and I was sliding a blade out of the packet and slicing into my own flesh. The blood was redder than I'd imagined.

"Judith," my dad said from the front seat.

My neck snapped up—I must have drifted off. I realized I was slumped in the back seat of his SUV. For a minute, I didn't know who he was talking to—he hadn't used my full name since I was a toddler and tried to stick my finger in a socket.

He didn't turn around to look at me as he dropped the bomb:

"There's a video of you having sex that went out to the entire Augustus student body early this morning."

My dad laid on the gas and now my head snapped back.

I knew then and there I'd never tell him, or my mother, what really happened.

Just like the night before, this car ride was one of very thick silence, except for a muttered "texted you your ticket" when we got to the parking lot. I got details of where I was going, the terms and conditions, once I got to the airport and was waiting to board, throat dry and scratchy but too fried to even take the ten steps to the newsstand across from me for a bottle of water.

I read it all. Texted you to tell everyone I was dead. Texted him back that I was destroying my phone, received one word in response. *Fine.*

Fine.

I wiped it clean, submerged it in the toilet, fished it out and buried it deep in a garbage can. Then scrubbed my hands, avoiding my bandage spotted with blood, before buying an extra-large bag of M&Ms at the newsstand. I ate them all without tasting even one.

And here I am.

I can't think anymore tonight.

I love you, Antonia.

CHAPTER THIRTY

Bronwyn

Principal Olive Murrell left a message on Cass and her mom's home voice mail, which I got after I returned from taking Cass to cheer, still shaking from our fight. She wanted to see me the following morning.

I knew it was over.

I didn't tell anyone. I wanted to talk about it with Cass, but she'd been in a shit mood lately. Not that I blamed her. I was surprised she hadn't officially quit as my campaign manager. At that point I was still officially running, but the drive I once felt to change Augustus for the better *and* pad my college application had slowly seeped out of me.

When I was in preschool, my dad and I watched *Days of Our Lives* and I don't remember much except the opening credits, with the giant hourglass and its steady stream of sand from top to bottom. My dad explained softly and gently that it used to mark time, like clocks do now. After the video I felt like the top part of the hourglass, slowly and steadily draining. Where the bottom was, I didn't know.

After my fight with Cass, I sat in the car outside the cheer gym because it had started pouring again and I wanted to wait it out a few minutes before getting back on the highway. Such a cliché, right? Pondering the consequences of my actions while I stare at water drops streaming down my windows as the sky goes from white to gray.

I couldn't believe I did this to my cousin. All of it.

No, I didn't force her. And I maintain that Cass is the one who took off her shoes and took out her phone when she saw Jude and whoever that was. Those were choices she and she alone made.

Except I could have stopped her, escorted her back downstairs and gotten her drunk for the first time like a good older cousin would. Or I could have taken us all home to the safety of my bedroom and card games, which Cass likely would have preferred anyway.

Cass looked up to me, always had. Trusted me to do what was right. And I've abused that practically from the first second I moved into her house. Even when I invited her to sit down with me and Porter, I wonder, was I unconsciously planting the seeds for what was to come? Befriended my cousin because down the line I knew she'd be good for a favor or six?

I knew she wasn't really in love with Porter, even when I accused her. I just wanted to assert that one last bit of power before it seeped out of me too. I knew they were friends, that he'd truly been kind to her with no agenda whatsoever. I never gave her the space to share with me how she felt about love and sex, if she felt anything at all.

Porter.

I had to do something about him too. It was all going too far. How hard had I tried, really, to talk him into going back on his meds? I had to admit that deep down at first I was thrilled, that this beta male of a boyfriend was rebelling against his mom and Big Pharma, while he who'd had several girlfriends was in a relationship with *me*. Again, sheer power. The sex was a bonus, as was his constant presence in my room.

But I realized then, looking at the rain, that though Porter loved me and I had no reason to question that, he might also be avoiding shit of his own by hiding out in my room, my bed. His mom, for one, who was going to catch on. And maybe even the shit going on in his head. We'd made our own little island in Cass's small house, taking refuge in each other and holding the real world at bay.

Except I wasn't sleeping, Porter wasn't functioning, and I may have ruined poor Cass.

It's over.

Just when I thought those two words—*it's over*—the sky cleared. I shit you not. The sun didn't come out or anything, but the rain stopped, and I could see more than six inches in front of me again.

Feeling virtuous and good for the first time in forever, I carefully backed out of the parking lot and inched back onto the highway, but not before setting an alarm on my phone.

Cass didn't want a ride home from me, but she would get one.

Along with a better apology if she was willing to listen. And if that didn't work, I'd bribe her with endless caramel Frappuccinos.

❖

I cruised home on nothing but optimism. Even the concrete driveway felt spongy against the soles of my sneakers—which were really Porter's—as I bounced out of the car and unlocked the front door. I headed to my room and noticed Porter wasn't napping on top of my covers the way he was when I left after I drove us all home from school. I'd kissed him on the forehead, murmured in his ear that I was taking Cass to cheer and I'd be back soon. He'd sleepily half-smiled and I felt almost maternal.

Now he was gone.

Still, my good mood remained. Maybe he called an Uber and went home for dinner. Even better, maybe he finally talked to his mom about getting a new doctor, or new meds maybe.

Yeah. This is gonna be fine. We're all gonna be okay. No matter what happens tomorrow in Principal Olive Murrell's office.

Even in that moment I was so naïve.

I remade my bed, pulling the sheets tight like I used to before the bottom dropped out, when my phone flashed with a call. An unknown number, probably a telemarketer, so I didn't pick it up, tucking the now crisp sheets under the mattress. They smelled a little rank, so I reversed the whole job, flinging out the linens like in a 1950s movie musical set in Italy, then carrying them to a pile by the door.

My phone dinged. Voice mail.

Curiosity piqued, I grabbed the phone from its place on the floor where it clattered in my fit of sheet flinging and held it to my ear.

"Little B."

I sank to the tip of the bare mattress.

Dad.

He gave each of us a nickname when we were born. We were all from the same surrogate but both Dad and Pop were always there for the births, stayed in Florida a few weeks. They timed it when I came along so my brothers would be on summer break and could come along too. I was, am, the product of meticulous planning.

He's still the only one who calls me Little B, because I was not only the youngest but the smallest in terms of birth weight.

Reception was scratchy, but I could make out my dad's awkward laugh, the one he always let out before giving a big speech at Pop's annual birthday party. About how much he loved and cherished all of us.

"I know I haven't been calling," he said. "And I'm sorry. This whole finding yourself deal isn't all it's cracked up to be."

No shit. I turned into a corrupt politician.

He kept going. "I guess I have Cheryl Strayed to thank, though?" Another awkward laugh. "Anyway, I never should have left you. I'm not sure what's going to happen with me and your pop, Little B, but I am sure it's time for me to come home." Another pause. A breath. Tears ran down my face. "I'll call you soon. Pick up this time, will ya?" Awkward laugh number three, then just before it cut off, my phone vibrated.

Another call was coming in, this time from Aunt Deb. Hands shaking, I clicked Accept.

"Bronwyn." Her voice was no-nonsense yet caring. I still didn't know my aunt very well because she worked so much, but I'd know her voice anywhere. It's perfect for a nurse: someone who will tell you exactly what's going on but will stick around to make sure you're okay, you're processing, and you're going to see it through. If I were a cancer patient, I'd want her taking care of me.

She'd never called my phone before, though.

"I'm at the hospital." Her words were short, clipped. "Cass took a fall at cheer."

"Okay," I said slowly, my head in two worlds: still with my dad and his awkward laugh, and here sitting on my bare mattress. "Do you want me to start dinner for when you get ba—"

"You need to come here." I heard the slightest tremor in her voice. "Cassandra's seriously hurt."

Oh.

Swallowing hard, I nodded. "Okay. I'll leave now. Thanks, Aunt—"

Rrrrr.

Another call, another unknown number, what the fuck now? Accept.

"Hello?"

"Bronwyn?" Another mom-type voice. "It's Janet Kendrick. Porter's mom. I found your number in the school directory."

"Um, hi." I looked wildly around the room, for my dad, for Cass, Aunt Deb, anyone. Nothing, just painted white walls offering me no answers, no comfort. Something told me I didn't want to hear what was coming.

"Have you seen Porter?" Her voice was quiet. She was a nurse too, but more of the maternal, cuddly kind, Porter's told me. So pregnant. I hoped she was sitting down.

"Um. What?" I made my way to the middle of the room, where my crumpled-up sheets were piled by the door. How long ago did I strip that bed, full of hope?

"We're—" She inhaled. "We're not sure what's going on, but he may be in withdrawal of some kind. And it's likely he's manic. He may not know where he is."

My heart was in my throat. Of course he was in withdrawal. Why hadn't *I* told Porter's mom?

Janet Kendrick rushed on. "They're looking for him right now, but I wanted you to know." Despite this devastating news, she sounded warm, reassuring. I wanted to wrap myself in that voice. "I'll keep you posted, honey, okay? And please call me if he reaches out to you. Anytime. My phone's on."

I opened my mouth to try to respond, but the phone went silent.

In the span of what, three minutes? Everything changed.

Just like for Jude when I hit Send.

I stood frozen and dumb in the middle of my room with nothing but a pile of sheets, desperate for someone, anyone, to tell me what to do next.

The phone rang again. It was him.

Chapter Thirty-One

Porter

"Was it ever about me?"

I do remember saying that to her. She was talking and talking and talking, but even in my most manic state I knew how to shut her up.

I know I technically couldn't help myself, but it still haunts me that the reaction I had to hearing the voice of my girlfriend was, shut up.

Bronwyn

I guess we *are* talking about the phone call again.

He told me it was my fault. And when I tried to ask him where he was, if he was okay, he told me to shut up.

At that point I was at a loss. He sounded high. Was he high? I didn't know. I just knew he was missing, and I had to find out where he was.

But when I asked, I just got it again.

Shut up.

Shut up.

Shut up.

I'm sorry, can we take a break? Just a few minutes?

CHAPTER THIRTY-TWO

Porter

Everything seemed like the best idea I'd ever had. Take a breather. Soothe myself with the rhythm of the train on the track. When I was a baby and wouldn't sleep, my parents would take me on car rides and all it took was a lap around the block before I was out cold. Maybe I remembered that? Wanted to soothe myself. And since I was practically an adult, I didn't have to tell anyone where I was going.

Little pieces have come back to me over the years. Being really mad at Bronwyn and forgetting I too was a part of this. But it was her idea! And I was sick of feeling like shit because of her rotten thoughts and plans and for what, in the end? A stupid school office we wouldn't even remember a year from then?

I guess a lot was going on in my mind that I'd be drinking, fucking, or brain-zapping away. I found out later I said something like, "Was it about me, or was it about fixing?" She'd always joked about being a fixer and apparently I internalized that. I didn't realize how much that weighed on me, whether she really loved me or whether she was trying to prove a point to Jude or herself or the world, I didn't know.

And it occurred to me to tell her everything I didn't even know I'd been thinking. Using my outside voice. I'm sure people were staring, if there were other people on the train at all. I remember the sun streaming through the windows and my voice breaking once or twice, like it hadn't since I was thirteen. That's it.

I didn't even think about my mom and dad. Calling around before going to the authorities. Who, by the way, immediately took it seriously because of my meds, or lack thereof.

All I wanted was to talk to Bronwyn. Tell her how I was feeling. Which at the moment wasn't good.

Bronwyn

He wasn't making a lot of sense, except when he was.

The parts that were supposed to hurt me, did.

Look. I know what state he was in. I didn't *know* know, I wasn't inside his head, I've never been manic. Hypomanic. But I did know he was missing and he'd reached out to me and I wanted to know where he was.

The problem was, Porter didn't know where he was. I could hear the clack clack of the train in the background, but we're a commuter town, that didn't narrow it down any. His words were garbled. Lapping one over another. But I could make out the parts I was supposed to hear.

All your fault.

You did this to me. You did this to us.

I hate you.

You killed her and you're going to kill me too.

And as he ranted, I lay back on the bed and took it.

CHAPTER THIRTY-THREE

Porter

I woke up in the back of an ambulance, not knowing where I was, barely cognizant of *who* I was.

No faces I knew, just green scrubs and paper masks. What was my name, they kept asking me. What day is today. Who's our president.

The first thought I had was, is this how it ends?

I wanted Bronwyn.

Chapter Thirty-Four

Cass

I fell on my head and woke up in traction.

Highest to lowest.

When I came to, I saw images behind my eyelids shiny as the trophies I'd coveted since I was three years old and stepped into this gym, tiny hand in my mother's large, rough one. She let go to introduce me to John. I was all on my own, from there on out.

Blinding pain drowned out the sound so the screams of "Don't move her!" and "Call 911!" the thud of sneakers on bouncy mat, the clear air as everyone backed away, faded to white noise. But the images, sharper than the hurt, remained.

My first bows, crisp and perfect, orange and black for Tigers, the tug on the roots of my hair as Mom fastened them. I only felt the pull for a second, before the bows became part of me.

The stunt I did last year, throwing a girl up and catching her effortlessly. Her smiling face as I lowered her to the ground, her bounce on the mat reflecting the *ping* in my heart, a moment I still think about before I fall asleep at night.

My cousin's sad and angry face in her car window, framed by gray sky and droplets of rain.

Fade to black.

Wake up.

Can't move.

CHAPTER THIRTY-FIVE

Antonia

It was Bronwyn's laptop. Of course it was.

Part of me wonders why she wasn't more careful.

Or maybe in the deepest recesses of her subconscious, to the extent she doesn't even realize, Bronwyn wanted to be caught all along.

Either way, I'm not about mining the deepest recesses of my ex-girlfriend's subconscious. Honestly, I don't even care about her place in the race for student body president, and I would bet not even Bronwyn does either.

Mostly I just want justice to be served, however Murrell chooses to dole it out.

Even more, I want Jude to come home.

I used to pride myself on not having real feelings. It's why I latched on to Jude's "Let's just be friends, high school relationships are stupid" thing. I genuinely believed it. Maybe because it's easier to go through high school stoic, as the impenetrable Antonia Marcus. Then Jude disappeared and everything changed. Then I found out what really happened, and my heart hurt so bad I wasn't sure I could go on.

Jude Cuthbert may not love me that way, but I sure as hell love Jude Cuthbert that way.

I set things right and I hope she'll be proud.

And when the time and place are both right, I'll tell her how I really feel.

Chapter Thirty-Six

Bronwyn

You don't think of "interrogations" any way but one.

You've seen true crime type shows, they're everywhere these days, so you know what I'm talking about. Yeah?

The bare bulb. The dank, gray-walled room behind two-way glass devoid of all humanity that still manages to smell like farts. The sweaty perp and screaming cop, both straight white men with more in common than they thought.

This wasn't it.

Principal Olive Murrell sported her usual crisp pinstripes and a demeanor that Gets Shit Done.

And I was just…Bronwyn, albeit an undone version, a Before pic. My hair was greasy because I'd planned to wash it that night, but more so because I couldn't stop running my perspiration-slicked hands through it. Because, yes, I was sweating even though it was an unseasonably warm April day and Augustus High's AC was on blast.

Because, after all, interrogation.

Principal Olive Murrell's office was a testament to the power and control that Jude and I had been vying for all semester. Have you been in there? No? Think *wood*. Sustainable and ethically harvested dead trees, and I could smell distinguishment instead of methane gas, along with the ting of Pine-Sol and my own BO.

I was still alone, and I knew that was purposeful on Principal Olive Murrell's part. Making me wait, stew in my own anxiety and bodily fluids, swallowing over and over until my throat, devoid of saliva, made my dry cough echo off the walls. I imagined she'd employ Teen Interrogation 101 that she learned in grad school, or straight up psychological warfare. She'd sit across from me, affixing me with a steady gaze, deeply neutral, letting me take the lead.

Augustus is a top-dollar magnet school in a cushy-ass burb. I wasn't tied to the organic oak chair, slats poking into my back. If I left, no one would physically restrain me because that's illegal.

My sweat abruptly dried and my teeth chattered, and the damn slats wouldn't stop poking. My cousin almost died, and my boyfriend was hanging on to sanity with a fraying thread.

I sat in Principal Olive Murrell's office and awaited my fate.

Were you ever in there, Calpurnia? Of course not. You're a good kid. Like I used to be.

A typical office with hard plastic chairs or maybe a very uncomfortable wooden bench isn't progressive enough for Augustus. Instead, we had expensive chairs across from a large and stately oak desk, which are supposed to invite discussion rather than accusations and punishment. Didn't really put me at ease, though. I knew why I was there.

And yet I felt strangely, almost eerily calm. I took deep breaths. Looked around at the walls of the school as I made my way down the hallway, as if for the last time. Before I stepped in and was waved into the inner sanctum by the secretary, I noticed a bright flash of posterboard.

Antonia's campaign poster. Rainbows, plus the trans flag. Good for them. Seriously.

"Do you know why you're here?" Principal Olive Murrell asked. Her voice was gentle, her dark eyes almost sympathetic. I was a "good" kid, good in quotation marks, who'd never once graced this office for anything related to discipline. I could tell she wanted to give me a chance to tell my side of the story.

Like Principal Olive Murrell, my dad has a law degree. Taught me to respect authority but also question it. To never talk myself into a problem that didn't need to exist.

So I asked, my voice level but respectful, "Why am I here?"

She laced her fingers together, placed them on top of the immaculate blotter that sat precisely in the center of her giant polished oak desk. I could smell the organic lemon furniture polish from here. We used to use it at home too.

After clearing her throat, Principal Olive Murrell said, "We heard from another student that you may know something about the, ah…" She looked down, then back up again. "*Video* that was emailed to the student body several weeks ago. Involving Jude Cuthbert."

I knew what I had to do.

The day before, I'd rushed to the hospital after my phone stopped blowing up. Cass was still unconscious, didn't come to until after Aunt Deb sent me home. We were both sobbing. I insisted it was my fault. She reassured me it wasn't. I think she was a little confused by how I could have caused her only daughter's possibly lethal cheer mishap. It hit me, then, how she knew none of what we'd been up to. Because she was working so hard, providing for herself, her daughter, their collective dream of shiny trophies and college scholarships.

While Aunt Deb and I kept vigil, Porter was found. Taken to the same hospital, a different wing: psychiatric. I wasn't allowed to see him and I thought about him every second. How I didn't put him on that runaway train, but I might as well have. His poor pregnant mom texted me every hour. Like Aunt Deb, she was clueless about our part in the Augustus scandal.

I'd spent the night tossing and turning, alone in my bed, alone in the house as Aunt Deb was spending the night by Cass's bedside again.

By the time the sun rose, birds chirping like idiots outside my window, I had reached a decision.

"Bronwyn?" Principal Olive Murrell's voice jerked me back to the present. "Do you have anything to sa—"

"It was me."

She sat back, trying very hard to conceal the shock on her face. And failing. Did I mention I was a "good" kid? "It was you," she repeated slowly.

I nodded.

And then, the second part I'd prepped for, what I knew she would ask. "Was there anyone else involved?"

You can do this, Bronwyn, I thought.

I shook my head. "No, Principal Murrell. It was just me."

Did she believe me? I've never been sure. If I were guessing, I'd say probably not. But what could she do? When someone confessed to such a heinous act, she had to go into prosecutor mode.

No point in making things more difficult.

"I wanted to win the election," I said, staring down at my hands, through with eye contact for the time being. "Also, Jude and I had had a falling out over…personal things, and I wanted to get back at her. I caught her at a party, and it went too far." Now I looked up. "That's all."

Here's the thing.

I know it's not my fault that Cass was injured, and that Porter went off his meds and into a physical breakdown. Even then I realized they chose for themselves how to deal with what we did.

But this whole ordeal wouldn't have happened if it weren't for me. I talked them into it. I questioned their loyalty, knowing they'd do anything to prove themselves to me. I wanted power, but once I got it, all I did was abuse it.

The two people I loved most were in hospital beds.

This was the bare minimum I could do to make things right.

After I closed the office door, I saw Antonia.

"Were you waiting for me?" I asked. They looked positively regal, their hair grown out enough for a fresh undercut, cheekbones as always on point.

They half-grinned. "Was it that obvious?"

And then I surprised us both.

"Thank you," I said. "You did the right thing."

Their eyes widened just the tiniest bit, but they nodded coolly. Always the put together one. "What happened in there?" they asked, jerking their chin to the office suite.

"Expelled," I said, then shrugged. "Deserved."

For the longest time, all I wanted was Augustus. The environment of excellence. The place that would tell me who I needed to be to succeed.

When I came into the office, though, I knew it was time to go. Both do my penance and challenge myself, spend senior year at a brand-new place. Figure it out for myself.

Antonia nodded slowly, before spinning on their heel to walk off into the empty hallway. Then they turned around again. Moved closer.

"I'm sure you can guess this, but all that really messed with Jude," they told me. "There's a whole story behind the…guy. Not mine to tell, but maybe she'll share it with you someday."

My heart sank. Jude was my best friend for most of my life. And I ruined hers because of some shitty comments about bisexuality. I wasn't as comfortable in my new, developing identity as I thought. Otherwise, why did I let Jude get to me so hard? Why did I go so far?

No more.

"She okay?" I asked.

They nodded, a hint of a smile gracing their beautiful face. "We've been talking."

Relief flooded through me, so powerful I had to touch the wall, so my knees didn't buckle. "I'm glad to hear that."

Their smile faded, replaced by that look of concerned empathy I remembered so well. Tone had the most compassion of any of us, probably. "How are your people? They weren't in school today."

"Okay." I nodded. "Laid up, but okay. Hanging in there." Like all of us. "Thanks."

And then it occurred to me. "Hey, Antonia? I'd love to see her when she's back." I could tell they weren't sure how to respond. "You know. If she wants to. Pass it on?"

They gave me a look I couldn't read and walked away for real this time.

The bell rang, and the hallway became a stream of humanity. Antonia was immediately lost in the crowd. I knew I should go to class—though what were they going to do, expel me?—but I wanted to do something else first.

After pushing open the heavy doors of what my dad once jokingly called "these hallowed halls of high school education," I perched on the concrete steps, feeling the coldness under my butt. I pulled out my phone from the back pocket of my jeans and dialed the number he left for me yesterday on another voice mail.

He picked up before the first ring ended, that gravelly greeting I'd known my whole life. The first voice I ever heard.

And despite myself, the terrible news I had to break to him, the confusion I felt, I smiled.

"Dad."

Cass

She visited both of us religiously. Like a martyr, at first. Ready to rend her garments or put herself on a rack or whatever martyrs do.

And we talked. A lot. The way we had when she first moved into our garage, when I was nervous and excited but mostly paranoid I'd look like a dork in front of my cool cousin.

I told her how I'd felt when we got our horrible new president. Scared like she was, but even more so because he'd made it clear what he thought of people who looked like me. How it kept me up at night, the horrible potential of that hate.

She was sitting on my bed with me, careful not to touch my various casts. I remember how surprised she looked. "You never told me that." I said, "You never asked."

She knew Porter and I were never involved. What I didn't tell her was that I *had* had feelings for him. I never acted on them, but Porter helped me realize that maybe I did want to date someone someday. Maybe sexual feelings and romantic feelings could be two different things. Maybe I could find someone who got that and we could be happy.

Porter was staying in the hospital for a while as well. They were figuring out a new treatment plan, therapy, medication he was helping to choose because only he knew how it made him feel. As time went on, they let him swing by for visits.

That day, Bronwyn brought Exploding Kittens. A brand-new set. And we played, just like on the garage floor, in my room, talking and laughing and bullshitting.

No conspiracy needed.

CHAPTER THIRTY-SEVEN

Jude

Tone, I'm coming back. It's time.

Talked to my dad and he actually agrees. He's going to stay in Florida a little longer, but is sending my aunt Charlotte, one of my cooler relatives, to stay in our guest room. I told him everything, which he took with the typical country-club manner that involves repression of feelings but also quiet action. I'm already signed up with a new therapist that specializes in sexual trauma.

I'm going to finish the school year online. Not quite ready for Augustus yet. Better to give it the rest of the semester, then summer, and hopefully someone else's sex tape will be headline news. Ha. Kidding.

And I'm going to talk to my mom. Not right away, but eventually. You only get one, right?

I thought I'd go insane in isolation. Like, truly unhinged. Though in reality I left my body that night in my room, when I cut myself in the bathroom and returned to my bed to bleed all over the white frills. Now that you and I have been talking every day, though, I can take walks and feel my feet on the ground. Smell the air: it may be cold on the coast, but you can tell spring is returning.

I wanted to die after my cousin dropped me off without even looking me in the face. And maybe in a way I *did* die, and I've been reborn. Okay, shitty metaphor and I know it. I'll tell it to you on our next call and I know you'll laugh.

God, I've missed your laugh.

That's the other thing, Tone. I don't think we're above dating each other. I think I wanted to keep my feelings for you, more intense than any I've ever known, at bay, because I didn't know how to handle them. Especially since I might not be a pure lesbian after all, whatever that means. But I think you'll understand that, and so I'm saying it to the air before I say it to you: I want us to be more than friends. We don't have to go to prom, but we can figure out a way that works for us. If you'll have me, scandalous and disgraced as I am, who still wants to change the world but needs a little, or a lot, longer to figure out how, where, when.

And then there's Bronwyn, who you've confirmed was my saboteur.

After I see you, I need to see her. I don't want to be friends again, exactly, but at this point we've all punished ourselves, and each other, enough. I want to hash this all out, face-to-face.

I know we just hung up, but I'm calling you back to ask one thing:

Please give her this number.

ACT V

Ut est rerum omnium magister usus.
(Experience is the teacher of all things.)
—Julius Caesar (the real one)

CHAPTER ONE

Bronwyn

This is how it really ends.

I breathed in roasted beans and baked sweetness as I entered the coffee shop. The same one you and I are sitting in now.

We picked the place because it was neutral ground. It was fairly new, in the next suburb over, as opposed to one of our normal hangouts back when we were tight. Easy to find, independent as opposed to corporate, and already building a name for themselves by way of chocolate chip cookies.

Maybe we'd split one.

Maybe we wouldn't.

I'd just left the hospital, two different wings of it, as I'd been doing every day that they'd both been there. First, to see Porter, who was responding well to a new course of meds. He'd been doing better since that night he scared us all, but they were keeping him a couple of weeks for observation and extra therapy, which he was okay with. Things were weird, but not as weird as they might have been. I was still deeply in love with him, and he with me, but we'd had some tough conversations we should have had months ago.

Topics included: why I was so set on having sex with him *that* way, like I needed to prove to me, to us, to the whole world, that we were a real couple, that I wasn't just experimenting. How I was determined to "save" him, was drawn to what I saw as brokenness in Porter when in reality, he is who he is and didn't need me or anyone to make him "better." His own insecurities about his bipolar and how that affected his life and relationships, not just with me but with his mom.

He'd be out soon. We were going to try again, going in with open eyes this time. In the meantime, we played Crazy Eights on his hospital bed. And okay, we made out before one of the doctors caught us in the act. No regrets.

Then I took the elevator three floors to see my cousin. My Cass. She was a true friend when I really didn't deserve one, and I privately vowed the day I got the three phone calls that changed my life, that I'll be the same for her. She'd been keeping up with assignments online, but I brought her a few textbooks, and a brand-new tarot deck. I found one with cheerleaders on Etsy, can you believe it?

She was teaching me to do readings as well. Her idea. My latest reading involved creativity, which was surprising since I'd always thought of myself as Little Miss STEM Overachiever. Even though the more I thought about it—when I wasn't sleeping, because suddenly I was back to eight hours a night—the more I realized I didn't have much of an identity at all. Outside of Augustus, that is. Obviously I was going to have to rethink that.

I went to an art supply store I'd never visited before and found myself drawn to a set of colored pencils. Threw down my debit card. Just because. Also picked up an application for employment, and I had an interview. Maybe it was time to learn something new.

Chapter Two

Bronwyn

It was a Saturday afternoon. The coffee shop had the usual suburban crowd, you know how it is. Moms in Lululemon sipping green tea and jiggling babies in strollers, people of various ages muttering at their laptops and hogging the two-person tables, junior high girls with multicolored hair extensions giggling as they quaffed frozen drinks with whipped cream.

I remember being that age, the boundless optimism and excitement about the possibilities of high school. Also, the stress. I was unnaturally stressed, already obsessing over my future.

Then I saw her.

She sat in a purple velvet armchair. On the tiny table between the chairs sat two lattes in mugs so big they were practically bowls, elaborate leaf designs in the foam on top. I knew from experience that the one closer to her was soy, and the other was almond milk, unsweetened. For me.

She didn't see me yet. I took the opportunity to study her, implant this new image in my mind. Her hair was longer. She was wearing skinny jeans and a She-Hulk T-shirt, her favorite. The one I always saw in my dreams. If I squinted, I could see a scar on her wrist, white against her tanned skin.

She smiled hesitantly. Gestured to the armchair and the latte, before carefully removing the backpack.

Jude Cuthbert and I met up to hash this out. Beginning to end.

Over the course of this afternoon, we sipped at our lattes nervously before eventually sucking them down like we used to, and getting another round, on me this time. I apologized over and over and over again, for what I did to her. She told me the whole story of who was in the bedroom with her. I apologized again when I heard it, holding back tears at first, before really letting the waterworks flow. My tears got Jude started on her own, at about which time we ran out of lattes again. I got two more, plus extra napkins and a cookie. No better time than the present to eat our feelings.

Before we ultimately crashed from all that caffeine and sugar, we talked faster. Jude told me how Antonia, Augustus High's new student body president by a landslide, was a lifeline for her during exile. She added that they were dating again. I tried to act surprised when, looking back, I'd totally seen it coming. Jude told me she was sorry for ostracizing me. She admitted she was covering up her own insecurities about her sexuality and how she herself might be changing. Evolving, just like the rest of us.

We talked about her mom. How Jude was getting more used to the changes. She was still mad at her parents for how it all went down. Which, fair. I thanked her for sharing what was really hard on her, which didn't excuse the crap she pulled but explained a lot. It was hard not to project that kind of craziness on the ones around her, especially when they were going through craziness of their own.

I told her how my dad was coming back the next week and how he found us an apartment downtown. Turned out, Dad had his own separate accounts and investments, all honestly procured. Not a fortune but enough to keep us afloat until he reentered the workforce. And I was going to work too—not because he told me he had to, but because I wanted to. Now I pull lattes in between college classes.

I told Jude how I wasn't coming back to Augustus. I'd offered to finish the year online like Cass and Porter, but Principal Olive Murrell took pity on me and was letting me stay until finals were over. It was only a few more weeks anyway, and I think it helped that I confessed and took full responsibility. Outside of Jude, Antonia, relevant parents and the principal, and my coconspirators, no one else at Augustus knew who leaked the video. They'd moved on to new gossip anyway.

And by now, I'm sure you know how this all ends, where we all are.

Porter and I are still together, at schools in the same East Coast city. His little sister is adorable and spoiled rotten. I know from social media and through the Augustus grapevine that I'm still on the fringes of that Jude and Antonia are still together as well. Jude and I don't speak, ditto me and Antonia. We all gave each other the space we needed until all there was left, was space. And that's okay.

Cass and I are still close. She got her scholarship and is at a community college with a championship team. They're in awe of her flawless full-fulls, as they should be. She's proudly asexual, but not aromantic, and is dating the sweetest *Star Wars*–loving trans girl you'll ever meet.

And of course you know what happened in the world, just a few months after Jude and I met up. Women, men, nonbinary humans overtook social media, day-to-day conversations, pop culture with a hashtag. Everyone had a story. What Jude went through is not an isolated incident but a worldwide disease that needs a cure yesterday.

Things aren't perfect, of course. But now we're paying more attention to who might be suffering because of someone's supposedly innocent actions, who may be blaming themselves, who'd been working through this shit for years. We do better together as we change the world in front of us.

But before all of that, I met Jude Cuthbert in this coffee shop.

She saw me right after I saw her. She cleared the seat opposite her, gestured to the coffee she got for us. I remember biting my lip, hard, tasting strawberry ChapStick. Now was my chance to run, to shirk my responsibilities once more, to escape what was undoubtedly going to be a really fucking hard conversation.

Instead, I dodged a yoga mom and her toddler and made a beeline for the table.

I took my jacket off slowly, one arm at a time. We took a collective deep breath. She spoke first.

"Hey."

"Hi."

EPILOGUE

Dear Calpurnia,

I've always wondered what happened to these kids. Because that's what they were, and that's what you all are to me. I remember that election, and that feeling of powerlessness, very well—as you put so eloquently in your introduction, it wasn't that long ago. But I could vote, I could donate, I could march and use my voice. Even though I work with students every day, I don't think I fully understood how the results of that election made you feel.

Until now.

Thank you for your extensive work on a very sensitive topic. So many times, with these projects, I wonder how much the student truly learns. In your case, however, it's on display in every word (the Shakespearean structure was an innovative touch, by the way). Even when you were a first-year, I got the sense you were a deep thinker who would be capable of taking on the world when the time was right. Validation has never felt so good.

Please come see me if you need any additional recommendations over the course of your final semester. Take a break once in a while, see how the sky looks. And if you're still in touch with the subjects of your project, let them know I remain, as always, in their corner.

Needless to say: A+. Never stop writing.

Enjoy winter break,

Ms. Strohm

About the Author

Lauren Emily Whalen is a freelance writer, amateur aerialist, and professional performer. She's the author of four books for young adults: *Take Her Down* and *Two Winters* with Bold Strokes Books, as well as the nonfiction book *Dealing With Drama* and her debut novel, *Satellite*. Lauren's short stories for teens and adults have been published in *BUST* Magazine as well as in three anthologies, including the holiday ghost collection *Link by Link*. She lives in Chicago with her cat, Rosaline, and an apartment full of books. Say hello at laurenemilywrites.com.

Young Adult Titles From Bold Strokes Books

Take Her Down by Lauren Emily Whalen. Stakes are cutthroat, scheming is creative, and loyalty is ever-changing in this queer, female-driven YA retelling of Shakespeare's *Julius Caesar*. (978-1-63679-089-3)

Two Winters by Lauren Emily Whalen. A modern YA retelling of Shakespeare's *The Winter's Tale* about birth, death, Catholic school, improv comedy, and the healing nature of time. (978-1-63679-019-0)

Boy at the Window by Lauren Melissa Ellzey. Daniel Kim struggles to hold onto reality while haunted by both his very-present past and his never-present parents. Jiwon Yoon may be the only one who can break Daniel free. (978-1-63679-092-3)

Three Left Turns to Nowhere by Jeffrey Ricker, J. Marshall Freeman & 'Nathan Burgoine. Three strangers heading to a convention in Toronto are stranded in rural Ontario, where a small town with a subtle kind of magic leads each to discover what he's been searching for. (978-1-63679-050-3)

#shedeservedit by Greg Herren. When his gay best friend, and high school football star, is murdered, Alex Wheeler is a suspect and must find the truth to clear himself. (978-1-63555-996-5)

The Infinite Summer by Morgan Lee Miller. While spending the summer with her dad in a small beach town, Remi Brenner falls for Harper Hebert and accidentally finds herself tangled up in an intense restaurant rivalry between her famous stepmom and her first love. (978-1-63555-969-9)

Bury Me in Shadows by Greg Herren. College student Jake Chapman is forced to spend the summer at his dying grandmother's home and soon finds danger from long-buried family secrets. (978-1-63555-993-4)

I Am Chris by R Kent. There's one saving grace to losing everything and moving away. Nobody knows her as Chrissy Taylor. Now Chris can live who he truly is. (978-1-63555-904-0)

The Dubious Gift of Dragon Blood by J. Marshall Freeman. One day Crispin is a lonely high school student—the next he is fighting a war in a land ruled by dragons, his otherworldly boyfriend at his side. (978-1-63555-725-1)

Jellicle Girl by Stevie Mikayne. One dark summer night, Beth and Jackie go out to the canoe dock. Two years later, Beth is still carrying the weight of what happened to Jackie. (978-1-63555-691-9)

All the Worlds Between Us by Morgan Lee Miller. High school senior Quinn Hughes discovers that a broken friendship is actually a door propped open for an unexpected romance. (978-1-63555-457-1)

Exit Plans for Teenage Freaks by 'Nathan Burgoine. Cole always has a plan—especially for escaping his small-town reputation as "that kid who was kidnapped when he was four"—but when he teleports to a museum, it's time to face facts: it's possible he's a total freak after all. (978-1-163555-098-6)

Rocks and Stars by Sam Ledel. Kyle's struggle to own who she is and what she really wants may end up landing her on the bench and without the woman of her dreams. (978-1-63555-156-3)